For Heaven's Sake
by
Dave Wickenden

Also by David Wickenden
<u>Laura Amour Thrillers</u>
In Defense of Innocence
Deadly Harvest

<u>Stand Alone</u>
Homegrown
Mad Dog
For these titles and other forthcoming stories,
please visit:
<u>https://davewickenden.wixsite.com/dave-wick-</u>
<u>enden</u>

Dedication

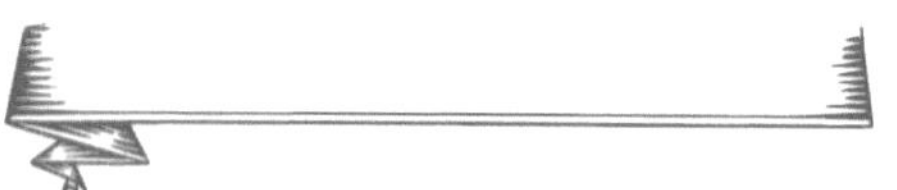

This story about Heaven is dedicated to two angels and loving mothers whom we lost during the 2020 Covid-19 Pandemic.

The first was my mother-in-law, Eliza Maria Stradiotto (nee Castellan), born May 24, 1934 who was confined not only to a wheelchair but also in a long-term Nursing Home. With the restrictions of the pandemic, her family, who (up to this time had) regularly visited her, was unable to check on her and bring authentic Italian meals. We feel that this isolation and possibly the thought of being abandoned helped speed up her decline. She left us April 5th,

2020. Even the funeral was restricted to ten people; the spouses of her grandchildren had to stay in their vehicles.

The second was my own mother, Betty Louise Wickenden, (nee Babin), born May 10, 1940, succumbed to the cancer she had been fighting for over a year. She passed quietly in her sleep on June 01, 2020. One of thirteen brothers and sisters, we were unable to have a service or internment until restrictions eased. Even then, only the immediate family was allowed to attend. Nieces, nephews and other friends were not. On July 22, 2020, she was laid to rest.

Both are missed.

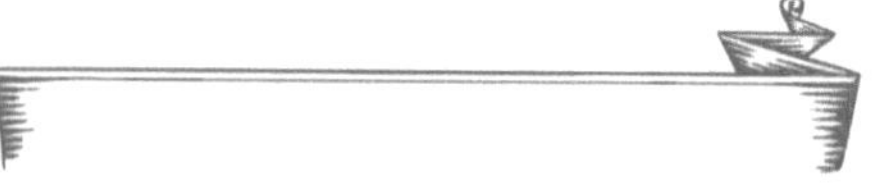

Acknowledgements

As always, Gina, who is my rock and never stops supporting me, I thank you from the bottom of my heart. To the rest of my family; you having my back, gives me the strength to keep banging on the keys.

A special shout out to a friend and fellow writer, Cindy O'Neil. Cindy took the time to edit my story and made it shine. She was a tough marker, but that was exactly what I had asked of her. Cindy and I met as school bus drivers and would talk about writing as we waited for the end of the school day and the exodus of kids. Any errors are mine.

I would like to thank Rob and the team at SelfPub-BookCovers.com[1] for the great cover for my story. They were professional and easy to work with. The end result was greater than I envisioned.

---

1. http://selfpubbookcovers.com/

Prologue

Smoke and dust obscured the battlefield. Muhammad stood panting, his weight on the guard of his sword. Weary-eyed, he took in the carnage that littered the field endlessly in every direction. The carcasses of both the enemy and his men lay in tangled heaps like morbid lovers. The battle's survivors were busy dispatching enemy wounded or assisting their brothers in arms. Monks offered conscious survivors water as they trudged among the fallen. That blessed coolness brought relief to ragged throats, scarred by the screams of fear and fury.

The enemy host had fled the field—for now. They would be back with fresh troops, of which they seem to have an endless supply.

Muhammad heard his name called out, and he turned towards the sound, his long black hair and beard flicking beads of sweat. The man approaching him had a look of sadness on his face. His eyes carried an expression of pain at the surrounding suffering. Muhammad knew how gentle a soul his friend was and felt sorrow that he was unable to shield him from the cruelty of war.

Clasping the other's arm, he pulled his friend into a huge hug, slapping him across the back.

"I am glad to see you alive, my friend," said Muhammad. "There was a time I thought they would break through our defenses."

The other man nodded. "Has it become desperate enough to send out the Sentinels?"

Muhammad's eyes swept across the surrounding destruction. With a deep sigh, he nodded. "They might have been prophesied but I fear what we ask of these children."

The other's eyes softened. "We must have faith."

Chapter 1
(Adam)

With a tortured crack the tree twisted from its intended drop and swung towards where my group and I stood open-mouthed at the spectacle. Before a thought could form, I felt myself being tossed aside like a leaf in a storm. I fell into a grunting tangle of arms and legs seconds before the enormous trunk hit the ground right where we had been standing. The ground shook with its weight and for a second, I thought it had hit me because I was unable to breathe with the weight pressing me to the ground.

"Get off me, you bloody behemoth," said Freddy, who lay beside me.

Understanding of what happened began to crystallize. Big Rob had used his arms to herd us together and tackle us out of the impact zone. The guy had saved our lives.

With a grunt, Rob pulled himself off me, and I could finally breathe. Freddy rolled away but managed to crush poor Ian as he got to his feet. I reached a hand down to help Ian, who gave me a shy smile.

"Quick thinking, Rob," I said, looking at the massive chunk of wood that lay only inches away. "We'd be dead if it wasn't for you."

Rob's face turned a bright crimson at my gratitude, and he shrugged.

A hand hit me in the center of my back, causing me to stumble forward through the cluster of ferns on the forest floor.

"What in hell are you idiots doing? Any of you assholes get killed on my watch, I'll kill you."

I looked back at the hateful face of the guard, wanting nothing more than to punch that overbearing bully in the face. The only thing holding me back was the fact that the others would share my retribution. So many times, the rest of us had to share the punishment of one of the other's transgressions. We understood that it was a way of centering out the transgressor, but they didn't understand that it unified us even more. We would not cave into their intimidations and threats.

My parents had bought the whole idea that this was a summer camp that would keep me out of trouble and that those here would guide me to a better way of seeing the world.

"It'll be nice," they said.

"You'll meet lots of friends," they said.

What they wouldn't say was that it was this or Juvie. They'd bought into the Judge's spiel that it was just like summer camp. Lots of fresh air and exercise, something according to the big man, which was missing in today's kids.

"A tired kid doesn't stay up till all hours of the night getting into trouble," Judge O'Brien said, looking over his glasses at me. "Adam, the bootcamp will keep you busy and teach you new skills. It'll also give you the time to consider your actions." They had caught me tagging the side of the police station. It hadn't been the first time. Judge O'Brien reached out and tousled my shoulder length, chestnut hair as if I was eight years old rather than fourteen. I wanted to hit the offending hand away, but knew that would only make matters worse, so gritted my teeth until I thought they'd shatter like glass.

But he didn't mention the crazy Camp Leader who worked us from first light according to the waking birds that fluttered from tree to tree until the first stars appeared in the darkening sky. Someone gave him the authority to abuse anyone of us for any imagined slight. He found exception with the fact that I had two different colored eyes; one a dark brown while the other was an icy, pale blue. I had earned a couple of slaps because it freaked him out.

With other kids, he found excuses equally unavoidable to rain his disdain on them.

The darkness brought out the bats, which fluttered against the evening sky to be lost in the lower shadows of the forest. They feasted on the insects that sucked our blood during the day, encouraged and drawn by the sweat that poured off our bodies as we dragged logs through the underbrush.

I could not count the number of times I had slipped in the evil smelling black muck that skirted the stagnant swamp, throwing up clouds of more starving bugs. The only blessing was the greasy soil created a stomach-rolling film on my skin, which held the cloud of black flies and mosquitoes at bay. They hovered around my head so thick that I had to keep my mouth shut tight as they would brave the gauntlet of teeth in an attempt to attack my tongue and gums. Many had a flavor for snot as they raced up each nostril whenever that opportunity presented itself, forcing me to ram slime covered fingers up my nose to extricate the fiends.

This caused the stink to become personal.

My fellow campers fared no better, and we staggered together like a horde of mindless zombies under the hateful glare of Camp Leader Dwight and his two brainless assistants, Dobie and Daisy.

The "3Ds." Dumb, Dumber and Dumbest.

In the distance, the metallic clang of the kitchen bell signaled lunch, and we pulled with a fresh sense of urgency. The work was demanding and our bodies screamed for nourishment to give us the strength to keep going. To fall in exhaustion only brought a swift swipe or a barrage of insults from one of the 3Ds. We weren't allowed to just drop our load and make for the camp. We had to finish hauling the eight foot log to where another crew dug a trench to accept the wood for the camp's palisade. Whether it was to keep us in or keep something out, none of us could hazard a guess.

As the length of log dipped into the damp soil, I dropped the canvas strap from my shoulder before the weight pulled me down. On the first day, I hadn't realized the danger, and it yanked me from my feet to fall with the descending length of wood that must have been at least seventy pounds. Fortunately for me, I rolled one way while it rolled another. It didn't crush me, but the rough bark chewed a line of scrapes across my ribs. When I showed it to Dwight, he laughed, "Teach ya to work more carefully. Get back to work. You'll live."

My crew comprised of three other boys who had arrived the same morning as I did, and together we staggered towards the beach, not bothering to pull off our shoes. I allowed myself to collapse full length into the water, relishing the coolness on my sun parched skin. After a minute enjoying that small pleasure, I stood and ran my hands across my chest and arms, making the water gray from the muck as it washed off.

Small hands ran up and down my back and looking over my shoulder, I saw Ian, the smallest of my team, wiping the mud off, his blue eyes intense as he surveyed my skin. Those delicate fingers could swipe anything that wasn't nailed down. Unfortunately, he hadn't noticed that camera that had caught him lifting food for his brother and sister at a local Wally World.

"Only bug bites left," Ian said with a giggle that sounded like a girl's.

I ducked under the water one more time to rinse the rest away, shaking my head to clear the water from my eyes. I pulled a hand across the top of my head, feeling the still alien stubble of the buzz cut, that we all received upon our arrival.

I returned the favor, brushing any remaining mud off Ian, and saw that Freddy and Rob were doing the same.

Freddy was a skinny, red-headed kid from some fishing village on the east coast. He was here because he had torched the fishing boat of a man who had messed with his old man.

"The sona'itch stole fish right out of my old man's nets, but did the law care about that?" he told us that first night as we got to know each other.

Freddy had to work more on Rob's broad back than Ian and I had. Rob was as big as a house. He reminded me of one of those Japanese Sumo wrestlers. At twelve years old, he was almost six feet and weighed over two hundred pounds. He was in here because he had beaten his mom's boyfriend to a pulp for slapping her around. When the cops showed up, dear old Mom stood up for the boyfriend instead of him.

"You're gonna have to check in between the folds, man," Freddy said, shaking his head with a sick look of disgust. "I ain't digging in there."

Rob spun around with a grace and speed that was mouth-dropping and threw his arms around the smaller, Freddy. He hugged the horror-stricken boy in a deep embrace so that Freddy almost disappeared in that wall of flesh. "But I love you, buddy."

He dropped the older boy unceremoniously with a huge grin across his round face, small dark black eyes almost disappearing in his dough—like features.

Freddy vanished under the water only to break the surface like a trout rising for a fly in a sputtering, coughing fit, his face red as a sockeye salmon returning to spawn. As he regained his breath, he stood with his fists clenched like he was ready to take a swing at the big boy.

Before the situation could escalate though, all our heads snapped at the bellow from shore. "If you love birds are finished, get your butts into the canteen or you'll work without lunch in ya!" Dwight stood on the rise above the beach, hands on his hips.

As one, the four of us trudged towards the shore, water dripping from our wet jeans and squishing out of our runners.

We followed Dwight towards the canteen which was just a covered area where two long tables and benches sat in the shade. Off to one side, Daisy was waiting with a plate piled with baked beans and two chunks of buttered bread. She handed the first plate to Ian, who looked at the contents in horror.

"Beans again?" he said. "Is that all you know how to cook?" As soon as the words were out of his mouth, his exasperated expression melted into a look of fear.

"Would you prefer nothing, you little worm?"

Ian seemed to shrink even smaller than his slight frame would allow. I put my hand on his shoulder and nudged him towards the tables as I reached for my own plate. I made eye contact with Daisy and gave her a wink and a smile. You'd think I had just proposed, because she blushed, eyes fluttering, and she gave me a shy smile which made her homely face look even more hideous.

They already took most of the spots at the table, but there was just enough at the far end and I steered Ian that way. They gave us an hour to eat and rest before the routine began all over again. Tomorrow, we would take our turn in the trench and the other group would haul logs.

"Thanks, Adam," Ian whispered under his breath as he stepped over the bench.

"Can't give them an excuse, buddy. I might not be there next time."

He nodded and shoveled a spoon full of beans into his mouth. I dragged a pitcher of water towards me and filled up four glasses as Rob and Freddy dropped their plates on the table. The only sounds in the canteen were the scraping of spoons across the plastic plates as each kid cleaned off every morsel, knowing there would be nothing else until dark.

I looked across the room, making sure none of the 3Ds were within hearing. Leaning forward, I whispered, "Tonight?"

All three of my team nodded slowly, each glancing at the other. We had planned our escape in ragged, one sentence steps as we hauled logs across the camp. It wasn't much of a plan, basically just a run for the nearest town, but we were all fed up with this bootcamp crap.

I couldn't see myself slaving in it for the next six weeks. It was only a matter of time before one of us got hurt or centered out for a beating from Dwight or the other guards. Just yesterday, Dobie wailed on a kid until he couldn't stand anymore. There was no reason for it that we could see. The kid was digging in the ditch and the guard just lit into him. Covered in his own blood, they had to carry him to the infirmary. He hadn't showed up for breakfast this morning.

The camp was in the middle of nowhere. We had passed through a rundown lumber town on the trip to the camp, and that was at least five or six miles away. We'd guessed that it would be the first place they'd look for us. But one thing Freddy had noticed and pointed out was the glow in the night sky, reflecting off the clouds on the far side of the lake. It had to be from a town we figured and might be a chance to leave the area if we could find a ride.

None of us ate the chunks of bread, but shoved them deep into our jeans, as we had the last couple meals. We had a pillow case stashed in the woods filled with bread and yeah; you guessed it, a couple cans of beans. Ian was able to snatch a can opener, so that was one less thing to think about. We needed anything we could easily carry because once we ran, we'd be hard pressed to find food in the wild. Except for Freddy, we all lived in cities. Living off the land wasn't something we knew anything about.

When lunch was over, we made our way back through the forest to the cutting area. Ian slipped off the trail to dump our latest offerings into a sack hidden under a deadfall. In seconds, he was back in line with no one noticing.

The afternoon dragged on while we made one backbreaking trip through the forest back to the wall after another. Time seemed to stand still, and I thought the day would never end.

I was pulled out of my exhausted stupor by the kitchen bell. Looking up for the first time and actually taking in my surroundings, I saw that it was almost dark. With a little urgency, we pulled towards the bell and the only light.

Even though it was part of imprisonment, it was a sanctuary against the surrounding blackness. I began to have second thoughts of making a run for it, imagining grizzlies or mountain lions just waiting for us to step into the shadows, ready to tear us apart in a frenzy of teeth and claws.

The fear was contagious as the other three boys began to lean into their harnesses with an effort that begrudged their previous efforts. Before long, the log was sliding along the forest floor at a manic pace that threatened to trip us in our panic, branches and leaves slapping our bare arms and backs.

We broke into the clearing, the breeze cool on our sweating skin, and seemed to strip the irrational terror from our minds. Suddenly, the load seemed more than we could manage and we staggered the last few yards before dropping the log unceremoniously to the sand.

I walked on shaky legs towards the water's edge to wash when I spied the glow across the lake. It seemed to come from the other side of the rise with no distinct light but rather just a reflection from over the horizon. I heard the others stop and gaze across the lake when suddenly as if timed; we all let out a surprised gasp.

A single light, like a firefly, rose high about the hilltop and spiraled back towards the ground, leaving a trail of light that reminded me of when you twirled a branch that had a live ember on one end. The moving ember blurred to make the orange light seem like a solid line rather than a single spot. What we saw was a spinning light that looked like an inverted tornado of light. As the light reached the ground, it rose up through the center of the cone to begin its descent once again.

Having seen nothing like it, I looked toward the others, but they all had an expression of awe and bewilderment that must have reflected my own. We looked at each other searching for an explanation, but by the time we turned back, the twirling wraith was gone, leaving the familiar glow bouncing off the clouds.

"Wh—What the heck was that?" Freddy stammered.

Before I could answer, another team of boys splashed through the shallows. Rather than bringing any attention on the area of interest, I dove under the surface to rinse off the reeking mud.

I wasn't sure what the strange moving light was and even as the water cooled my skin, I felt a colder hand tighten around my guts as if warning me away. After the quick wash, we made our way to the canteen to wolf down the same gruel they had been serving all week, again saving the hard-crusted bread.

Lying in my bunk waiting for lights out and our chance for escape, the rising and descending light show played over and over in my head. In an hour or so, we would be heading towards that strange and troubling mystery and the idea was unsettling, but I couldn't exactly say why. Some inner voice told me I didn't want to know.

Chapter 2
(Adam)

I was startled awake as a hand tugged on my leg. Forgetting where I was, I sat up and slammed my forehead into the bunk above with a clunk. Stars filled my vision in the dark dorm room. Holding my head, I heard a suppressed giggle and knew it came from Freddy.

A wave of nausea shook me as I reached down for my shoes, and I had to sit still for a moment till it passed. I prayed that I hadn't given myself a concussion.

"Come on," said Freddy in a tight whisper.

Forcing myself to stand, I followed the thin outline of my fellow inmate across the dorm to the rear door. In the gloom Rob's massive form almost completely hid Ian. The little guy had his face pressed up against the cracked door. Peeking over his head to ensure no one waited to swoop down and end our escape before it actually started, I pushed him through the doorway. The others followed.

Compared to the interior of the cabin, the night seemed lit up. The moon was not quite overhead, but the entire clearing was visible. Deep shadows stretched from the trees towards the lake and we moved in their covering embrace. There was no wind and the only sound was the hum of the insects over the croaking of frogs. Occasionally there was a faint splash of some aquatic creature eating or being eaten out on the lake.

Light from the administration building bled across the pathway. Through the un-curtained window, we could see the 3Ds sucking on tall boys. A blue haze of cigarette smoke hovered over the trio as they pushed cards around the table.

We casually skirted the light that fell across the trail, not really concerned about being seen. They'd only see their own reflection staring back at them if they did look up.

Once past, we waited hunched down in the shadows as Freddy ran for the pillowcase of supplies. It took only minutes but felt like forever before he came flying down the trail, the flash of a white bag bouncing across his path.

We picked up the pace, running along the hard-packed beach. Where the shoreline allowed, we ran through reeds and bulrushes, scaring up frogs that fled towards the water's safety. I almost screamed out loud when some waterfowl exploded skyward right at my feet. The sudden movement sent me reeling as I threw myself in the opposite direction. The memory of bears and other carnivores flashed through my mind before I heard the panicked quacking of the duck, realizing it must be as scared as me.

Behind me I heard nervous chuckles, and I was about to snap a retort to cover my wounded pride when Rob's huge hand helped me up.

"You okay?" he asked in a low tone. My anger bled away from the concern in his voice.

"Yeah, thanks."

"Go a little slower. No sense busting a leg or ankle."

He was right. It was important to put as much distance as possible between us and the camp before first light, but it wouldn't do us any good if we ended up unable to continue. As it was, we probably cut a trail a blind man could follow.

The shoreline pulled away to create a small bay, and I indicated the point across the water. "You guys up for a swim? It'll hide our tracks and cut some distance."

Everyone agreed, and we entered the water. Swimming slowly so that no one got separated, we crossed to the opposite side. Freddy held the supply bag high above his head and halfway across, I took a turn to give him a break. We clung to the rock face of the point to catch our breath before pulling ourselves around the abutment rather than climbing the steep grade in the dark. Staying in the water, we pushed a parallel path with the shore to avoid leaving any tracks.

The first blush of daylight saw us on the opposite side of the lake. With the slight fading of stars, the songbirds started calling each other cautiously at first but with ever increasing joy of welcoming the new day. For a city kid, I could not believe the number or variety of bird-calls that filled the morning air. Back home, all we had were robins and pigeons if you noticed them at all. But here in the wild, it was like a Dolby True HD Surround system. The lone, haunting cry of the loon was my favorite as it echoed across the water.

The water had drained us of body heat and I pulled off my wet clothes and hung them on the branches of a tree to drip dry. The others followed suit. We sat shivering on the beach waiting for the sun's heat to revitalize us while we avoided looking at each other's nakedness. I sat rocking myself with my arms around my knees, trying to retain what heat I could. I was starting to feel the exhaustion of being awake most of the night, especially after yesterday's labors.

The first kiss from the sun felt amazing, and I basked in the early morning heat. I must have nodded off while huddled there, because the next thing I knew, I was sprawled across the sand beach with Freddy hissing at me to stay low.

"Crawl to the trees," he said in a nervous voice.

An angry yell magnified across the water. I couldn't make out the words, but I recognized Dwight's roar before I twisted my head. Squinting against the glare off the water, I could make out a group of inmates struggling to launch a boat. It must have been the large wooden one that was half hidden in the tall grass behind the latrines. I'd be surprised if it even floated.

I crawled towards the tree that held my clothing and rose high enough to snag them. I must have been out for a while, because they were nearly dry. The shoes were another story, but it would be better than running barefoot.

Just inside the forest, I found the others quickly dragging their own damp clothes on. In minutes, we were fully dressed and peering through the trees at Dwight's armada of one. Low in the water, the boat struggled to maintain a straight line, but it became clear that it wasn't heading towards our side of the lake—yet. Rather, it hugged the shoreline as if Dwight was concerned about the craft's sea-worthiness.

"There," said Rob, his husky voice low as he pointed over my shoulder. "On the shore."

I looked past the boat to the far side and caught a flash of the pale yellow of the guard's uniform shirts. I could only see the one which made sense. It was either Daisy or Dobie, leaving the other to hold the other kids in place. I could guess who was staggering through the cattails that clogged the beach, considering Daisy did all the cooking.

"They're following our trail," I said, nodding. I slapped the big guy's arm. "We'll see how well they track through water when they hit the bay we swam across."

His chuckle caused his huge form to shudder. His shoulders looked like a mountain that was being shaken by an earthquake.

The others were watching the scene across the lake as well. Freddy seemed to be bored while Ian fidgeted like a bird that might take wing at the first threat.

"Let's make tracks," I said. "Might as well put as much distance between us and the "D's" as we can before nightfall. No telling what we'll run into be-fore then."

Not waiting for any argument, knowing they would follow regardless, I turned into the grade and scrambled up the incline. There was no way Dwight could have spotted us through the heavy growth and the distance, and he didn't dare venture across in that wooden death trap.

The pine needles made the climb treacherous as they slipped under foot where they covered the smooth granite in thin layers, leaving scars in the surface a satellite could follow. We were practically crawling on our hands and knees because of the hill's steepness. Ian and Freddy scurried on either side of me and without it being declared, we were racing towards an outcropping of rock thirty yards above us. Sweat rolled freely down my face, stinging my eyes. I could only shake my head like a dog after his bath, because I needed both hands to haul myself forward. My heart hammered in my ears and I struggled to gulp more air to fuel the sprint.

I could feel Ian fall behind, but Freddy was holding his own, staying locked with me for first place. Together we both lunged the final few yards. My foot slipped as hidden rocks rolled from under my weight, causing me to lose momentum. Freddy used my slip to his advantage. With a ragged gasp, he threw himself over the lip of the outcrop, seconds before me.

He won our little race, but there was no celebration. Both of us lay on our backs staring through the overhead branches, our chests rising and falling uncontrollably. It took minutes before I could even raise myself to one elbow to look over at Freddy.

"Good run," I said to him. He nodded his thanks and fell back, still exhausted.

I rolled over and looked down the slope in time to give a hand up to Ian, whose face was red with exertion. I pulled him over the edge and he collapsed between Freddy and I.

"Hey, guys?" an indistinct voice seemed to whisper all around us from no particular direction. As the other two looked above us, I leaned over the edge just as the nervous voice cried out again. "Fellas?"

I couldn't see him, but recognized Rob's voice.

"Up here, buddy," I yelled down suddenly worried that my voice might extend farther down the mountain than I intended.

"Wait," came the weak reply. "Please."

I looked out through the branches towards the lake, but even though I could see the sun reflecting off the surface, I couldn't see any sign of Dwight or his ragtag navy. He was out there, that I didn't doubt. He should not be able to see us, hidden by the tree-covered mountain. He had boasted often enough that there had never been a successful escape from the camp while he ran it, so I figured he wouldn't give up too quickly. We could only hope to reach the camp or town indicated by the glow we had seen and then decide our next move once we found what was there. Hitching a ride to a bigger town would open more opportunities for four teens on the lam.

My stomach growled to inform me of its idea of what the biggest priority was.

It took almost an hour for Rob to reach the ledge where we waited. He made the climb on his hands and knees, literally pulling himself up the incline. His entire face was beet red and he could only climb in ten to fifteen-foot intervals. I began to worry that he'd have a heart attack and my mind scrambled on what I would do if he did just keel over. It's not like we could carry him—up or down the mountain. But it's not like I could just leave him.

Rob was like a good hound. Once he declared himself your friend, nothing on earth would ever break that bond. He'd be like the mutt whose masters died; sleeping beside the grave until someone took him away and chained him elsewhere. He'd never give up on one of us, and there would be no way I'd cut and run.

I think Ian would be the same. He might be small, but he would stand.

Freddy might be different, and I wouldn't know until the situation unfolded. But the way he lit out after the fisherman that sabotaged his father's catch, I would bet he had what it took to back you up.

The four of us only had each other. Both our families and the law looked to us like lost causes with little to offer. They kept judging us by the standards they either grew up with or those reflected in society, but not in today's lenses. They never looked deep enough to find any worth just as we were.

Once Rob's breathing calmed down, we passed out chunks of bread and stuffed the stale pieces into our mouths. Without water to soften the crust, it took some doing; I left the last piece stuffed in my cheek like a wad of tobacco. As meager as the meal was, I felt it re-energize me.

Without being told, we all rose and began to pick our way towards the mountain's summit. This time Rob set the pace.

Having seen this mountain from the bootcamp's shore, we knew that the trees would thin out the last third of the way. The top looked like it might be all rock, with a scattering of wind-bent trees and shrubs.

We kept moving in spurts, stopping only long enough to catch our breath. I was sweating continuously and could not fathom how Rob lumbered forward without complaint. Not that any of us had enough breath to hold a conversation. What was starting to take its toll on all of us was the lack of water. The shade from the trees helped, but we needed to replace the fluids we were sweating out. Our dehydration would ramp up as soon as we were out in the open.

The sun was directly overhead, and I felt scorch bleeding through the trees.

"Hold up, guys," I gasped. I dropped to the russet bed of pine needles. No one argued as I felt rather than saw each of them drop nearby. We lay there panting like tired dogs for what felt like an eternity. As was becoming the norm, the first one to stand up and look around was Ian, who was as high-strung as a Chihuahua.

He moved further up the hillside till he crested a large outcropping of rock and looked back towards us. With his hands shading his eyes, he looked down the mountain and then scouted our path forward. With an excited yell, he began waving us forward onward.

With a grunt, I rose to my feet and both Freddy and I lent a hand to help Rob up. He didn't look too good, and he staggered as he stood reaching out to Freddy and me for balance.

"Whoa," he said swaying for a moment before he became stable. His skin was flushed but dry where mine was still damp with perspiration.

"You all right, big guy?" Freddy asked, his eyes flickering to me in concern.

"A little light-headed there for a minute." He grimaced and raised a hand over his eyes. "Ahh—feels like my head's going to explode."

"Sit back down," I said, helping him settle back against the trunk of the tree. "You just need more rest. That was a heck of a climb."

"You guys should just go on," he said. "I'm just slowing you down."

"Forget it, Rob. We're in this together."

"Yeah," Freddy said, backing up my words. "No one gets left behind."

I looked back up the slope, but Ian wasn't in sight. I admit I was a little annoyed that he didn't wait, especially with Rob's condition. Sighing, I looked at Freddy and indicated that he stay and keep an eye on our friend. "I better go and see what he found, so he doesn't get too far ahead."

Freddy nodded and settled beside our large friend.

I turned and climbed the rock face, feeling the heat on my back immediately. As I climbed, I tried to wrap my mind around the problem with Rob. This climb would be extremely difficult for him. I had to use my hands to support myself as my feet felt for purchase against the granite. When I reached the top, I might be able to spot an easier route that wouldn't be so difficult for a guy his size.

It's not like he was out of shape. The weeks slaving for Dwight's palisade had made us all buff. Rob was a powerhouse, but endurance was his weakness.

Pulling myself up, I scrambled to the top of the ledge and stood. Looking back, I could see the prison camp across the water, but no movement showing where Dwight and his crew might be. Turning, I saw that the land dropped into a shallow bowl of a valley that had been hidden from our view by the ledge I stood on.

I smiled as I saw that Ian had found an answer to our immediate problems.

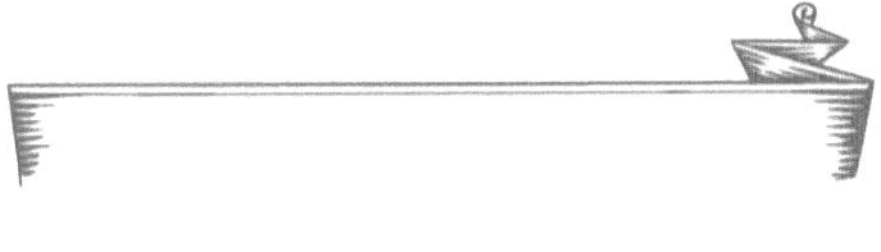

Chapter 3
(Adam)

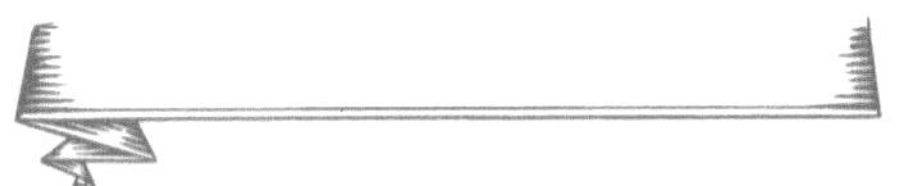

It took over two hours to help Rob maneuver around the rock face through a saddle in the hillside that allowed easier passage. All three of us took turns supporting him while he staggered forward, eyes squeezed tight against the pain in his head. The bright sunshine only made it worse, so we became his eyes.

When we finally arrived, Rob dropped to his knees and crawled to the pool of water that Ian had found. He lay lapping the water like a dog.

"Not too fast, buddy," Freddy warned. "Drink slowly or it might all come back up."

I used my hands to pour the cool water over the back of Rob's neck and head, hoping it would help cool him. He moaned in pleasure at the sensation.

Ian and Freddy wasted no time to strip and wade into the clear pool that was about twenty feet across and twice as long. A stream that dropped from further up the mountain fed it. I could see no exit point for the water from where I stood, but didn't want to leave Rob to explore further. A curtain of tall reeds surrounded the water with a few bushy cedars staggered about. It was under one of these that Rob finally dragged himself and fell fast asleep in its shade.

I joined the others in the pond, enjoying the chill that coursed through me. The quick drop off of the pond's bottom surprised me. One minute I was standing waste high, the next I dipped under the surface. Regaining the lip of the underwater ledge, I took a deep breath and dove, exploring the depths. My ears popped as I descended; enjoying the cooler atmosphere the deeper I went. The light fled, and I was soon staring into blackness. With my chest straining near its limits, the need for a fresh breath began to build. I began to arch my back to angle towards the surface when I glimpsed a flash below me. I stopped moving, my curiosity overwhelming the need for air.

The glow, which seemed to come from a far deeper part of the pool, began to rise toward the surface. It grew in size and intensity as it came closer. Only then did I feel a sense of panic grow as I realized that I was in the path of this unknown object. I pushed away and upwards, kicking my feet madly to gain the surface as much as to escape this phenomenon.

A dread began to fill me, my mind screaming that this was not a part of nature but some malevolent being that would drag me down to the depths for all time. Clawing at the dense liquid that pushed around me, I was desperate for the light and sanity above. My lungs starved of oxygen, burned with a demand for release. I allowed some air to escape between my clenched teeth in an effort to satisfy in exchange for a bit more time.

The surrounding water grew lighter, and I was not sure if it was from nearing the surface or from the glow rising towards me. I risked a peek downwards and realized the light was closing on my position and I pushed even harder, my pulse thumping violently in my ears.

Just as my body began to rebel and risk breathing the cool water in an effort to ease the pressure, my hand caught the ledge and I pushed through to the surface with a grunt that broke into a scream as I felt a feathery tingle wrap around my right leg. The spent air tore from my lungs, but before I could draw in another life-giving breath, I was tugged downwards.

The need for air was so great that my body reacted to fill the vacuum in my chest and automatically sucked in a mouthful of water. I immediately began to convulse as the water entered the windpipe towards my lungs. In a real panic, I struggled upwards even as my chest spasmed for oxygen. However, whatever had dragged me under had other intentions and I felt that same light yet powerful grip raise past my hips and engulf my upper body.

Even as I lay drowning, the panic receded enough that I could recognize the glowing object as a skull. Dark pits for eyes and two small orifices where the nose should be and a clenched mouth of teeth. Its stare bore into me as if searching my soul. In horror, I watched that horrible mouth open to expose a cavern of madness and in my mind heard a scream, *"NOOO!"*

It released and pushed away from me in a panic that mirrored my own and everything went black.

I CAME TO COUGHING and vomiting water while it felt like my back was being used as a drum.

Being as weak as a kitten, I could do nothing but endure the torture.

"Easy, Freddy," I heard Ian's warning. "I think he's coming around."

The blows to my back stopped, and I felt hands roll me over. This caused another bout of coughing, as what water I had spit up tried to retrace its path back down my throat. I lay there on my elbows as my breathing settled, the sun warm on my back. Finally, I rolled over and sat up to find all three friends waiting for my recovery, sharing similar worried expressions.

"What the heck happened to you, Adam?" asked Freddy.

I shook my head, not knowing what was real or what was brought on by a near death situation. The image I remembered could not have been real. It had to be from being oxygen starved or something.

"You came shooting out of the water," Ian said, "only to go down again."

"But the second time you came up," Freddy said, "You flew through the air and landed on the shore. It was like someone had shot you from a cannon." His eyes were wide as he remembered. "I mean, you didn't touch ground for twelve to fifteen feet."

I stared at him like he was mad, but considering what I thought I saw, I wasn't so sure. My eyes flickered to each of my friends and with a fear they'd mock my story; I closed my eyes before I told them what I had experienced under the pond's surface.

I watched a kaleidoscope of expressions morph across their faces as they listened to my tale, their eyes bouncing from me to the pond and occasionally to each other. Wide eyes and slack mouths advertised the shock, wonder and fear that coursed through them.

No one showed scorn or disbelief.

Silence filled the shallow valley, broken only by the gurgle of the moving water.

Freddy broke the bubble of apprehension by stating, "Maybe we should keep moving while it's still light."

"Ah—yeah," stammered Rob. "The water and rest did me some good. I'm ready." He slowly rose to his feet, testing his balance before letting go of the tree trunk.

"Adam," Ian said with some hesitation. "You good?"

I nodded and allowed him to help me to my feet. We backed away from the water, almost expecting another attack to materialize, but nothing disturbed the calm surface. No one said anything, but we were feeling the same thing. Young punks that stood up against bullies, rebelled against the rules or did what they liked, would never admit, let alone say it aloud.

We were scared.

WITH NO ONE DECIDING, we let Rob set the pace. We found a game trail that worked its way up the face of the mountain and followed that. It only made sense that the animals would know the best ways to move about. However, the higher we climbed, the more rock we crossed. Less soil meant fewer trail signs, to the point that we were clueless to the best route. We were no longer leaving any sign of our passage, and if Dwight made it as far as the shallow valley, he'd be hard pressed to follow further.

The sun was starting to tumble from the sky when we reached the crest. Panting, the four of us stood taking in the view. A gentle breeze climbed the mountain drying the sweat from our bodies and it felt so good I almost groaned.

Far across the lake, the camp was the size of a postage stamp. The clearing looked small beside the vastness of the forest that surrounded it on three sides. There was movement along the shoreline, but I couldn't make out what was happening because of the distance. I could make out the different marshes that spotted the lake, including the one we dragged logs through just yesterday. The lake curved away further in the distance, hiding its full shape.

"Down," Freddy hissed.

We all crouched for all the good it did. Standing on the top of a mountain with nothing but blue sky at our backs, we must have stood out like a pimple on a donkey's butt. Following Freddy's pointing hand, I watched as Dwight, his hand shielding his eyes, looked up towards us. He raised a fist towards us and although the distance was too far to hear him; the rage was clear.

"How the heck did he find us?" Ian asked, the fear in his voice clear.

"Doesn't matter," I said, patting him on the shoulder to reassure him. "We ain't going back. We'll lose him in the dark."

Chapter 4
(Adam)

We crossed the summit as the last light left the sky. Before it was too dark to see, Rob found a trail that wound down the backside of the mountain. Stumbling on tree roots, we followed the trail by feel more than anything. Branches reached out to slap us in the face, leaving scrapes and bruises in their wake. Mosquitoes drove us on, the drone of their buzzing promising days of scratching if they caught up.

Ahead and over the trees, we saw the glow of what we suspected was a town. Fortunately, our path continued in that direction. Eventually we spied a light between the trees that grew brighter as we moved forward.

The trees ended abruptly, and the trail dipped down a graded bank that had obviously been cut by heavy equipment. They had leveled the entire area to create a flat clearing to accommodate several buildings. The largest was the tall headframe of a mineshaft, reaching forty feet above the clearing. Each of the buildings were lit by huge floodlights creating virtual daylight in the entire area.

"So much for the town we thought was here," Freddy said the disappointment mixed with anger. "Now what?"

At a loss, and to give myself some time to think, I said, "Let's look around."

"Maybe there's some food," said Rob.

We split up, each trying the doors of the different buildings or looking through dirty windows to identify what it might yield. Two of the porta-rooms seemed to be bunk houses, with stripped mattresses sitting on steel frames. There was no evidence that anyone had been living there for some time. The stairs and landing going into each unit was covered with a thick covering of dust mixed with pine needles and leaves.

Ian let out a muffled yell. We all ran to the building he had been scoping to find an open window on the side of the building. How he had reached it was anybody's guess, but he had somehow leapt six feet up to the edge and wormed his way inside. Seconds later the front door was flung open, and he stood grinning like a madman.

"Dinner is served," he yelled, his voice cracking.

We scrambled inside to find the building had been the canteen for the camp. Several stoves, a large grill, and two large refrigerators lined one wall. A number of tables ran the length of the building with benches on either side to accommodate a large group of people.

In an exaggerated tone of a maitre d' he said, "For your dining pleasure, we offer a succulent course of canned spaghetti in a marinara sauce." He held up a large can with a flourish. "If someone can figure out how to turn on the gas, we can eat it warmed."

"On it," Freddy said, rushing out the door.

A few minutes later, we heard him yell out, and Ian turned one of the burners on and was awarded with a ring of blue flames.

"Freddy, you're the man," Ian yelled. Ripping his backpack off, he scrimmaged through it until he pulled out the can opener he had lifted from Daisy's kitchen. He attacked the can and in minutes had the entire can heating in a large pot.

I found four bowls and utensils and brought them to the counters. Before long the four of us sat on the steps of the canteen, each shoveling down noodles and sauce.

"Now why couldn't they serve this once in a while instead of the steady diet of beans," Ian whined. "At least it would air out the stench of farts."

After the second bowl, I was feeling content and sleepy.

"Should we chance getting some sleep or put more distance between us and the D's?" I said, hoping someone would be as tired as I was.

"It's 11:15 now," Ian said, looking down at his watch, the light reflecting his slight features. "I could set an alarm for whenever you want. That way we can get some rest but get out of here long before dawn."

I looked over at the other two. "You guys okay with that?"

"Yeah," Freddy said, "but I think at least one of us should keep watch. Dwight looked mad enough to try that climb at night."

"I could use some rest," Rob said.

"Okay, we'll sleep until 3:30, cook more food and leave by 4:00 AM. I'll take first watch," I said.

Rob agreed to take the second and Freddy third. Ian would take the last watch and cook up breakfast before waking us. Rather than try to break into the bunkhouses, Ian and Freddy stretched out on two tables in the canteen. Rob, not trusting his size to the flimsy furniture, settled himself on the floor. In minutes, all three were out of it, leaving me to watch for Dwight and crew.

Even with the harsh floodlights, I felt my eyelids drooping and had to get up and walk around so I wouldn't nod off. I crossed to the head frame; cables as thick as my wrist running from the structure's top to a large pulley wheel. A large diesel motor stood dormant beside the wheel.

The door to the headframe was a massive sliding door that was padlocked to keep out curious people not unlike myself. I wondered if the elevator cage stood on the surface or if the shaft was open to the depths below. From under the door were, twin steel rails, covered with a light patina of rust. They ran over a loading chute for offloading ore into trucks to carry down the mountain.

Moving to the next building, a massive Quonset for equipment, I pulled back the heavy, weighted canvas tarp that served as its door to see the outline a front-end loader. The rest of the interior was completely black, so I moved on.

Beyond the equipment building, I found a yard full of abandoned ore cars, excavator buckets, loader shovels. Some were left to the elements, but others were covered with vinyl coverings. This opened the question as to why the mine had been closed. Had they had depleted the ore? Or had it become unsafe? As my mind ran over these questions, another thought came to me which was more relevant to our situation. If the miners had to bunk out at this mine, just how far away was the nearest community? We could end up walking for days before finding our way to a town or worse, the road that descended the mountain could circle around to meet the road to the prison camp. We had limited food and no water unless we came across a creek or another lake, but nothing to carry it in.

Note to self: check out the canteen for water jugs.

Pressing the button on Ian's watch, the numbers flashed on and I saw that I had another fifteen minutes before I could lie down. Turning my back on the road that led away from the mine, I ambled back towards the others.

I eased myself onto the steps and sat watching the numbers count down, not wanting to deprive Rob of even one minute of sleep. The big fellow must have been hurting after today's climb.

When the numbers hit the one-hour mark, I stood up and reached for the door. From behind me, I heard a low hum that grew louder by the second. I swung around to see the door on the head frame slide open on its own; the padlock laying the in dirt.

From within the darkened maw of the building, I spotted a reddish-white radiance rising out of the ground. As it fully emerged, I had to squint from the brilliance of the glow. It levitated across the ground like a silent hovercraft, except for a hum which you felt and heard, like it was part of you.

Suddenly, it lifted like a space rocket going straight up a hundred—no—a thousand feet in seconds. As it reached its pinnacle, it tipped over and glided back to earth in graceful spirals.

This is what we saw last night!

I turned to open the door to call the others out, but saw their faces pressed against the canteen's windows, eyes wide and mouths gapping as they watched from the relative safety of the building. My head snapped back around to find the globe of light had come to a sudden stop, hovering in mid-air like a glimmering humming bird. I heard the door behind me crack open and felt a hand on my shoulder.

"What is it, Adam?" Ian said in a tight whisper, a mixture of fear and amazement.

I just shook my head. The others crowded the door, their shuffling loud in the quiet of the camp and I stepped off the stairs to avoid being pushed off. We stood there watching this remarkable light show as the globe continued to sit in the sky like a star that had become fixed to the night. The spiral trail that had followed it from on high began to fade from its highest arc and slowly the spirals lost their brightness before disappearing completely. Only the globe of light remained, vibrating in place.

Without warning, it dropped toward the earth in a swooping downward arc before becoming level with the ground and sped directly towards us. It came at such incredible speed that we had no time to run. Cringing with eyes tightly closed, I braced for impact, thinking I would be dead. It took a second before I realized that it had not shot through me. Even with eyes pressed tightly closed, I could see the brilliance through my eyelids.

With a hand shielding my eyes, I cracked one and then the other to find this ball of light inches from my face. Although it was still brilliant, the intensity did not blind. I could see that the ball spun on itself, first one way and then another. The color became less white and more of a soft pink like the pedals of a rose. I could feel no heat emanating off the light.

"You came," said a voice in my head similar to how the horrible skull had screamed. The difference was that there seemed nothing to fear. I felt no animosity from this thing as I did the other. I did not hear the voice through my ears but it seemed to vibrate deep within my brain.

"Whoa," I heard from behind me, not knowing which had spoken. I glanced behind and from the stunned expressions on my friend's faces, they had all heard it as well.

"We must hurry," the voice said, the sense of urgency causing me to back away, only to bump into one of the others. *"The Scavengers know that you are close."*

With little warning, the globe pulsed bright white again. Before any of us could move, it circled the four of us once, twice, three times, the trail of its passage tightening around us so it crushed us together as if tied by a large lasso. My arms pinned to my side; I could not break free. I could feel the others squirm, but they were equally trapped.

The globe pulled the noose tighter as it lunged towards the open headframe. With a lurch it yanked us off our feet, not to be dragged but to fly through the air after our captor. I watched in terror as the globe dove down the mouth of the mine shaft.

I screamed in panic; sure we would fall to our deaths never to be found in this abandoned mine. The others joined my chorus and our wails echoed a hollow tune down the mine's granite walls. Falling and falling, I thought we'd never reach the bottom, but continue on to pop out like a bad cartoon in some field in China. I tasted the canned spaghetti and had to swallow hard to keep from painting the shaft with it. The walls were lit by the luminous trail left behind the globe, the same that held us tightly in its coils. The rock face flew past us as we dropped like a stone. My throat burned from my vocal protests but renewed when the sphere of light suddenly spun in a different direction and disappeared down an unseen tunnel. Knowing we'd never be able to change directions as quickly, my chest tightened, and I squeezed my eyes shut so I wouldn't see the stone floor rushing towards me.

With a snap, I felt us change direction; the noose extending and softening to absorb our weight and the shock of the ninety-degree turn. Breathless, I opened my eyes to once again see the globe racing ahead of us. This time instead of speeding down a dark hole, it sped towards a light that made the globe look dim. The new light, seemed to fill the entire tunnel, both in width and height. The light rippled as if made of liquid being pushed by a breeze. As we neared it, my head tilted so I could watch our progress, I could see the tracks for the mine carts disappear into the shimmering light.

I almost cried out, when suddenly, unbidden, I recalled the phrase, "Walk towards the light," meaning death. Was that where the orb was taking us? Was it going to kill us? Or worse? But what about the Scavenger?

Chapter 5
(Adam)

The second the globe of light pulling us disappeared into the brightness, its tether to us increased pulling us at an unfathomable rate of speed. We entered the bright liquid, engulfed in the blinding pool, our screams silenced as a rush of calm settled over us. It might have lasted a minute or a century; I had no sense of time. It could have lasted an eternity or as quick as the flash of a spark. The feeling of speed also disappeared, leaving us suspended, but still held tightly by the orb's tail.

With the same suddenness, we popped out of the light into a world that reminded me of the cartoon where the character digs a hole and ends up digging to the other side of the world

Under the familiar sun and sky, a multi-tiered pagoda broke the horizon; its flashes of gold and green easy on the eye. A multitude of people, many wearing the Asian conical hat, gathered around a huge series of ponds and waterfalls, hand feeding multi-colored Koi. Speckled among the multitude were fierce Samurai, their faces covered with vicious face pieces and swords at the ready.

We were still traveling at a breath-taking speed, so in seconds we left the Japanese and encountered an island that held a vast table that seemed to stretch the far horizon, overloaded with food and drink. On either side, Viking warriors, with horned helmets and bare swords gorged themselves on ale while striking out at their neighbor. The air was full of drunken laughter and the clash of steel on steel.

Large long boats floated beside the island, horrifying dragon-headed prows foretelling their purpose.

Seconds later, the burnt ruins of an Islamic Mosque stood with its dome partially caved in. Dark oily smoke still escaped skyward as Saracens worked side by side with modern-day suicide bombers, the explosives visible across their chests, to shore up their defenses. The damage was fresh and others were helping the wounded move to a safer area.

With another snap, they were before a massive cathedral that reminded me of Notre Dame. Another cartoon memory had me expecting to see Quasimodo swinging from the bell tower, but there was no bell tower. It lay in a heap at the base of the church, smoke and flames keeping the faithful at bay. I could hear the solemn drone of the Franciscan monks that clustered together in prayer. Templar's stood at the ready by the thousands, their broadswords unsheathed, glittering in the sunlight, waiting in vain to give their lives "In the Glory of God."

Next, a massive golden Buddha rose above the vista, the only blemish was the soot-colored cheeks that seemed to come from the burnt ruins that lay at his feet. The monastery had been totally flattened, its lacquered walls feeding the flames. Monks dressed in crimson shawls decorated with bright yellow, moved among the ruins chanting together in acceptance of the inevitable.

We passed a perfect replica of both Stonehenge and the Acropolis, totally unblemished, while hordes of English archers and Spartans stood guard. A squad of Greeks hammered their short swords against their shields in salute at our passing.

"Is any of this real?" Rob asked. It was the same question I think we all were pondering.

"It looked like the Muslims and the Christians were still going at it," Freddy said as he tried to shake from his bonds.

We hadn't died or been killed, so I held my opinion to myself, figuring someone in authority would soon give us an explanation. Not to say that I wasn't a little freaked out, just the same.

The globe began to slow as we reached a clearing that was surrounded by thrones, each occupied. Behind the clearing, three massive pyramids rose, blocking out half the sky. The distance between the sphere and the four of us, still trussed up tightly, shortened and then the trailing light loosened, and pulled away the multiple wraps. We collapsed in a heap with the suddenness of the release. It felt like my body was still moving at light speed. The globe gained in brilliance and circled the clearing, and in my mind, I heard it speak again.

"Holy Ones, I have found the one you ask me to seek. There was a Scavenger nearby and from the boy's mind I sense they know of him."

"Thank you, Guāng. You have done us a great service," said a dark-bearded man who tilted his head in tribute. His voice was deep yet soft. The man was dressed in a black robe off-set by a white turban.

Guāng rose and flew behind the man to spin in place as if awaiting further orders.

Turning his attention to the four of us, he raised his hands in welcome and said, "Honored Guests. Your trip must have been very unsettling. I am Muhammad. Allow me to welcome you to Heaven."

The expression of shock or horror must have been displayed on our faces because Muhammad said, "Be at ease, my friends. We will explain all, but rest assured that you are not dead." He turned, his hand indicating those who sat in the many thrones that made up the circle, "Behold the leaders and Prophets of Earth's religion; past and present."

I followed the circle and recognized some of the deities that surrounded us. For me, the most recognizable was a long-haired man in a simple robe. I had seen countless images of Jesus from the weekly trips to church with my parents, but none had captured the gentleness and kindness of the eyes that fell upon me. He nodded at me with a soft smile.

"I do know you, Adam," I heard in my mind; the voice tearing away my fear and leaving me at peace.

I pulled my gaze from his radiant face and moved to the others. I recognized the Egyptian god, Amum-Ra by his human body with the head of a falcon and shivered when those dark eyes fixated on me. Beside him, a massive old man sat with a patch over one eye identifying him as Odin. It amazed me to see a four-armed blue figure, dressing in an open vest and sheer pantaloons. I wasn't too sure about him, but thought he might be Hindu. He was nodding to something that Buddha was saying.

A massive woman stretched beside one throne. She stood as she doubled the size of the chair. Humongous breasts hung down her ample belly and her other features seemed small in the oversized body. I had seen similar carved figures of Mother Earth, but never thought she would be so huge in actual life.

There were a multitude of others I did not know. A few I recognized by their attire as being a god of South America or Africa. Some smiled with love in their eyes while others exposed sharp, deadly grins full of pointy teeth that evoked fear and dread.

My friends had a mixture of questionable and fearful expressions on their faces as we turned back to face the man who proclaimed to be the Prophet of Allah.

With a warm smile, Mohammad said, "As expected, this is all overwhelming. To help you understand what has happened and how you came to be here, I have enlisted someone you know, Adam. Prepare for something of a shock."

Looking in the direction he indicated, I saw the man's outline against the brilliance of another globe of light, this one a pale yellow. Even without seeing his face, I recognized his step and my knees weakened and I would have fallen if Rob had not stepped forward and grabbed me.

"Heck, Adam," said the man in the voice that caused me to sob, in confused grief and loss. "Looks like you've seen a ghost." He stopped a few paces from me, but his face was a blur as I cried with total abandon. He stepped forward and pulled me into his embrace and for the first time in two years, I smelt the familiar scents of Old Spice and pipe tobacco that was part of my Grandpa. I wept hard against his shoulder and he held me tight until I was done.

When he died of cancer, I could not shed a single tear and it had almost driven me mad. I didn't understand why I could not weep for the man who had always had time to listen to me. Grandpa was my best friend and confidant. He understood me and accepted me as I was, unlike my parents. And yet, I could not let go. I took to roaming the streets at night when sleep wouldn't allow me to escape my grief and pain. Within two years, I imploded and was sent to bootcamp.

"Come here, my boy," he said, holding out the familiar checkered handkerchief to wipe my eyes. "Introduce me to your friends."

"This is Rob, Ian and Freddy," I said with a shaky voice. "Guys, this is my Grandpa Bill."

After everyone had shaken hands, Grandpa said, "I have a place set up near here, where we can have a sit down while I fill you in on what's been happening and what you might do to help."

We walked through an apple orchard; the bent branches heavy with ripening fruit. The row we followed opened to an inner clearing which boasted a large bonfire surrounded by chairs. The scene was right out of my childhood. I had sat at this exact fire pit where Grandpa would enthrall me with tales of heroes and battles between good and evil. I walked around the flames and Grandpa laughed at my bewilderment.

"Nothing is impossible, here in Heaven," he said, and to prove his point, he reached out and a tall glass materialized in his hand. "Strawberry shake with real berries, if I remember right."

I reached for the heavy crystal-clear soda fountain glass as if it were the grail, afraid that it would disappear if I made a mistake. I sipped the red and white straw and savored the flavor. It was as perfect as I remembered.

Grandpa pulled a different shake for each of my friends according to their favorite flavors and soon we all sat on the chairs around the fire, contently sucking on straws.

From behind his cabin beyond the trees, a group of dogs came rushing at our group; tongues hanging and tails waggling. A few cats sashayed behind them with a little more dignity, tails held high. The herd of animals circled us, jumping up and offering kisses. It was a happy reception until I recognized one of the dog's as Grandpa's Border Collie, Scooter, who had died before Grandpa got sick.

"Is this...?"

He gave me a huge smile. "Of course, these are all the pets I had over the years. What did you think happened to them when they died? They were all waiting for me to arrive." He leaned towards me and in a conspirator's voice said, "Best part is their food and water are self-filling and their droppings disappear in minutes. No more picking up poop."

That had everyone laughing.

Once the animals settled, Grandpa told us a tale as wild as any he had ever told in the past, but assuring us that it was all real.

Chapter 6
(Adam)

"As you saw when you arrived," Grandpa said, stirring the fire with a stick, "Heaven houses all the religions of the world. This is because the God we followed was the same God the other faiths followed. He was just represented in the image that made more sense to the different cultures around the world." He shook his head sadly. "You can imagine the waste of all those who fought and were killed in religious battles and wars throughout the Earth's history, only to arrive here to find out they died for nothing. But that is man's folly."

"Heaven is massive, as you would guess. Having to house all those who had lived before, it has to be. No one knows just how large it is, but no one has ever reached the end or circled the globe; if it's like the other planets. There are massive cities and endless wild lands. The ancient people prefer to live with those from their times, which makes sense, I guess. It is a true wonder."

He leaned forward on his knees and clasped his hands in front of him, "Now what you don't know is that God created thousands of races and worlds across the universe. Each one has its own piece of Heaven. In his wisdom, God kept the different sections of Heaven separated because the differences between the races are so very different."

He reached behind his chair and grabbed a chunk of wood from a pile and threw it onto the fire, sending a shower of sparks skyward. He leaned forward and look at each of us before he said, "That was before someone found a rift."

I felt a chill run through me, suddenly remembering the glowing skull from the pool. It and the rift had to be connected. I felt the association more than knew it for certain. I couldn't explain why.

"You see," Grandpa said, "When you enter Heaven, you can continue to pursue the same interests that you enjoyed during your lives. Because Heaven is so massive, the world's explorers continue to seek out the far corners of our existence, either together or separately. It was a North American fur trader, a man originally named William Decklan, but who was given the name 'Nitawahtaw', One who wanders, by the Cree, that found the gateway."

Unaware of what he had found, he passed through the riff into another section of Heaven; one that held a race of alien warriors who worshiped violence. It did not take long before the inhabitants of that section of Heaven captured him. They tortured him for days before allowing him to escape. In his delirium and pain, he led them to the entrance to our section of Heaven."

I glanced at my friends and all three sat with wide eyes and mouths slack as they absorbed the story. I must have had a similar expression.

"Grandpa," I said, "if the people in Heaven are dead, how can they be tortured or killed?"

The old man smiled gently before he said, "You come here whole, except you don't have to worry about dying, at least not until the Kleptons showed up. We never grow old or get sick or go hungry. It's never too cold or too hot. Until lately, it was a true paradise."

Freddy's brow was creased as he asked, "But how can you torture someone who is already dead?"

"Because we were born again when we arrived in Heaven," Grandpa said. "Just like the Good Book told us."

"But what happens if you're killed here in Heaven," Ian asked, the fear in his voice echoing my own.

Grandpa shook his head slowly, "We just don't know."

"But if God is all powerful, why can't he stop the Kleptons or close the riff?" I asked.

"Now we get to the root of the problem," Grandpa said with a sigh. He reached a hand out and his old pipe appeared in his hand, smoke already curling up from the bowl. Pulling a breath of the cherry-flavored smoke he favored, yet had caused his cancer, he looked deep into the flames. Other than the crackle of the fire, no other noise intruded the silence of the clearing and I was almost ready to prod him to explain what he meant when he said, "You're right. God could fix this in an instant. Except he's no longer here."

"Where—" I began to ask, but he cut me off with his hand.

"He left a millennium ago with no explanation other than to leave a prophecy etched into the wall of His house that foretold of a time of unrest and pain. It also said that a small team of mortals and immortals would be led by a young hero who would be known by his blue and brown eyes, which are known as the eyes of Heaven and Earth."

My head snapped from him to my friends and back again. "You don't mean me?"

Those calm, gentle eyes I had known all my life held mine; sizing me up before he nodded. "We have been waiting for you and your friends. It was why the Sentinels have been standing guard outside the portals between Heaven and earth, watching for you."

"But I'm no hero. Heck, I was in bootcamp up until last night," I said praying they had the wrong guy. "I know nothing about fighting, especially an alien race."

"Adam," he said in a soft, patient tone. "Hundreds of Sentinels around the world stood guarding as many portals and you are the only mortal to answer the call. Even the Scavenger recognized you for what you are." He reached over and tapped my knee, "And there's more, Adam. The prophesy said that the blue/brown-eyed boy will lead the band with his three earthly friends; a thief, a scrapper, and strongman. It speaks of four more warriors which you will have to choose from those assembled from Heaven's greatest heroes."

My friends and I exchanged glances, and I saw both fear and pride being called upon for such a task.

Rob leaned forward, his huge arms resting on his knees. "Does this prophecy mention what we must do?"

"It only says that you will bring balance back to the Heavens," Grandpa said, fidgeting at the lack of details. "The Deities believe that the first goal is to find the Staff of Moses, which the enemy stole in the initial attack. With it, they might seal the riff. If the Kleptons figure out its powers, they might tear down the boundaries of all the Heavens, including the veil between Heaven and the host planets. If that happens both mortal and immortal beings throughout the universe would be at the mercy of the Kleptons."

A maniacal laugh bubbled up my throat, threatening to drown me in the madness I was hearing. I felt my hands start to shake and my vision began to dim. Sounds seemed to become so acute, that it seemed I could hear the scraping of fabric every time I took a breath. I felt myself begin to give into the stress and anxiety when cold water hit me square in the face, drenching me. Looking up, I saw Grandpa pull a second glass of water out of thin air, concerned yet determined.

"I'm okay," I stammered, my hand up to ward off the second drenching. Using my other hand, I squeegeed the excess water from my face, flinging droplets towards the fire.

Before I could say anything further, a long drawn out sound broke the still air. It was a high, steady melody that seemed to come from all directions. My eyes flew to my Grandpa's horrified expression.

"Gabriel's horn!" he said as if it explained everything. Seeing our bewildered expressions, he added in explanation, "We are under attack."

As one, we rose expecting to be overrun by alien hordes, each of us looking towards a different direction for threats.

Grandpa took charge of our group with his quiet assurance. "We need to join the others. Follow me."

We trailed after him in a frenzied rush, each bunching against the other, our fear pushing us forward. We would have run helter-skelter if not for Grandpa's reassuring demeanor. It was like he was purposely keeping to a slow gait so we would not panic. Once again, we passed through the rows of the apple orchard, but this time we each grabbed the lowest fruit and stuffed them into our pockets or backpacks as a provision to our next meal. Who knew when we would have the next opportunity?

We broke out into the opening that should have been the large courtyard where we had met the Deities, but it had transformed to a parade ground with troops of every nation on earth mustered in their own cohorts.

Legions of Romans stood in silent discipline beside Vikings who slammed their swords against wooden shields while screaming their death oaths to Thor, who strode back and forth of the barely controlled horde. Ranks of Chinese warriors dressed in medieval armor and the green communist uniform. Among them savage looking Mongols with long flowing mustaches and beards pranced in place on short-legged horses that barely lifted the men off the ground.

Hundreds of thousands stood waiting for the invader. Their eyes were locked on the far horizon, and looking that way I saw a shadow of movement in the distance. It looked like a dust cloud that seemed ready to steal the very air we breathed. It rose hundreds of meters into the air and seemed to stretch across the skyline.

I yanked my eyes away from the menace when I felt a tug on my arm. Grandpa was guiding us to a podium that stood to the side, its rich wooden frame engraved with banners from all the different religions. A handful of Deities stood on the podium, and I recognized Mohammad and Jesus of Nazareth in the forefront. They led us up the set of steps and the two approached our party with tight smiles.

"I take it you had enough time to explain our peril, Bill?" Mohammad said more a statement than a question.

"They know the most important parts."

Jesus stepped before me and held out His hands. The minute He took mine into His, I felt the fear and doubt leave me. "Trust in yourself and your companions, Adam. The God of all Gods has declared that you will save us from this enemy. He knows so much more than all of us combined."

He reached out and touched each of my friends in turn and I could see the tension leave them. They stood straighter and more relaxed.

"We send some of our most trusted Captains and their best men and women to accompany you to the original riff," Muhammad said, pointing to a smaller group that stood aside from the massive armies of Heaven. "They will help and guide you, but do not mistake who is charge of this band, Adam. You have been appointed leader by our Supreme Ruler. Get to know these warriors and learn from them. When it's time to enter the world of the Kleptons, you will have to choose only four to accompany you into the other Heaven. We dare not go against what God has foretold."

With a wave of his hand towards the group, he gestured for me and the others to move towards the group of our personal guard. Four columns of twenty warriors stood at attention, a leader in front of each group. He escorted us to the first group and Mohammad introduced us to a thin man clothed entirely in black.

"Meet Master Hattori Hanzo. He led a Ninja colony in the 16th century, as was allied with the Shogun Tokugowa. He and his men are masters at infiltration, sabotage and stealth. As you must penetrate the Klepton territories, his skills will be of huge advantage to your party."

Hattori bowed low to us. His dark eyes looked stern and were all we could see of his face. A long sword was tied to his back and lay across his right shoulder for easy access. The left shoulder held a long wooden bow, a quiver of black arrows tied just behind his hip. The four of us bowed back in silent respect.

Crossing to the second troop, Muhammad said, "These men are Nepalese Gurkhas, led by Gopi Pradad Rai. The world knew these men and their ancestors as some of the most famous warriors in WWI and WWII and fought alongside the British. They are experts in all types of warfare but are famous because of their knife work." He indicated the eighteen-inch curved knife on the man's hip, the infamous kukri.

Indicating the next group, a band of Native Americans stood at ease. A horse stood at each warrior's side, painted with bloody hands, their manes decorated with eagle and hawk feathers. "Boys, meet Puhihwikwasu'u, War Chief of the Comanches. You can call him Iron Jacket. He and his horse soldiers were the best horsemen of the American plains."

I nodded at the man, but there was no change in his demeanor, in fact it was like I wasn't worth his attention. I knew we would get along famously.

The fourth and final group stood in a loose group rather than rigid military lines. The warriors were tall, thin black men. Most were bald, or they had cut their hair close to the skull. A white chalk-like paste painted their faces, so they looked like skulls. Each soldier carried only a tall wooden staff that was only three quarters of an inch thick. They were dressed in only a blue or purple shawl worn over one shoulder or bunched up around the chest to create a loose robe or kilt. Behind the group, two women stood quietly. The first thing I noticed was the large disks that stretched their lower lips away from their faces. Each disk was elaborately decorated. They each had different headdresses; one looked like dried yellow fruit, while the other had rings with a long tusk hanging on either side of her neck. Both wore a similar shawl over one shoulder, and I had to look away when I realized that one breast stood bare.

Muhammad waved his hand over the group. "These are the Suri, from southern Ethiopia, and are considered the most dangerous fighters in the world, led by Kwegu. They call those long staffs donga and they are deadly in the experienced hands of a warrior. As it is beneath a man in their culture to cook and farm, the two women will accompany the troop, but be forewarned; they are as dangerous as their men."

Freddy raised his hand as if in school. When Muhammad turned to face him, my friend said, "They look ferocious but how are we to understand each other? I only know English."

Amusement danced in the Prophet's eyes. "My son, you needn't worry. You are in Heaven. Regardless of what tongue the others speak, you will understand them and they, you."

"Cool!"

"Now the horde approaches and you must leave for the riff. Our armies will hold the enemy here to gain you time. Make haste."

They brought four horses forward, and they helped the boys into their saddles. A fifth horse pulled up and a barrel-chested man with a full beard wearing leathers pulled up.

"I am William Decklan, but you can call me "Nita" which is the short version of my native name. I was the first to find the riff and I will be your guide."

"Glad for your help Mr.—er, Nita," I said.

"Then let's get crackin'," he said, tugging on the horse's reins, leading the way.

The familiar blinding light of Guāng zipped from the group of Deities and settled over my right shoulder, his presence reassuring.

We followed, all of us looking back to see each of the four groups of warriors wheel around to follow. The Comanches didn't wait but spread out to either side of the column, and a few moved ahead as a forward guard.

Behind us, we heard the roar of warriors as they met the lead elements of the enemy's armies. I was almost sick to my stomach as I took in the massive horde that drove towards them. I was slow to relax, even after the forest we entered cut off the sight and sounds of the war behind us.

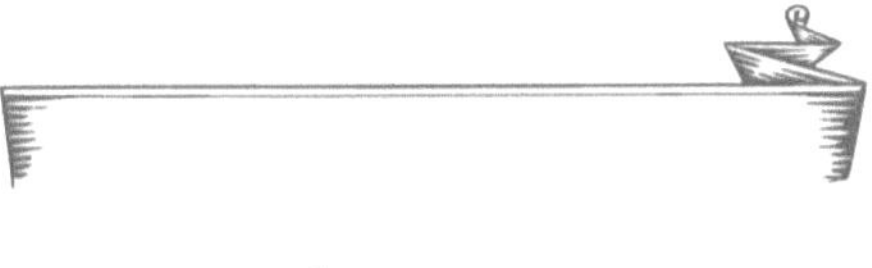

Chapter 7
(Adam)

The landscape seemed to change every hour or so as we followed Nita's broad shoulders. No one talked while we traveled and the only sounds were the birds that sang out in alarm at our passing and the thuds of the horses' hooves in the soft soil. We rode every time the land opened up but walked our horses through forests or across rocky terrain. Being new to the saddle, I appreciated the breaks as my butt and thighs ached from the long stints on horseback.

We stopped beside a fast-moving brook to allow the horses and ourselves a drink of icy cold water. Afterwards I questioned Nita about the route we were taking.

"Why don't we just have the Guāng carry us to the riff, like it carried us from Earth to Heaven?" I asked. "Wouldn't that be faster?"

He nodded flicking excess water from his hands before rubbing them across his leather pants. "It would, but the enemy would sense us immediately. As denizens of their own Heaven, which has similar characteristics, they would feel the use of divine power. They would travel towards us in a similar manner or at the very least figure out what we have planned. By moving without Heaven's power, they stand less chance of finding us."

"How long will it take to reach the riff?" Freddy asked stretching the tension from his lower back.

"Normally it would take a week, but we're not taking the most direct route in case it's being watched." The mountain man dipped a water skin into the water for a minute before tapping in the stopper with the palm of his hand. "Fill your own water skins which should be tied to your saddle horn and get ready to ride. We still have about four hours before we make camp."

True to his word, we rode for most of the afternoon before entering a dense cover of cedars that sat at the base of a sheer cliff. Three Comanche warriors sat around a small smokeless fire and pointed to a rope for us to tie up our horses. Bundles of grass had been cut and piled as feed for the animals. We copied Nita and the other horsemen to remove our saddles and rub down the sweating horses before dropping our exhausted and aching bodies in the soft bed of cedar scale leaves.

One of the Suri women brought us food served on a wooden plank. There was rice and strips of dried meat which took a lot of chewing but released delicious flavors as it softened. The other leaders of the different war parties joined our fire to eat but very little was said until the same woman came to take our empty plates from us.

I noticed her bottom lip hung loose and drooped to below her jaw, empty of the disk I saw earlier. "Thank you. It was very good," I said trying to keep from staring at her bare breast which was exposed. I could feel my face redden at my discomfort.

She smiled, obviously enjoying my discomfort then turned and winked at Kwegu, the Suri chieftain. He laughed out loud, "My wife, Nabala, thinks you cute Adam, but will cover herself in the future to avoid embarrassing you and your friends. We understand you are not accustomed to our ways."

The other warriors chuckled under their breaths and I wished I could hide my face.

To change the topic, I asked, "Why would the women cook for us when they can just wish for a meal? My Grandpa pulled milkshakes right from the air."

"For two reasons," Kwegu said, his white teeth flashing in the reflection of the fire. "That little bit of power might be picked up by the enemy and lead them to us. But more importantly, my wife would thump me if I ate something she had not cooked with her own hands."

"Well said, husband," came a voice from the dark. "The Suri women must take care of their warrior husbands otherwise they would starve to death and crumble to the ground, like children." Her harsh laughter cut through the night and Kwegu bowed to me as if there was no room for argument, but he was all smiles.

From inside his robe, Hattori pulled a clay pot and poured a small amount of liquid into a small cup with painted leaves on its side. He raised the vessel as a toast and threw back the contents in a quick single swallow. Turning towards me, he passed the pot and cup to me and I took them and repeated his movements. As the liquid splashed against the back of my throat, I felt the immediate burn and fell into a coughing fit.

"It seems that tonight is a night of firsts for our young leader," said Hattori his thin lips pressed tightly together to avoid laughing at me, but mirth danced in his dark eyes.

I passed the pot to Ian who poured his own ration and drank with more caution, but the sudden intake of air exposed his shock at the liquid's bite.

"What is it?" Freddy asked as he took the items next.

"Sake," said Hattori. "Japanese rice wine."

"Cool." With no hesitation, Freddy poured and tipped the amber liquid in one fast swallow. His face darkened but had no other issue with the liquor.

Neither did Rob who passed the pot to the next person around the fire.

Once we had all sampled the rice wine, Hattori looked at me and said, "We have eaten and drank together as brothers. In the future when we are called upon to fight, we will fight like brothers." He gestured to the other chiefs. "We would like to suggest that each of us take one of you within our war party to teach you how to fight and protect yourself."

"I would appreciate that. I have no experience in fighting, especially with weapons," I said.

Freddy looked especially excited, where Ian looked nervous. Rob looked comfortable, and I knew he was open to learning new things

Hattori shifted his attention to Ian. "They tell us you are skilled at stealing. The Ninjas are the greatest at stealth and infiltration. We can teach you how to be invisible."

Ian's eye grew large and he nodded with excitement.

Kwegu spoke next, this time to Freddy. "You are a scrapper. The Suri love to duel. It is difficult and can be painful but we can show you how to best any enemy."

"Do I get one of those fighting sticks?" Freddy asked pointing at the long, smooth staff that leaned against the tree behind the Ethiopian.

"But of course. It is the first weapon all of our warriors must master."

"That's sick!"

Iron Jacket stood and placed a hand on Rob's massive shoulder. "Tomorrow you will learn to master the horse and learn the battle strategies of the Comanches. We will also teach you to hunt and track."

Rob just nodded.

The last war leader was the thin dark-skinned man who sat quietly on one leg while the other was bent before him. He sat watching me as if wondering if I was worthy. "Adam, I have fought alongside British, Canadians and Americans against the Japanese in Burma. We will make a good team, I am thinking."

"Thank you, Gopi Pradad Rai. I will try not to disappoint you."

"As our leader, you may address me as Gopi," he said tone indicating that he felt resentment that I, a mere boy, was to be the leader.

"You do me a great honor."

He nodded but said nothing and I couldn't help wondering if I hadn't already failed some test of his. I felt the heat of anger of being dismissed so easily and was determined to take everything he could dish out.

"Good," said Hattori. "You will eat, sleep, train and travel with your new brothers and sisters. It is time to get some sleep, for most of you." He looked over at Ian. "For you, your training will start now."

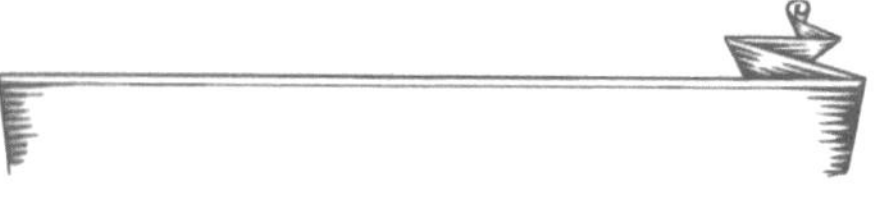

Chapter 8
(Adam)

Two hours of knife training upon waking had both of my arms aching. I struggled onto the saddle of my horse that had to be held by one of the others. However, looking back along the line, I realized that the Gurkhas were without horses and marched in three columns, as did the Suri warriors. Sliding off the horse, I gave the reins to Rob who was to ride with the Comanches. I walked back and fell into the rear of the column, but not before Gaje, Gopi's son who had led the morning training, threw me a wink. Guāng spun in place at my side giving a soft glow in the morning light.

"Good morning, Adam," said Guāng, inside my mind.

"Ah...good morning."

The man beside me nodded. "Good morning."

"If you talk to me with your thoughts, I can hear them," said Guāng. *"That way, our conversations are private and it won't look like you're talking to yourself."*

"Like this?" I tried.

"Perfect. When you wish to speak with me start the sentence with, Guāng. This way I will know I am the target of your conversation. It also keeps your thoughts private as I would never trespass your inner thoughts."

"So, what are you?"

"I am a messenger. In your faith, you called me the Holy Spirit. God sent me with the messages to people of your faith."

"Whoa... that's pretty incredible." I shook my head as I was having trouble wrapping my mind around all these revelations. *"So, why are you here?"*

"To help you anyway I can and then to speed back with news once you have entered the riff."

Minutes later we started moving at a quick pace. The Gurkhas followed the teachings of the British Army when it came to forced marching. They used long strides when marching for a distance of four hundred yards and then jogged for two hundred. This allowed the troop to cover a lot of territory without exhausting the soldiers.

Not for the first time was I glad they had toughened me up during my time at the bootcamp. The weeks dragging logs through the bush had hardened slack muscles to that point that even though the marching was rigorous; I could keep up.

We stopped for an hour under a canopy of leaves to eat a light lunch of rice and dried beef that had been cured in a sweet teriyaki sauce. Although I saw Freddy and Ian in their groups, we did not get the chance to talk. Ian was curled in a ball fast asleep. I knew he started his training last night, but had no idea how late it lasted. There was no sign of Rob and

I figured that he was with the Comanche outriders and wouldn't come back before the troop stopped for the night.

"Don't drink too much water, Adam," said Gaje with a warm smile. "You will end up with cramps. Just enough to rinse your mouth. When we stop to make camp, you can drink until you float."

We continued the march under a clear sky. It was warm but a steady breeze kept us comfortable and my mind ran through a thousand questions regarding Heaven. It looked and felt just like the earth with one sun. Were we just on another planet or was it a parallel dimension? And the idea that God was missing. How does that work? Did He just leave our universe to journey to another or was He creating others and was too busy to return? He must know what we are facing otherwise He would never have left this prophecy in the first place.

The column stopped so suddenly that I walked into the man in front of me and if not for helping hands, we would have both gone down. We stood in a tense group and I noticed that most of the men had their hands on their knives. Others held bows at the ready, arrows already notched. Other than the breeze rustling the knee-high grass, I could hear nothing. It was like the entire world held its breath. With no commands, the column had compressed into a rough square, all eyes and weapons pointed outward for any threat. Guāng's glow was muted and he hovered just above the grass as if he did not want to bring attention to us.

The man beside me indicated that I should scan the area behind our position as the rear flank. Not knowing what I was looking for had me jumping every time the grass swayed or a bird fluttered by, imaging an army creeping under its cover to surprise us.

From the head of the column, the muted clomps of shoe-less horse's hooves reached the rear column and glancing back, I saw one of the Comanche warriors trotting alongside the square of soldiers. A single horse trailed behind him. He stopped and conferred with the Gurkhas leader, Gopi before moving down the line.

"Adam, they need you up front. There has been a development."

I swung my head towards Gopi who nodded his permission to break ranks. The Comanche warrior extended a leather rein towards me and once I mounted the animal, turned to lead us forward. I felt the eyes of every warrior on me as we passed and couldn't help feeling unsettled. These were the finest fighters in the world's history and I, an untrained and untried kid was to be there their commander? I felt like a fraud. Why was I chosen? There had to be another person with two different colored eyes who was the real leader of the prophecy. I knew nothing about fighting. I would get us all killed.

In minutes, I dropped off the horse to stand with Iron Horse and Hattori. Pulling his face scarf down, Hattori bowed his head towards me. "We have just received a scout's report of a sizable force of the enemy to the north-east of our position," he said pointing in the direction. "They have a large group of prisoners. Do you wish to free the captives or avoid detection?"

I was taken aback by the question and my expression must have shown it. Hattori's stern expressions seemed to tense while Iron Horse snorted and rolled his eyes. I knew I had no experience but they must have known of it as well. I felt a surge of anger at their derision.

"Can we attack with the assurance that none would escape to tell of our location?" I said trying to rein in my frustration. I needed to act with a cool head or they would treat me like a child. "We can't afford to allow one to get away. It will lead their entire army to us and we would be finished before we even reached the gate."

The glitter in Hattori's eyes was the only indication that he was pleased. "Hai! My men and the Gurkhas can enter their camp after dark and wipe them out before they know we are among them. The

Mori and the Iron Horse's people can cut off any who try to flee."

I looked at the grim-faced Comanche and he nodded his head. It was the closest thing to a conversation I could hope for from the warrior.

To avoid detection, our marching column had broken into sections and took parallel paths to get ahead of the slower marching group who had to herd their captives along. The Mori, who could run like the wind, took a heavy loop to the south and had disappeared from sight in minutes. We took a shallower angle, while the Ninja continued on, but walked rather than take the chance of being sky-lit. Guāng swayed back and forth through the grass, his light almost muted to avoid being seen. The pace increased and though I was freely sweating; it was not an all and out fast march. They could not allow the trek to wear out the men who would have to carry out the attack. Because of the pace, the breaks were more frequent and although I was only rinsing my mouth rather than downing it, I soon ran out of water. My pride wasn't tested though as others also drained their canteens.

DUE TO OUR LACK OF skills and training, Hattori suggested that my friends and I stay with the supply train and spare horses. The approach, he explained, had to be done with absolutely no noise if the attack stood a chance of success. The enemy force was almost twice as large as ours, but he assured me that if they could close on the camp without detection, the numbers would mean little in the dark. One man from each of the warrior groups stood guard around us in case the worst happened. They each sat with their backs to a tree waiting patiently to hear the outcome of the battle.

The four of us were quiet even though we had a lot to share of our own different experiences with the various warriors and fighting styles. The stress of waiting the outcome of the ambush was agonizing and I couldn't sit still. I paced between the trees, my ears straining to hear the sounds of battle.

"Be at peace, young one," said my Gurkha bodyguard. "Not hearing anything is a good sign. When we do hear the clash of swords, then it means the enemy is aware of our people. Let it be just before the kukri slides across their throat." In seconds of closing his eyes, his breathing indicated that he had fallen asleep like he had not a care in the world.

I shook my head amazed that anyone could relax at a time like this. I felt so helpless. This was my first tactical decision, and I was on the hook for anything that went wrong. Everyone of our men that might fall tonight was because of my choice. A decision I made because I felt slighted by the contempt of two seasoned fighters.

From the darkness, the screams were our first sign that the fighting had begun followed by the clanging of steel on steel. But the cries of pain and fear were unlike anything I ever had heard before. It sounded like high-pitched croaking like a frog that had been thrown into a boiling pot of water. The tortuous din drove ice through my veins and I looked at the bodyguards, who still sat relaxed, but obviously listening to the distant clamor with interest.

The fighting noises faded away in increments, with a sudden barrage of metal on metal followed by either silence or a scream of pain and hatred.

"Your plan seems to have worked well, young one," said my sentinel. "Congratulations."

I spun around and said, "How in hell can you tell who won, from here?"

He smiled and tilted his head to search for my face in the dark. "Because none of those screams were human."

His words stopped me cold as I realized he was right. All the cries of pain had been the high-pitched croaks of *alien* soldiers. An enemy I had not yet laid eyes on, other than the Scavenger back in the pool on the mountain.

The night seemed to last forever as I continued to pace. Ian and Freddy were asleep on either side of

Rob, his huge blanket acting like a tent for them as they cuddled for warmth. The four bodyguards suddenly rose and gathered their own blankets without a word. I stared at them confused.

"Our escort has arrived," said a young Suri, his smile bright in the darkness.

I had heard nothing.

"Hello, the camp," came a call from the darkness. "I am alone and my sword is sheathed." Seconds later a shadow materialized among the trees. One of the Ninja drifted into the clearing, his face scarf lowered and hands held out to show he held no weapon.

He bowed to me before approaching. "My master, Hattori has asked me to inform you that your plan was a resounding success. We have eliminated the enemy and it is safe for you and your party to advance." He bowed again. "We must hasten so we can move the hostages to a new location before we set camp."

"Thank you for the news," I said. "We're ready."

I headed for the packhorses when one guard said, "Leave it, Adam. They'll want you up front right away. Your friends will help us move the horses and supplies."

"Thank you," I said eager to see the results of my first order.

I followed the young Ninja out of the trees. We jogged across a large open area of tall grass towards another dark island of trees in the distance. As we closed on the large stand of trees, we could see flickers of torch light. My companion slowed and put out a hand to stop me. Raising his hands to his mouth, he whistled a low bird cry into the darkness. From the clumps of grass rose a Suri warrior, his spear at the ready. He acknowledged us with a nod and lowered himself back into cover. We trotted ahead until we were among the trees. I could hear voices ahead of me, the tones suggesting forceful commands and questions.

As I pushed through the final shadows, I tripped over something underfoot and landed face first in a clump of bushes; the branches tearing at my skin. One soldier carrying a torch helped me up, but not before his flickering light exposed an alien corpse. It was like something out of a bad horror film and I scurried back in shock, my hand on the handle of my Gurkha knife.

The soldier chuckled and gave the corpse a kick before he said, "The creature is quite dead, you don't have to worry about him." He waved his own kukri, its blade covered in a sticky silver film. "I killed this one myself. He didn't hear my approach at all."

"G-good job," I said staring at the hideous corpse. Indicating the torch, I asked, "May I?"

He handed me the light and I brought it closer to the dead body to get a closer look at the enemy. It had a humanoid form, but that was where the similarities ended. The back of its head and back was covered what looked like a hard shell. I pulled my blade and tapped the head with the hilt and heard a hollow clunk.

"The creature is completely shielded by that armor," said the Gurkha soldier. "Even the Ninja's famous steel cannot cut through. To kill these things, you have to go after the soft spots like the throat or between the smaller plates of armor that surround its abdominal areas."

Returning my gaze to the body, I saw what he meant about the chest and stomach armor. The smaller plates allowed for more flexibility for movement but also yielded a way past the shield. Even so, the accuracy of its opponent's thrust or cut would have to be precise.

Other than its two main arms, there were four more jutting out from either side, the appendages ending in small sharp pincers. Looking upward, the mouth was made up of four interlocking pincers, like that of a huge spider. Above that two large black eyes protruded from its head, supported by thick tendons.

"It looks similar to a lobster," I said in surprise.

The Gurkha laughed and said, "Except this little girl would prefer to eat you."

I gaped at the man.

"Oh, you didn't know that," he said pointing at the eight smaller arms alongside the creature. "If you get too close, they hold you tight with these claws while they eat you alive, starting with your brain."

I felt my stomach heave and had to swallow hard repeatedly to keep my meager supper down as I imagined the thing feeding on a human. I pushed myself to stand beside the soldier partially to hide my discomfort but also to distance myself from this disgusting life form. I don't think I could ever eat sea food again.

"You called it a girl," I asked. "How can you tell?"

"They're all female." He said spitting toward the corpse. "They lay their eggs within a host victim. After they hatch, the young devour the host from the inside out."

He laughed again at the expression my face which most likely looked like I'd be sick, if it matched how I felt. I turned away, allowing my gaze to sweep the area. Four or five fires pushed back the night and I could see many of the captives sitting in groups, a look of relief in most of their faces.

Ninja and Gurkhas moved through the groups handing out food liberated from the enemy. I spied Hattori and made my way to him. Seeing me, he bowed low, surprising me.

"Adam-san. Congratulations. Your first battle order was a complete victory," he said bowing once again.

"Casualties?"

They killed a few of the hostages in the fighting, but none of our fighters. There are a few injuries, but they will heal quickly."

A sigh of relief escaped and he put his hand on my shoulder. "Adam-san, a leader must sometimes put his people at risk. They will fight to the death as long as it helps you succeed. It is good you value them, but the warriors here decided to aid you in your quest whatever the cost."

I nodded. "What about the captives?"

"They have told us they come from several small communities attacked in raids by the Kleptons. There seems to be war parties roaming the lands. We will have to be vigilante if we are to avoid them."

"And these people?"

He shrugged. "We will leave the food stolen from them, but they will have to fend for themselves. They would only slow us down."

I nodded looking at the number of children that sat with their parents. I turned toward Hattori and said, "Have your men casually drop the idea that we march north."

He looked across at me and for the first time smiled. "Shrewd as well."

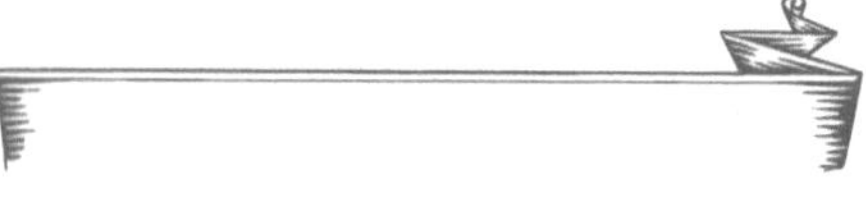

Chapter 9
(Adam)

The questioning cries of the birds and the lightening of the sky were hinting of the dawn when we left behind the captives we had freed. We were all exhausted having been on the go for a day and a night, but we had to put distance between us and this battleground. We moved unhurriedly in a northerly direction for an hour before one of our rear outriders rode in to confirm we were not being followed.

The column made a wide turn towards the west and then south until Nita, the mountain man confirmed we were back on track with the route he had planned to take us to the riff. Heading west again, we marched beside a large hill that stretched east west. Just as we could see where the hill dropped to the plane, Nita turned the march towards the mountain and into a curtain of trees. The faint trail we followed only allowed two men to walk abreast, so it took some time for the entire party to leave the open ground. We walked along the sheer cliffs then abruptly turned into a cutback between two rocky segments that looked as if a giant hammer had hacked them apart.

Nita guided his horse carefully across the broken ground, allowing the animal to move at its own pace so it would not spook. The trail cut back again and opened to a hidden valley surrounded by tall cliffs. Water fell across the far wall and I could see a sizable pool at the base of the rock. Stunted trees, among rich grass, dotted the valley.

"How's this for a safe camp?" Nita said as we trailed past him.

Safe indeed. With the one entrance, a few men could hold off an army, but on the same hand, a few enemies could trap us till we starved. I kept my mouth shut though, hoping the guide knew his business.

"We can have fires here as the smoke or light will not be seen from the outside," he explained. "And the water is clean and cold."

We spread out in our small groups and after arranging a guard schedule, curled under our sleeping blankets in exhaustion.

WE STAYED IN THE VALLEY for two days making sure everyone was well rested. It also gave the three injured warriors, two Ninja and a Gurkha time to heal. Iron Horse had sent out riders to watch for any sign of raiding parties but none were spotted.

Gaje continued with the lessons. He continued to focus on the kukri but introduced the bow.

"In my homeland, archery is a national sport and people come from hundreds of miles to compete every weekend all across the area. Since we cannot fight with the modern weapons here in Heaven that we were trained with while alive, my brothers and sisters have gone back to archery." He held up the fighting knife. "This is for close combat." Raising the finely made bow he said, "This is for distance—once you have learned how to shoot."

He taught me the proper way of holding the bow and notching the arrow. There were so many subtle things to remember that it took over an hour before I could hit the target. I spent as much time searching for arrows in the grass as I did shooting. The welts on my forearm grew redder, even as my fingers cramped from holding back the string until I was ready to release.

The down time also gave Rob, Ian, Freddy and I a chance to compare the fighting styles we were learning. Ian looked like he had always worn the black, loose garments of a Ninja and was so proud of his Ninjato, the straight Japanese fighting sword.

"I'm only allowed to use it for defense of a real attack until I can master the wooden Bokken," he said passing the heavy practice sword around the campfire so we could feel its weight.

"Damn," Freddy said holding the sword at arm's length, "you could do some real damage even with the practice sword. That's heavy."

With his arms held from his body, I could see the welts that covered Freddy's arms. "What the heck happened?" I asked in shock.

He bent his arm and ran a hand lightly over the raised skin. "Mistakes. Every time you make a mistake in stick fighting, your opponent lets you know." He threw his head back and crowed, "You should see the other guy!"

I rolled my eyes at his bravado but was concerned for him.

"Don't worry, Adam. I'm a fast learner." He raised both hands in reconciliation. "This is their way of teaching. They all have gone through the same training and it makes them tough as nails. As ferocious as they are in battle, they are a happy people who love to laugh and joke." He looked around the fire at each of us. "I enjoy their company."

I nodded and didn't argue. I could see he was being honest.

Like me, Rob was learning how to use a bow. Unlike me, they taught him how to shoot while riding. "It's all in the timing," he said pulling his arm as if he held a bow. "When you aim, you have to wait for the moment all four feet of the horse are off the ground, before you release your shot. It's at that moment that nothing can jar your aim."

"My God," I said looking at him in awe. "I've been working on shooting standing still and I can barely hit the target. To do it from horseback would be impossible."

"Tosahwi, whose name means White Knife, never misses. He's fantastic," Rob said nodding his head. "But don't feel bad, Adam. I'm getting better, but I still haven't hit the target that many times. Tosahwi has been shooting for almost two centuries now."

I had never considered that. Even though the man had died in the 1800s, he still followed his way of life here in Heaven. No wonder he was such a great shot.

I chuckled and said, "I guess we have more practice ahead of us."

"Have you noticed," Ian said after throwing another chunk of dried wood on the fire, "How different the adults here treat us as compared to back home?"

"No comparison," said Freddy.

"Even with this prophecy in place, they've accepted us as equals, not kids," Rob said leaning forward with his elbows on his knees. "If we fall, it's expected we get up or be left behind. But when we succeed, we gain respect and a place in the tribe."

I had to agree. I felt the hostility from Gopi and Hattori at the beginning, but by accepting the most menial tasks without complaint and working hard, they have grudgingly accepted me. My taking charge of the decisions of the raid also helped gain me some distinction, but I wasn't naïve enough to think they would not judge me the next time we faced an adversary or brutal choice.

By the time we reached the riff, I had to decide on which four warriors would accompany us across to the Klepton's version of Heaven. But unless I proved myself during our passage to the gate, no warrior will accompany me on his or her own accord. I had to show these mighty, accomplished fighters that I was up to the task. In fact, all four of us had to.

Looking around the fire, I could see that each of my friends was doing his very best to learn the ways of the different fighting cultures we had attached to. Ian's fatigue, Freddy's welts and Rob's sore backside were living proof of that as were my cramped fingers and tired legs from all the marching.

I felt proud of myself and my friends and knew that as scared as we were of this monumental task, we would be there for each other.

As the fire's embers began to cool, each of us knew it was time to get back to our own training group. We hugged each other, slapping each other's backs. Rob almost crushed me in the warmth of camaraderie.

Chapter 10
(Adam)

I ron Horse and his men slowly moved through the switchback rock cut that led out of the hidden valley. They left in twos: fifteen to twenty minutes apart. They would spread out and scout the land before the rest of us left the relative safety of the sheltered valley. We all were rested and eager to move on. Our water bags were cool against our skins having been refilled prior to breaking camp.

When the all-clear signal came, we rose in silence and moved in pairs, the dew still cool and fresh on the grass. The now familiar breeze greeted us as we stepped between the trees and onto the plains. Other than the high cliffs that hid our camp, a sea of grass unfolded for as far as the eye could see. As we marched, we spied hidden valleys and cuts in the land that held ancient waterbeds that waited for the rain to fall. Rob told us that the Comanches used these lowlands as a way to move across the land undetected, never sky-lighting themselves. In an environment where a tree could be seen for miles, it was prudent to stay hidden. In all the time we traveled those rolling fields of grass, the Comanches were never visible unless they wanted to be.

Marching forever west, we crossed the grassland, dipping into the valleys and up onto the plains. We were not worried about being spied as the Comanches were all around us ensuring there was no threat to our forces. The light breeze kept us cool until we dipped into the valleys where it was noticeably warmer, sheltered by the rolling hills. But the valleys allowed a chance for cold fresh water.

In the far distance, columns of black smoke rose high enough that it was visible. Whispers carried through the company that it might be raiding Klepton parties. It was common knowledge that they were running rampant across the back country and small communities that dotted the wild country.

"Only burning flesh creates that kind of black smoke," Gaje said in a harsh whisper.

We traveled in silence; each man captive to his own thoughts. At first, I found this stressful as my mind kept imagining the worst scenarios possible. I could almost see all of us dead, ambushed by the Klepton horde. My imagination was making me frantic and eventually I refused to think about the endgame. I struggled to stay in the here and now, concentrating on my immediate surroundings and while in camp, I would exhaust myself with knife, bow and hand-to-hand practice.

I could feel my muscles strengthening and my stamina growing from all the walking. I grudgingly had to thank the '3D's' for starting my transformation, not that I would ever admit that to any of them. I certainly didn't miss the hostility and malice. As long as we pulled our weight and worked at learning the skills being taught, the other soldiers treated us as equals. There was laughter during the meals, not the scared avoidance of punishment.

After a long day of marching, I was happy to see two of the Comanches waiting in one of the ravines to guide us to a good spot to camp. After following the stream that cut through the valley for an hour, we pulled into a shelter glen of cedar trees that grew beside the waterway. The heavy growth gave us plenty of cover and we all helped to gather dry deadwood for the cook fires which would be lit after the sun went down to avoid any telltale smoke line that might lead an enemy force towards us.

Once that chore had been completed and our bedrolls spread out, we began our training regime, starting with the bow, before moving to the knife. Calluses had formed on my fingers that pulled back the bowstring and it hurt less every day. Gaje had formed a guard for my forearm to absorb the slap of the string. I could finally hit the target more times than not and was feeling good about my progress.

With my arms aching, my brothers and I made our way to the stream where we washed before supper. The darkness hid my nakedness as I washed the sweat from my body. There was a low murmur of voices as the men spoke about the training or about the land we crossed. After pulling on our clothes, we made our way to the cook fires and were served by the two Suri women, both fully clothed to my relief. Before I could sit down, Gaje crossed over and told me my training wasn't over yet and that I was to meet him at the edge of the camp once I had eaten.

Curiosity competed with the exhaustion of the day's efforts. After eating and returning my washed plate to Nabala with a nod of thanks, I walked through the camp, nodding at the other warriors. Within minutes I stood under the cover of the trees before an open area. Other than a soft scratching of leaves rustling by the wind and the gurgle of the stream, there was no sign of life. I looked back to-wards the camp for Gaje or one of the other Gurkhas who was to teach the new lesson.

With no warning, a hand reached over my shoulder and I felt the cold kiss of steel on my throat. I froze.

"You'd be dead, Adam," Gaje said in a quiet whisper. "You need to attune yourself to the night and be able to move without noise. In my father's fight against the Japanese, his men became feared by sneaking into an enemy encampment and slicing the throats of every soldier while they slept. Tonight, you will learn to move like a ghost."

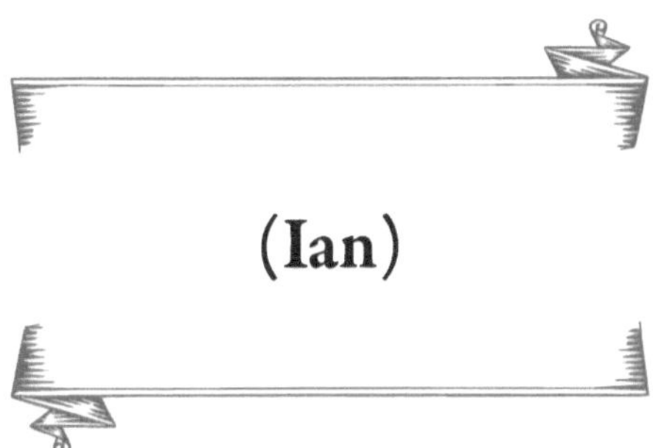

(Ian)

Like the others, I marched. Every day, my feet moved me forward with the troop, but I in a stupor, not seeing the scenery. One foot in front of the other, a zombie on the only road moving forward.

I was so exhausted and wished only for a night that Hattori allowed me to sleep until the break of dawn. I never imagined I'd view the rigors of the bootcamp as luxurious. To sleep in to 7:00 A. M. was only a pipe dream now.

Regardless of how tired I was, I was attaining some skills that Hattori and his men were teaching me. Tonight, they tasked me with approaching one of the Gurkhas guards that stood watch while the men slept. Dressed in my black shozoko, which covered my entire body, leaving only the eyes visible, I crept through the grass and approached the camp. I knew one of the other Ninjas was somewhere in the dark observing my technique. After my attempt, they would break down my efforts and explain to me how I could improve my approach or withdrawal. If detected, I would fail the exercise.

I crouched beside a clump of bushes for what felt like hours, waiting and listening for some sign to show where the guard was situated. Finally rewarded, I heard a suppressed yawn, off to my right, I paused. I waited until the second yawn came through the still night air. On my hands and feet, I moved forward, feeling the ground for anything that might snap or rustle as I passed. I slowly moved branches to one side as I parted the stalks of grass with steady hands.

One would think that moving quietly and not exerting one's self would be easy, but the time it took to approach the guard saw me sweating. The concentration, fear of discovery, and my own self-doubt caused my clothes to stick to my skin. More than once, I had to wipe the sweat from my eyes with careful, slow movements so not to make any noise.

It was strange, I thought, that during these exercises, my fatigue was gone. I was on high alert.

Finally, I saw the man's outline, a shade lighter than the shadows of the tree he stood beside. From my pant pocket I pulled out the folding stick. With minute movements, I unfolded the tool till it was three feet long, topped with a single feather that hung from the tip. I opened my left chest pocket, and meticulously opened another tiny jar and placed it on the ground before me. I dipped the feather into the jar, letting the bright yellow power in the jar adhere to the plume. Setting the stick aside, I closed the jar and returned it to its pocket.

From a prone position, I pushed the stick towards the guard until the feather touched the fabric of his shirt. My Ninja instructors had taught me that only the slightest touch was enough to transfer the yellow power trace to the target. With the same care, I inched the stick back towards me and collapsed it before returning it to its pocket. I lay still and allowed my heart to slow, before I retreated the way I came.

Gliding through the grass with the same methodical care, I froze when I detected movement coming from the camp. It was headed straight towards my position. The soft rustle of fabric against grass was barely discernible but after hours of sneaking about, I'd tuned out the normal and regular sounds in the night.

Peering through a clump of grass, I spied an open area of ground and a shadow broke from the far side. It stopped and lay there in silence, watching and listening. I saw a glint of steel to one side, the light reflecting from the waning moon outlining the distinct shape of a Gurkha blade. Was he hunting me or was he doing his own training? A thought came to me and I had to struggle to keep from chuckling out loud.

I had successfully tagged the camp guard and passed the requirements of my training mission. If I could tag the man in front of me, it would show my fellow warriors that I held potential and that their training had not been a waste of time.

I readied the marking stick again and waited in the silence for my new opponent to make his move. When he made his move across the bare ground, I began to push the stick forward between the stalks of tall grass. The angle he was moving would have him pass within a foot from my position. Keeping my face low so that there was no chance of the moon light exposing me in the darkness. The shadow moved closer in similar slow movements that they had taught me and it seemed to take an eternity for him to cross the open ground between us. The difference was they had taught me to go around such open spots; to stay hidden within the cover of the grass.

As the man passed by my position and began to enter the grass, I let the stick drop to just above his shoulders. I could see the yellow feather drag across the man's back as he wiggled further into cover. He would have a long yellow track down his jacket to prove my success to my new warrior brothers. I listened as he moved away before gathering my gear and moving towards the rendezvous where I was to meet my instructor.

By the time I reached the spot, I could feel the exhaustion dragging down on me. I had to struggle not to allow myself to make careless mistakes that might cause a sound. Inside the cover of a cluster of trees, I stood to find Hattori himself waiting for me.

"You did well tonight, my little thief," he said in a tight whisper. "You surpassed the original goals of this mission and tagged another." He put his hand my shoulder and pulled me closer so that his breath tickled my ear as he told me, "Wait until you see who it was you tagged. You are progressing well." With a warm squeeze of his hand, he said, "Get some sleep."

With that, he was gone. Even though I was learning, his disappearance unnerved me. Looking at the stars to ensure the direction of the Ninja camp, I moved forward silently. As I approached the sleep area, I heard a muted snap that seemed to come from my left. I froze in place and waited in a crouch. After a few moments, I was about to continue when I heard it again. It wasn't my imagination.

Someone was out there.

The first thought was it might be the Gurkha warrior I had tagged, but although I was able to mark him, he moved with a silence that equaled my own. I had been lucky only because I saw him before he saw me.

Moving in the direction of the sound, all thought of sleep disappeared. My senses expanded; I could smell the faint acrid smell of a dead animal further along the valley and could hear the soft swoop of an owl overhead.

I followed the valley, keeping in the dense shadows of the trees. The sound repeated itself a few more times and as I came even with the last one, I realized that it come from above the lip of the valley. Something or someone was moving on the prairie.

Taking my time so I would not make a sound, I climbed the incline on hands and knees. I could see the lip of the hill against the lighter darkness of the sky that was lit with vastness of the universe.

I eased my head over the lip of the cliff only to be grabbed by the throat. Something crashed into my head and I knew no more.

Chapter 11
(Adam)

I woke tired and groggy from crawling around the camp in silence, trying to imitate the movements Gaje had taught me. As I moved towards the creek to rinse the sleep from my eyes, I heard grunts of mirth around me. When I looked around, the other warriors averted their eyes or turned away to hide the smirk on their faces.

Bewildered by their actions, I was too tired to care. I bent over the water and splashed frigid water over my head. The shock helped wake me fully.

"You look like a skunk," a voice said from behind me.

Still crouched, I turned to see Gopi standing with his arms crossed a serious expression on his face.

"My son tells me that your training has been going well Adam, but it is obvious that your stealth and night movements require more practice," he said, impatience heaving in his tone.

"I don't understand," I said completely at a loss.

"Take off your jacket."

Still unsure what I had done wrong, I slipped my jacket off and handed it to him. He stretched it out with the back of the coat facing me and I was shocked to find a yellow line drawn from below the collar down to the waist. I raised a hand tentatively to the mark and it transferred to my fingers, a dry power like caulk dust.

"The Ninja tag is a sign that one of them was close enough to touch you without you sensing them." His eyes bore into mine. "But you are a beginner and can be forgiven. Expect another student to train with you the next chance we have. They also tagged one of our guards, a fully-trained soldier, and there is no excuse for that."

He tossed the jacket at me and turned on his heel. I couldn't understand why he was so upset. I had just started this training. He couldn't expect me to master it in one night. I felt my anger mount at being treated like a fool.

"Don't let him get under your skin," said Gaje pushing through the undergrowth. He took the coat, and while wiping the worst of the powder off with a handful of grass, "There's more on your butt, but you'll have to clean that off," he said smilingly.

"Why does Gopi hate me so much?"

"He doesn't. He was livid when he discovered they had tagged one of his favorites. Seeing you marked added insult to injury."

A black clad Ninja trotted towards us. He bowed deeply to me. "Adam-son, Hattori sends his complements and asks if you have seen young Ian?"

"Not since last evening."

"After his training last night, he was headed for our camp to sleep, but his bedroll has not been disturbed and we can find him nowhere."

I FELT HELPLESS SITTING in camp while the Comanches searched for Ian.

"Iron Horse and his men are some of the best trackers in the world. If anyone can find him, they can."

"But I want to help as well," I had said to Hattori.

"I know you do, but as Iron Horse hinted at, we could destroy any sign without meaning too. We have to trust in his expertise and swallow our own feelings. Waiting is hard. I would suggest that you continue training. It will help pass the time and get your mind off your friend." He stood and nudged me with his foot. "If you wish, I could show you how to avoid being caught unaware again by a Ninja scout."

My eyes swung to his bemused expression.

"You and the guard were marked by my youngest trainee."

"Do you mean—?"

He nodded. "Ian is a fast learner."

I chuckled at the thought of Ian beating me at this high-stakes game of hide and seek. Wait until I see him.

"I'm game. Teach me."

The morning flew by under the rigorous and relentless stealth training. Nothing was left to chance with the Japanese warriors. I was taught the fundamentals of camouflage and concealment. After lunch, I was taught how to move on all fours like an animal, low to the ground. Concentrating on hand and foot placement to avoid making noise. The Ninja used the elements themselves to help blend their movements. They would wait until the wind bent the tall grass to hide their own movements. They explained the deep breathing exercises and how it slowed the heart, yet fed the bloodstream with a strong supply of oxygen. I would practice in breathing through my nose and exhaling through my mouth. I was also shown vigorous exercises to build up my leg muscles so that I would eventually be able to leap higher which helps to scale a wall or climb a tree.

When they finally stopped for supper, I was exhausted. Although Ian was at the edges of my consciousness, the heavy training had helped. Freddy met me as I walked into the main camp.

"No," he said the anxiety visible in his expression. "What happens if he's gone? How are we going to fulfill the prophesy? It spoke to all four of us, not three."

"I don't know, but let's not give up yet."

After eating, Freddy and I waited while darkness fell. The mood in the camp was somber, almost like we were all collectively holding our breath.

I must have nodded off at some point, because I was startled by a cry off in the darkness. Freddy and I both jumped to our feet. Out of the gloom, the white blaze of an appaloosa bobbed between the trees. Iron Horse's features materialized and to my relief, the pale face of Ian looked around his shoulder. As he came even with the camp fire, Ian slid off the rump of the animal and we rushed to greet him.

There was a gash on Ian's head, just over the temple. Crusted dried blood matted his close cut, brown hair.

I grabbed Ian in a fierce hug. "I'm so happy that you are okay. What happened to you?"

Iron Horse answered for him. "He was surprised and knocked unconscious by a Mormon sheep farmer. The man thought he could trade Ian to the aliens in exchange for his family who had been captured yesterday a couple miles north of here. He will betray no one else."

With that curt answer, he pushed his horse towards his end of the camp.

I looked back at Ian, but he lowered his eyes. He must have witnessed the man's death.

"Come on," I said slapping Ian on the back. "You must be starving."

Chapter 12
(Adam)

I t was late afternoon a few days after Ian's adventure, when we entered one of the depressions in the land to find Iron Horse waiting for us. As the troops were assigned duties for setting up our camp, I was called into a war meeting.

Wasting no time, the somber native said, "There are three Klepton raiding parties ahead of us. My men report they are killing most of the people they find, however, some they are being collected for mating."

I felt a wave of disgust go through me and my stomach heaved. I swallowed hard.

"Once again, we can avoid these groups or attack to save the hostages," Iron Horse said. "But it will alert the raiding parties to our presence, as the hostage camp is also where they are storing their supplies." With a stick, he marked three spots in a loose triangle with a fourth in the center. "This is the layout of their camps."

I could feel the eyes of the Captains as they waited for my decision and I tried to ignore it and concentrate on the rough diagram before me. "How far apart are these camps? Would they hear the sounds of battle?"

"No, they are spread out across the plains. These two," he said pointing at the two closest to his feet, "are doing most of the attacking, while this one is acting as a rearguard."

"And where are we on this map?"

He tapped his stick behind the rearguard.

I studied the map and my thought went to all I had learned and saw since joining this band of warriors. A dozen plans surfaced and I rejected them until one seemed to make the most sense. I looked up at the men and said, "Using the same tactics as the other night, I would suggest we take out the rearguard and then the supply camp. If Iron Horse and Kwegu's men can contain anyone who flees, we can set up an ambush for the other two parties when they return for supplies."

The four Captains exchanged stern glances and I felt like I'd let them down in some way. Iron Horse finally broke the silence. "Good plan."

My chest filled with pride and I knew I was grinning like a dumb kid, but I didn't care. "Master Gopi, do you feel I have learned enough to be part of the attack? I've never been in battle before and feel it something I need to experience."

His eyes stared at the ground as he contemplated my request. For long seconds I held my breath before he gave a curt nod. "You will follow the lead of my son, Gaje and must promise to do exactly what he says. Losing you would destroy any chance we had in stopping the Kleptons."

"Thank you."

"Don't thank me. I'm not doing this as a favor, but because I have no choice," he said his eyes suddenly vulnerable. "I would kill a hundred enemies to spare you the pain of your first kill. There is no turning back after that." He turned on his heel and walked away leaving me wondering what he meant.

AFTER OUR EVENING MEAL, each warrior checked and rechecked our weapons. My wooden practice knife was exchanged with a real one, its blade razor sharp. I twirled the lighter blade in a blur and realized the heavier practice knife had strengthened my wrists.

Because we planned to attack during the night, there was no need to bring our bows, yet we took the time to wipe the weapon with a thin coat of melted tallow to keep it from drying out. The strings received a coat of beeswax to protect the fibers. All those who used the bow, either carried them by hand or tied them to the saddle, unstrung. This was to keep the bows relaxed until needed. It took seconds to restring the weapon and was done so while advancing the enemy. We would be leaving them with the supply horses, but this daily maintenance was a more active routine.

The others rolled themselves in their blankets to catch some sleep before it was time to move against the rearguard camp. My mind would not settle down long enough for sleep to find me and after much tossing and turning, I rose and left the camp so not to wake the others.

Guāng followed behind me. *"Is something amiss, Adam? You seem troubled."*

I shook my head. "Just nervous about the attack. I want to save those people, but at the same time I'm worried that it might ruin our chances of reaching the riff."

"Trust in yourself. You would not have been chosen if you were not up to the task."

"Do you mean everything is fixed?" I asked, turning to see Guāng's muted omnipresent glow.

"Not at all. You have the potential of doing this task and more, but you must stay true to your heart. The fact that you want to help those captured from the horrors they face speaks much of your heart." His light shifted to a lava limpish warm glow as if casting comforting thoughts.

His words gave me repose and I found myself breathing deeper. We continued to the small spring that sat in the center of the camp and filled my water bags after I brushed my teeth with a supple twig. From a pocket, I pulled out a number of wild mint leaves the Comanches had gathered for tea or fresh breath, and stuck them inside my cheek.

As I rose, Gaje and his father walked into the clearing.

Gopi nodded. "I see you are ready for the action. Remember to stay close to my son and apply everything we have taught you about moving quietly."

"I will do my best to make the Gurkhas proud."

He gave me a tight smile and moved towards the spring to clean up.

Gaje smiled and put his hand on my shoulder. "As much as I am glad I do not have to smell your bad breath, I would suggest you get rid of the mint. In the quiet of the night that scent might give you away to an alert sentry."

"I never would have thought about that. Thank you." I spit them out and rinsed my mouth to rid my mouth of the taste.

Around me the camp began to stir. Without any given orders, the warriors prepared themselves for battle. There was very little talking as each man checked the placement of his gear to ensure it wouldn't make any noise.

The Comanche and Suri left first so they could circle the camp. After a time, Hattori and Gopi waved the rest of us forward in two columns which would travel directly to the staging area of the attack. Behind us, a few soldiers remained at the camp to protect the supplies and the Suri women. Guāng bobbed up and down in a gesture of farewell.

"Trust in yourself, Adam."

I nodded and swallowed hard to depress the fear of heading into my first battle.

Chapter 13
(Adam)

Crawling slowly through the dark, I was glad for the slight breeze that pushed the long stalks of grass towards me. It would muffle any sound I might make while blowing the smell of my sweat away from the enemy camp. Knowing that I could face one of the daunting aliens in a pitched fight, stretched my nerves taut as a bowstring and I was drenched with sweat.

Ahead of my position, I could make out the outline of a guard, the light of a campfire highlighting him from the darkness. It was him I was moving towards. Through hand signals, Gaje had showed which sentry was mine to kill.

I could sense the quick scurrying of small rodents in the grass as they fled my approach. That they could sense me made me wonder if the alien might also know I was approaching. He gave no sign as he shifted from foot to foot, probably to stay awake.

I had to decide how to attack him. Gaje had given me a lesson in the Klepton's anatomy with regards on how best to dispatch them. He had walked me through both frontal and rear attacks. As I edged closer, I guessed the creature to be taller than me. A rear attack would have me reach around the alien's head to slice his throat if I could get my knife between his armor plates. My best shot would be a frontal attack. I would see my target and attack either from below or straight on. But that would mean that I'd have to crawl to its feet without it knowing.

Inch by inch, I closed the distance to my target, taking care to check the ground before me with a light touch to find anything that might make a noise or trip me up. Every time I did, it would take minutes to painstakingly move the object from my path.

Finally, I crouched within a foot of the monstrous alien. With minute movements I reached to my chest and carefully dragged my kukri out of its felt-lined sheath. Gripping the handle in my right hand, I placed my other hand on the blade's back, right at the curve. Counting slowly to myself to calm myself, I readied to launch my attack.

From off to my right, came a soft grunt of pain. The alien heard it too and his head swung in that direction. Using the distraction, I burst upwards, aiming my blade towards the crack in the Kleptons' armor plate below his throat. It slid along the plate below and plunged under the lip of the next. I felt a slight resistance as it cut through the membrane that sealed the creature's skin. As warm liquid gushed across my hands, I ripped the knife across its massive chest, even as her inner arms reached and pinched at me trying to pull me into its deadly embrace. The kukri finished its arc under the chest plate and scratched across the underside of the creatures' arm. I danced away to avoid its hulkish carcass from landing on me.

I wiped my knife with a handful of grass, but couldn't rid it of the slick goop of the Kleptons' body fluids. Of course, my hands and clothes were covered with its noxious stench.

My heart was racing as adrenalin pumped. I almost jumped from my skin as a hand clapped me on the back. I twisted and raised my blade ready to attack. It was Gaje; his grin visible in the shadows.

He motioned his head towards the camp and for me to follow. It took all my will not to let out a bark of scared laughter. Wiping the worst of the viscera off my hands and onto my pants, I took a better grip on the knife's tang and keeping low, I followed my friend towards the camp.

We reached the edge of a clearing to sounds of clashing steel on steel. Several lumbering Kleptons advanced on a pair of black-clad Ninjas, their razor-sharp Ninjato swords held at the ready. In a blur of shadows, the two warriors set upon the enemy, even though outnumbered. With what looked like a choreographed dance, the two delivered a blistering assault on the heavily-armored aliens. The swords grazed or bounced off the carapace until they closed with the enemy to deliver lightning strikes with the tip of swords. These attacks drove first to the underarms of the massive claws and then at the tight openings between the armor plates. The creatures squealed and staggered into their own kind as their rancid viscera poured out from between the plates. As their fellow arthropods tried to move around them, the two Japanese warriors used the distraction to press the attack. In seconds another pair were down and dying.

Gaje pulled me towards one Klepton who was issuing orders through her dual mandibles, in a series of clicks and snaps. He motioned me to hit low as I did the last guard while he distracted the alien who, through its actions appeared to be an officer.

Keeping to the shadows, we made our way to crouch directly behind her. When I was ready, Gaje struck the creature across the back of head with his kukri before jumping back. As fast as Gaje was, the Klepton almost caught him with her massive claw as she swung around with stunning speed for such a massive creature. Its eyes were on Gaje and it didn't even see me until I ripped my knife through its chest. In a last breath movement, the alien reached and grabbed my free arm with her claw and bore down. The pressure was excruciating, and I was sure she would snap my arm off like a twig. My other hand moved without thought and jabbed my blade between the two incisors, stopping them from closing. For a moment, I thought the claw would crush my steel blade with its brute strength, but the pressure slowly lessened as its life's blood left its body.

Gaje jumped to my side and needed to use his feet for leverage to open the claw enough so I could extract my arm from that death grip. I rubbed the offended skin both to soothe the pain and to motivate the blood to flow again. My friend helped me to my feet, and we surveyed the camp to see that the fight was over as fast as it had began. Warriors moved through the clearing dispatching wounded aliens or assisting our own wounded. We had lost one of our soldiers and three other had minor injuries.

I suddenly noticed the gore painted across my clothing, hands and knife and with a shudder. I staggered away from my friend and vomited into the underbrush. I rinsed my mouth out with the water bag that was being passed among the men, but was still queasy.

Hattori and Gopi moved among the men, speaking with each group, exclaiming their pride in the efforts of their troops. Seeing us, they headed directly our way and both bowed respectively to me. I was taken aback by the display.

"A great triumph, Adam! You've been bloodied and were victorious," Gopi said so every soldier heard his praise.

"Thank you," I said uncomfortable with the attention. "But this is just part of our plan. We must move on the main camp before dawn."

"Good point. We'll give the men a time to recover and then begin our advancement towards the hostages." His facial expression told me I had passed some test. I wasn't sure what it might have been, but his attitude towards me had changed.

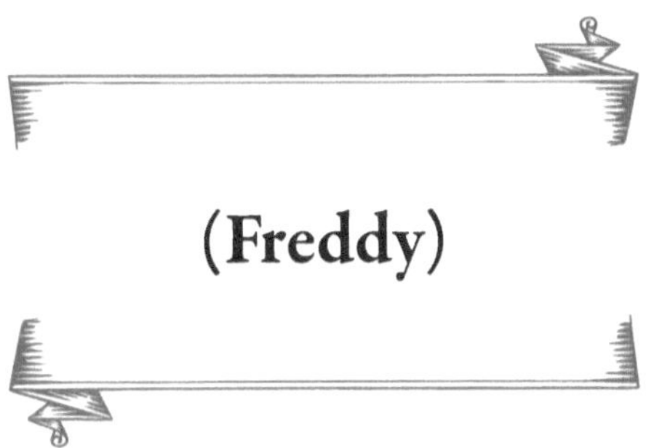

(Freddy)

The main camp proved less defended, and we swarmed the small guard that kept the hostages contained. I sat near a clump of branches to breakup my shadow when one of the remaining Kleptons ran towards my hiding place to escape the carnage of the attack. Although her armor gave her flexibility and ultra protection, she sounded like an elephant during the rutting season. The two antennae scanned for threats as she lumbered towards me. I waited to the last moment, until I saw the top of her head over the grass that I crouched behind. I wedged the base of my spear into the ground and stood so the enemy could see me. I kept the leaf-shaped metal spear point just under the swaying grass, so the alien would not see the danger.

Thinking me an easy kill, she charged me—exactly what I wanted her to do.

The ground moved as her huge form lunged at me. I had to stand firm. To flinch or turn in the way I hoped to escape this behemoth would give me away. When her massive chest towered over me, blocking the sky, I lifted the spear tip to chest level, pushing the butt of the spear deeper into the dry soil.

With arms stretched wide to corral me into the snapping lower arms that extended from her abdomen, the alien had no time to react to the sudden appearance of my weapon. The leaf-shaped blade slid over two armor plates before the Kleptons' momentum and weight forced the tip into the vulnerable areas of its innards. The shaft of the spear snapped in two as the monster over ran my position, collapsing in a shuddering heap of flesh and carapace.

Looking in horror at the putrid slime that covered my hands from the creature's innards, I had no incentive to retrieve the spear tip.

It was my first kill and I screamed a raged victory cry. I was pumped at the way I used the skills the Suri taught me to take down an attacking opponent. In all my elation, I had left my guard down and a second Klepton rushed me.

It caught me flatfooted as this seven-foot-tall monster ran straight towards me. I was now unarmed, except for my fighting sticks. I ripped them from where they sat on each hip. Both flexible and strong, each stick was about two feet long, and at the base and was about one and a half of an inch thick.

Over the past few weeks, I had been on the receiving end of these crude but effective weapons, but now I was hoping to dish out some effective damage.

I wasn't sure if my sticks would impact the rushing monster especially with all its armor, but with no choice, I ran forward to meet her charge. As we closed, she raised one of her large claws to crush me to the ground. I threw myself at the alien's legs and braced for impact. Those hardened limbs cracked against my spine causing me to see stars, but I heard rather than saw the Klepton trip and fall face first into the dirt before tumbling over onto its back. It sounded like wooden wind chimes being tossed by the wind as the armor clanged on itself.

It was all I could do to rise to my feet, the pain in my back was excruciating. I only had one of my sticks, the other lost on impact. I scrambled to find it, impeded by my pain it took me longer than I liked.

The Klepton was squirming to roll itself over so it could gain its feet. As I moved towards it, the creature swung its claw, attempting to crush my legs. I jumped back, crying from the pain in my back.

Warily, I circled the beast, so I stood behind its head. It swung first one and then the other large claw, but I held back waiting as it tired itself out. The Klepton sputtered several clicks towards me and I guessed she was cursing me or trying to explain what she would do if caught me. It was a good thing I couldn't understand because I didn't need the distraction of becoming angry.

Timing my strike with the fall of her claws, I reached in and struck one of her extended eyes with my hardened fighting stick. The anthropoid let out a high piercing scream that hurt the ears. She was thrashing madly in pain rather than trying to stand up. Using the other stick, I swung at the other eye, but caught part of the carapace as she rolled back and forth. I waited until her movements slowed and tried again, but she raised one of the smaller arms and caught my stick in its pincer. With a twist, it pulled the weapon from my grip. I launched a second swipe with the other stick and heard the arm crack at the elbow; as my lost stick fell beneath my opponent. A painful grunt came from the creature and it settled to wait for my next attack.

I only had one stick left and even if I managed to blind the Kleptons' remaining eye, I still could not finish the kill. Even though it was my enemy, I wanted to kill her clean. It made me sick to see her suffer even though I know she would do the same to me and my fellow humans given the chance.

With no choice, I stepped away from the prone enemy and raised my fingers to my mouth, to whistle a long and loud trill that carried in the night. To my disgust, I found that my fingers were covered in the body fluids of the first Klepton I had speared. While I waited for one of my Suri brothers to arrive, I spit out a river, trying to clean out my mouth.

In minutes, I had two warriors join me from either flank. They took in the two enemies I downed and began to dance vigorously around me, praising me as a great hunter. With some effort, I finally stopped their celebration to explain that I could not dispatch the second Klepton because my spear had broken.

"Freddy, you must use my spear. It would do me great honor. You must count the kill," one hunter said handing me his spear.

I nodded my thanks and walked around the beast so I was at her feet, raised the spear and rammed it between its chest plates. The creature stiffened and then convulsed for a few minutes until it became still. Pulling the spear loose, I took care of cleaning the blade of the stinking viscous before returning the weapon to its owner with my thanks.

The two began dancing all over to my embarrassment. Their cries and singing attracted more warriors, and I had to suffer more celebrating.

"You've become a man and a warrior tonight, my friend," said Kwegu when he arrived, his strong white teeth bright in the darkness.

He gave an order and two Ethiopians began chopping through the armor of the first creature I had killed. After much effort, they retrieved the spearhead from the corpse and returned it to me.

"In the morning, my wife will craft a new spear for you, so you will be ready to fight again."

"Thank you, Kwegu."

"No, my friend, you do me honor. You have proved yourself an equal to every Suri warrior."

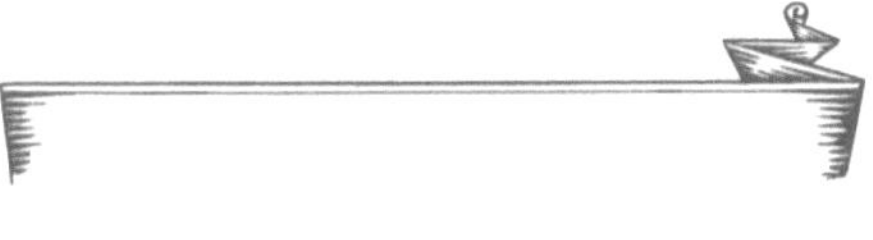

Chapter 14
(Adam)

The morning light saw one hundred and thirty-two people eating their fill from the stolen supplies. The survivors had been forced to carry their own food to keep them alive until they were needed to feed the aliens. Two of the survivors; a man and a woman, were watched closely because they had been reported to be impregnated by their Klepton captors and could release several immature aliens at any time. The two begged the warriors to kill them, but the leaders were at an impasse on what to do.

"The humans will die, regardless. Killing them now will also kill the brood within them," said Iron Horse his perpetual scowl seemingly to hold more weight.

Hattori agreed with the Comanche while Kwegu and Gopi sided with leaving them live in case the seed hadn't germinated. "If something went wrong, and the seed was dead, killing these two will waste precious life."

Because of the stalemate, they called on me to decide. I was horrified at being the one responsible to make the choice. Each explained their reasons.

Begging time to think before deciding, I asked the Captains to continue the work of preparing the ambush. We still had two sizable raiding forces to contend with and needed to be ready before they showed up.

I first walked to the simple shelter that housed the two. It was just a lean-to meant to keep them comfortable while they awaited their fate. Four soldiers guarded them, just in case the aliens began to hatch. It would be their job to kill each of the off-spring before they could escape or attack our people.

I walked up to the shelter and sat across the fire from the two victims. Guāng hovered over my right shoulder and his presence gave me strength. I needed to know these two as individuals. The idea of killing fellow humans was horrifying, but I hoped that the more I knew of them and their feelings, the better armed I would be to make this irreversible decision.

"Please tell me about yourselves and how you can be sure they have infected you," I said.

"I'm Bray and I am... or I was a horse farmer. That was until they raided us. Those aliens butchered my entire herd, and I was helpless to stop them. I can still hear their screams as they died. Afterwards, one of the Klepton leaders had me stripped, and they drove a hollow spear-like appendage into my stomach." He raised his shirt to show an angry red wound just over the belly button. It was partially healed but looked painful. "She injected me with something, which we later heard was how they multiplied. That was two weeks ago and now I can feel them moving inside, getting bigger." He was rocking, holding his stomach, tears of fear silently sliding down his face.

The woman's lip was quivering as she undid her blouse and opened it with no regard to her nakedness. I tried to avert my eyes as she pointed at an area of her stomach where she too carried the mark of injection. The wound seemed better healed but to my horror, I could see movement beneath the skin. It rippled and bulged in a couple of different areas across her abdomen.

"Please... please kill me before they start feeding. They're starting to wake." She was shaking violently, and the man put his arm around her and pulled her to his chest when she broke down completely.

I don't remember rising or leaving that place. I staggered through the clearing and out onto the plains. For how long I stood there I didn't know. It was only when I heard my name being called did

I actually see my surroundings. Guāng spun before me, his soft light ebbing with concern.

"*I am here to help you, Adam.*"

"How can anyone ask me to make this decision? I'm just a kid, not a murderer."

"*It would not be murder. They were both dead the minute it impregnated them. Having them killed would be an act of mercy.*"

I began to sob uncontrollably as the weight of responsibility crushed me. Suddenly, I felt warmth infuse me and some grief and pain diminished. Turning toward Guāng I saw that his glow extended over me. It didn't take away the feelings that threatened to overwhelm me, but they became manageable.

"Thank you," I muttered taking a deep breath. Guāng spun quietly allowing me contemplate what needed doing. The decision might have been mine to voice, but it wasn't a simple decision. As Guāng said, it was an act of mercy to put them out of their suffering.

Turning, I strode back into the camp and sought out Hattori. "Can you promise to dispatch them with as little pain as possible?"

His dark eyes softened, perhaps understanding what I was feeling. "Hai, neither will feel a thing."

"Then see to it, quickly. And be ready in case any of those things are still alive."

He bowed deeply, a sign of respect and marched away to fulfill his orders.

I stood there, my guts turning at the choice I made. Ordering the killing of these two pathetic refugees might be a mercy, but I couldn't help feeling like a coward to make another man do the job. I don't know if I was the right person for the task because my skills with the knife or sword were so new. But no matter how hard it was, I had to be present to witness an act that came from my decision.

Closing my eyes to the horror I might witness, I walked behind Hattori biting almost through my lip, struggling to gather myself.

I heard Hattori advising the refugees of my decision as I approached the lean-to. Upon hearing the verdict, the woman collapsed while the man sobbed in silence. As they recognized my presence, the man clasped his hands before him and bowed to me. "Thank you, Master," he cried.

The woman looked up and seeing me, her eyes full of tears, nodded to me and performed the sign of the cross.

Hattori had the two kneel facing away from each other so they would not witness the death of each other. Both bowed their heads in acceptance of their fate, their bodies relaxed, as if this was a welcome release for them.

Beside them, Hattori drew his sword in a smooth, controlled movement. From his uniform, he drew a flask and poured the contents over the blade to cleanse it. Taking a rag, he carefully dried the blade. He slowly raised the sword into position so it stood high over his shoulder ready to descend towards the man's bare neck. His eyes flickered to me for a final acknowledgment.

I held his eyes for a moment that seemed to elongate, before nodding.

Without hesitation, the sword flashed downward and neatly carved through the man's neck, severing it from his body. Hattori's blade turned in an arc and continued in the opposite direction without pause to decapitate the woman, even as the man's body collapsed and went still. There was no expression or cry of pain and I was sure they found peace.

If this scene would not haunt my remaining days on earth, the next would sustain all the nightmares of a lifetime.

From the woman's corpse, came a wet ripping sound and multiple creatures ruptured from the dead flesh. They looked like miniature replicas of the Kleptons but were the size of jumbo shrimp, their carapaces still soft and vulnerable. They scattered in multiple directions to escape the cold, cruel blade of Hattori, which flashed left and right with the lightning precision of a Teppanyaki chef. The Ninja archers skewered two which had escaped Hattori.

Silence settled on the clearing as the warriors ensured that there was no more threat. With a sharp order, Hattori's warriors cover the two bodies and knocked down the lean-to before putting it to the torch. I stood frozen as the flames consumed both victims and prey. Each soldier dropped a branch on the burning pyre as they left the area so there was enough fuel to completely release the brave souls.

Finally, it was only Hattori and I standing guard. He walked to me and put his hand on my shoulder and gazed deep into my eyes. "As hard as this was, Adam-san, you did right by these two. And they knew it. Hold that tight to your heart."

He walked off as I dropped to my knees and wept.

WE LOADED THE NEWLY released refugees up with as much of the surplus supplies as they could carry and pointed towards the largest settlement, which according to Nita was an actual city, New Chicago.

"It lies on a massive freshwater lake similar to Lake Michigan back on Earth, thus the name. All these riverbeds we've been crossing, drain into it."

"It's not a big as the real Chicago is it?" Ian asked watching them disappearing in the bend of the dry creek bed.

"Not yet, but it's growing so a man can hardly hear himself think," the mountain man said. "I visit from time to time, but I'm always happy to leave. I need wide open spaces and sound of the wind through the grasses.

"How long will it take them to get there, Nita?"

"If they have no problems, they should reach the outskirts in three days. Four if they drag their butts."

All the men had begun the preparations for the ambushes. We knew the general direction they would come from so set up our traps and conceal-ment facing those directions. Rob and all the other Comanches were scouting both enemy camps and would fall back as they approached our position. The only worry is that they'd return together, but the Captains assured me that the surprise attack and the orchestrated assault they'd planned would anni-hilate the raiding parties, even if both attacked to-gether.

Although we all worked hard in preparation for the coming battles, there was much laughter and clowning around among the soldiers. Every few min-utes, one man would trip another only to be running like the wind to avoid the retaliation from his victim or his friends. One fellow threw a pail of water across the backs of a group of workers, but then had his pants filled with sand while the others held him down. He had to strip to get the fine grains of sand out. This brought more laughter from the crowd.

"When the men are bored or anxious, the devil comes out," said Gobi a strange grin on his face.

"Were you like that too?" I asked looking up at him where I weaved long handfuls of grass into a frame of twigs that would be used to hide myself.

"As long as there have been wars, men have done this," he said subtly avoiding the question. "It is a way of ignoring the fact that he might be killed soon. We all handle it differently, but laughter helps. With Iron Horse and his men keeping an eye on the raiding parties, I know it's safe for the men to blow off some steam. I just wish we had a lake to play in."

It surprised me he opened himself to me, and felt I must be doing something right in his eyes. I needed his help to accomplish this mission. Was it the hard choices I've had to make as the celebrity leader this group? Or was it I followed everyone of his orders without hesitation? After this morning, I had little patience for any of these games. The only thing that might help is the coming battle. I wanted a little payback for those two tortured souls.

Chapter 15
(Rob)

Never in a thousand years would I have thought I would sit on a gorgeous American Indian Horse. Brought from Europe by the Spanish, it was a combination of Arabian and Appaloosa. It had the stamina to travel all day at a trot which covered a lot of distance. My thighs ached for the first few days and I felt that I never would master riding, but suddenly, all the teachings of my Comanche brothers came together and I was riding with confidence. Using my knees more than the reins to control the horse, she followed my lead without hesitation.

She was larger than most of the Indian horses; dark gray with a blaze of white on her forehead and socks. To me, she was the most beautiful creature in existence. I think I took as much joy in brushing her with handfuls of dry grass as she did in the attention. I named her Moonbeam.

"You take care of the needs of your animal," said Peta, Iron Horse's son and my trainer in everything Comanche. "Even before you take care of yourself. Without your horse, you would not last long in the plains."

Peta and the others wore my fingers off practicing with the bow, one of the Comanche's main weapons. Although not a marksman, I could hit the target more times than not. When I was feeling good about my new talent, they told me to practice shooting from horseback. While we scouted, Peta would set up targets which I was supposed to hit, but I found it impossible to draw a bead while bouncing on the back of a running horse.

"I've explained about the moment when all four of your horse's feet leave the ground. It's only for a second, but nothing will disturb your aim at that moment. Look for that calm spot. Don't force it, just let it happen," he instructed.

Over and over I rode waiting for the sweet spot. I had almost given up when—boom—I felt weightless! Moonbeams' body floated for just a fraction of a second and then it was gone. The pounding hooves hit the ground in a steady tattoo.

From then on, I felt that moment more often, and I started hitting the target while at full gallop. It would be a long time before I could shoot like Iron Horse, but I was improving.

I was learning how to track as well. All the teachings were from memory. The Comanche had no written language. They passed their knowledge down from one generation to the next through word of mouth or stories, and they taught me the same way. Every animal track we saw, they expected me to memorize.

"See how soft the soil is beneath the track?" Peta said. "This animal passed by here within the hour. If the soil was drier or more brittle, it would suggest a longer time period. You must train your eyes and fingers to tell the difference."

Some of the training wasn't as much fun as the others. Peta had me breaking apart clumps of animal droppings. "Like the tracks, the wetness or dryness of the droppings tells us how old," he said. "What it consists of gives us a hint at what the animal is eating which gives us a clue as to where we might hunt for him."

The Comanche studied everything in their environment not only to survive but to gain the advantage over the enemy.

The riding and walking - you need to give your horse a break - and the small, but basic meals had made a difference. There was a new lightness to my step and for the first time since I was little, I could see my feet. This life suited me; I think.

Over the weeks we cut the trail of the Kleptons many times and Peta would force me to tell him what the signs told me of their movement.

We had been trailing the movements of the raiding parties. Using the folds in the land, we moved unseen by the enemy. During the first close encounter, the troop marched past our hidden position in a clump of cedars; I detected a scent stronger than the pungent cedar bows.

"That greasy smell is from the Kleptons," said Peta.

"Smells like rancid oil."

He nodded. "Remember that smell. It might save your life one day."

We could see that this raiding party was breaking camp. The few humans were being pressed as mules, carrying staggering bundles of supplies. The Kleptons headed toward the main camp moving at a slow pace.

"Rob," Peta said, "you will bring news of their movement to Adam and the other commanders. Remember your training and do not allow yourself to be seen, but be quick. This group should reach the other camp by mid-day tomorrow." He clapped his hand on my shoulder. "Now go!"

It was a test, I know. I had all the training and now the responsibility to bring the word to our warriors without being detected. Immediately, I pushed my knee to Moonbeam's flank and left the clump of cedars. I let the mare choose her way as she had greater senses in the dark than I did. She steadily moved through the trees and navigated into one of the hundreds of gullies. She moved confidently up stream taking us in a roundabout from the Klepton's raiding camp. As we hit the prairie, I signaled Moonbeam to a steady mile devouring gait. We used every dip in the land to camouflage our movements.

We slowed up as we entered the last valley where our friends waited. I walked Moonbeam carefully so not to raise an alarm.

From above me, I heard a rustle in the leaves . I felt the razor-sharp edge of a blade press against my throat.

"I'd ask, 'who goes there,'" said a voice I knew so well. "But of course, I would recognize you anywhere, big guy."

My assailant pulled the mask from his face— Ian was grinning from ear to ear.

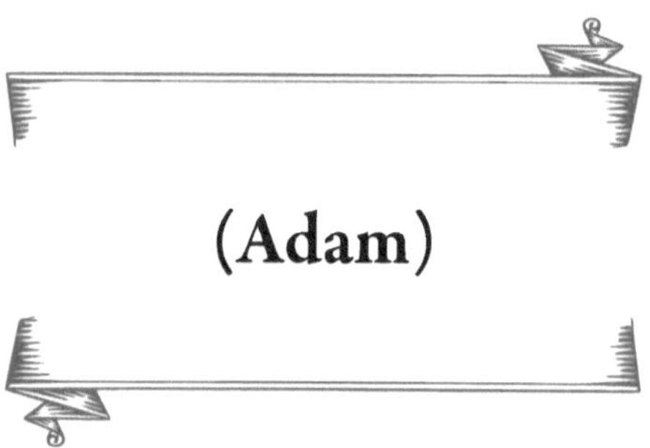

(Adam)

I watched the approaching column of Kleptons march into their camp from behind my grass woven shield. The Suri women had taught our warriors to craft these for camouflage in plain sight. When completed to Kwegu's wife, Nabala's specifications, each shield passed for a single clump of grass in a field of grass.

The enemy marched with confidence, pushing the collection of supply laden hostages ahead of them. If they wondered why their brothers standing guard at the entrance of the camp did not wave back, it didn't seem to make them suspicious. Gopi had a group of us prop up a few of the dead anthropoids up with the help of some tree trunks and branches. They looked alive to us from a distance, and we could only hope it would fool the raiders. If they picked up on the reek or slime-spattered armor, we might be in trouble.

Making a rough count, it looked like the raiding party comprised thirty soldiers. In the center of the line, there were two aliens that were completely different from the others. They were about eight feet long and were completely black. Their backs were covered with what looked like a hard carapace shell, but the sides seemed to be unarmored. Each looked like a massive earwig. Even their heads were free of protection. Each had two feelers in front of their mandibles while the long-narrowed claws served as both guard and weapons.

Looking towards Gaje, he mouthed the words, "Wizards. Careful!"

Wizards? How could I be careful, if I've never heard about them? What are they capable of? I crashed from total confidence to what-the-heck-am-

I-doing-here situation. My nerves were zapped right back to when Guāng yanked us through the depths of the earth.

It was the 'Wizards' that sensed something wasn't right. With an ear-splitting screech, the column slammed to a stop just short of the trap we'd set. The two wizards both stood on their hind legs as if smelling for danger. Their antennas were moving back and forth in front of their bulbous, black eyes.

For several tense moments, the two Wizards clicked and clacked between themselves, but finally they dropped to the ground in a more relaxed manner and the entire column began shuffling forward again.

We had decided it prudent to allow the humans to move through our lines before attacking. We intended on keeping the humans safe. They staggered under their heavy freight and I could not be sure that any of them even were aware what they walked into.

As they passed our position, we waited until the line of Kleptons followed and rose to Gopi's sharp whistle, driving our knives under the shield plate of the monsters. Screams split the camp as blades found their way past the armor plates and deep into the vulnerable vitals. Noxious fumes enveloped us as alien bloods oozed down our weapons. In seconds, we had decimated the first ranks of the raiding party to a mass of dead and dying.

Looking over the next rank, I watched as the Ninja who had been hiding in the trees dropped weighted ropes over the heads of the last rank. Once tightened, the lithe assassins threw themselves off the treetops in an arc that pulled the ropes tight like a noose around the enemy's throat. Comanches ran forward and added their weight to that of the Ninjas pulling the monsters off their feet to hang from the tree limbs like tainted fruit. Together the warriors took their time, shoving their blade tips through the thin carapace between the armored plates while the enemy dangled like a soap-on-a-rope.

The middle ranks pushed to help either their forward troops or their rear allies, depending on which way they turned. As they charged to help their brethren, we stretched two sets of rope taut through the grass from opposing sides. In the chaos, the Kleptons didn't see the hazard and tripped landing in the dirt. Half of them fell on their backs shuffling helplessly, unable to turn over and raise themselves up for the next assault.

The Suri bound through the tall grass like gazelles, carrying newly-crafted spears that were twice their normal length. After Freddy's experiences during his first battle, the tribe members had altered their tactics to attack from a farther range to avoid the Kleptons being able to strike from a ground position. They used those longer spears to reach in and jam the leaf-shaped metal spearheads under the armored plates with no fear of the thrashing giant front claws. We decimated two-thirds of the force within minutes.

On the outskirts of the battle, the Comanche were circling, containing the combatants and firing towards the enemy at every chance. Each hit to their armor sounded like hollow bamboo wind chimes being battered by a windstorm.

The two Wizards rose vertically on their back legs, to survey the battleground. They clacked at each other then simultaneously emitted sonic blasts bowling over anyone in their path. Other than stunning the warriors, it had no lasting effect that I could see.

Across the field, I noticed a Klepton towering over one lone Ninja. From his slight structure instinctively, I knew it was Ian. I was too far to help and I screamed a warning. I thought I was hallucinating from fear when out of the edges of my vision came a massive warrior on horseback. Just as the monster raised its massive claw, the rider jumped from the saddle and threw himself at the alien. A flash of steel arced downward before they settled in a heap.

Running forward, I arrived in time to help Ian up and see Rob using a tomahawk with more savagery than I thought possible from the gentle giant.

The axe rose and fell in a blur. Rob stood, towering over all of us. The creature that had threatened Ian lay convulsing in its death-throes. For a minute, I wasn't sure if he saw us. He was covered with alien blood and guts.

"You guys okay?" he asked without pause and I could only marvel at the difference a few weeks had made for my friend. The kid who always had to re-strain himself so not to hurt others his age, had been given license to let go. With full force he was permit-ted to hit or slam anyone who attacked him and he was reveling in it. I could only pray it would not go to Rob's head and he had become worse for it.

Without waiting for an answer, he turned and lumbered towards the two Wizards with no thought to his own safety. He took a hit of a partial sonic blast and it tossed even his great bulk to the side. Shaking his head to clear it, he rose slowly. He hun-kered down; an angry bull ready to charge. He hit the first Wizard, plowing right through it with such force that it didn't move again.

The second and smaller of the Wizards threw its hind end in the air and fired a star-light flare from its tail, skyward. The light rose thousands of feet above the prairie, before it exploded in a blossom of crimson like the world's best fireworks. As beautiful as the pyrotechnic seemed to be, it sent a cold chill through me.

We had announced our presence to the Klepton hoard.

Gopi, dropped his knee on the hard carapace of the Wizard while he savagely drew his kukri across the alien's unprotected throat. It thrashed briefly as its body fluids drained out.

The others recognized the implication also, as both Iron Horse and the Suri leader, Kwegu, called for their men and raced towards the remaining raiding camp, while we finished off the last of the remaining Kleptons.

Gopi and Hattori yelled at their men to hurry and gather our gear. The wounded were attended to immediately. We found that for the first time; we had suffered some casualties. They lay two Gurkhas out beside each other with as much respect as possible, but the one Asian had most of his head torn off from a Klepton's massive claw. As gut wrenching as it was to see men I trained with and eaten with lying dead when they were breathing just moments ago, it was worse for their companions. They had been brothers through two lives. Gaje began a Tibetan chant and the entire group joined him while they worked. These merciless warriors went about their duties with tears scaring their faces as they chanted their goodbye to their fallen comrades.

Chapter 16
(Adam)

The last of the wounded had been attended to when Iron Horse returned with Kwegu bouncing behind him, his horse lathered and blowing hard from the run. Releasing the reins, he dropped to ground with the agility of a much younger man. His grim expression conveyed bad news.

"They fled the minute the signal went up," he said the frustration clear in his voice. "Headed north at a fast pace. We might catch them in a couple days if they'd slow down, but my guess is they are running to a much larger contingent."

Gopi looked at Nita and said, "Is there somewhere we can disappear without leaving a trail? Once they reach their comrades, they'll be heading back with a vengeance."

Nita looked towards the western horizon as if looking at a map only he could see. After a minute, he nodded. "There is a place, but it will be a long march, especially with a hunt party at our backs." He scanned the faces of the other Captains. "You've all seen how fast they can move when they want to. It'll be a close race, depending how long of a lead we have."

"There there's no time to waste," Gopi stated. "We've suffered some casualties and we need time to send them on their way. Kwegu, one of them was yours."

"Who?" he demanded his eyes wide in shock.

"Kirinomeri."

A groan came from the Ethiopian leader and he ran his scarred hand over his bald head tried to control his emotions. "My brother's son," his eyes welling with tears. "Oh, how will I face him?" he muttered, walking away in sorrow. His wife, Nabala ran across the clearing to console him, but he held up a hand, halting her. She stopped and stood helplessly with her arms wrapped around herself, staring after him.

While Kwegu dealt with his grief privately, we still had to rush the make-shift funerals for our dead. With Nabala's help the dead soldiers were cleansed and placed on a pile of dead wood that all the soldiers had gathered. They placed their weapons in their hands or across their chests.

The remaining Comanche and Suri warriors arrived to find the funeral procession ready. When the Suri were told of Kirinomeri's passing, a horrible wail rose over the clearing. It was then that Kwegu returned and took charge of his people, swallowing his grief.

Hattori brought both Gopi and Kwegu in front of the funeral pyre. "Brothers," he said in a loud voice for everyone to hear. "We have lost three of our people today. Remember, they died as they lived, with a weapon in their hand. There can be no greater death. We will grieve them in our own secret hearts and in doing so they will live on."

He handed a torch to both Captains and stepped back as they lit the pyre. The dry wood ignited with a rush, engulfing the pile and the corpses in minutes. The heat drove the leaders back, stumbling into their men. For seconds the only noise was the fire snapping and crackling until it became a roaring furnace pushed by a breeze.

Hattori gave the order to get into ranks and the men slowly moved into their assigned positions in the column. Both Kwegu and Gopi were the last to form up as they lingered near the blaze. Without further word, the Comanches spread out on horseback to act as a guard while the rest of us began marching westward once more. I wasn't the only person to look back at the black oily smoke blotting the sky.

THEY KEPT THE MARCH at a fast clip. The Captains talked to the troops as they marched, explaining that they were headed to a place where we would lose any enemy pursuit that might already be bearing down on us. The soldiers took the news in stride. They knew the capabilities of the Kleptons and realized the need for speed, especially if they were racing from a superior force. I'd been told that the enemy could really hustle their troop movements, but hadn't witnessed it. To me they were slow and clumsy whenever we'd attacked them. Of course, I hadn't realized there were different aliens until I encountered the Wizards.

During one of our short breaks, I asked Guāng about the enemy.

"There are four different creatures that we've seen to date," he said. *"You know the Kleptons, of course. They seem to be the infantry; tough, armored and there seems to be a vast number of them. As you have*

*said, they seem cumbersome, but they can roll them-
selves into a ball, like an Armadillo and roll across the
land at incredible speed. This is what your Captains
are worried about."*

I pictured an armadillo, with all its armor,
rolling into the ranks of our soldiers and I shuddered
at the devastation that it could inflict.

*"You've also met the Wizards, who can throw balls
of sonic force at their enemies. They are considered
leaders."*

"Do they have any other powers? They're certainly not as armored as the Kleptons."

*"Normally, they're protected by the Kleptons. We
had surprise on our side this morning, which is why
we were successful in defeating them. It doesn't happen
regularly."*

"You mentioned two others?"

*"Yes. Our soldiers have fought against two special-
ist soldiers. One is a flier. It resembles a Dragonfly but
spits a glue-like substance that splatters the immediate
area. Any of our soldiers that either step into it or are*

covered in it, are essentially trapped in place to await slaughter. Time is the only thing that seems to help. The substance dissolves after an hour's time."

"Finally, the one you encountered in the pond, back on earth, the Scavenger." Guāng said, his glow being replaced with a replica of what I encountered in the depths of the natural spring halfway up the mountain in what seemed like a life-time ago.

"We don't know if it has any offensive powers or just acts as a messenger, like me."

"It was able to grab me," I said shuddering at the memory. "But it let go when it looked me in the face."

"It saw your two-colored eyes and knew that it saw its destruction."

"Do you mean that the aliens know about the prophesy?"

The sphere bounced up and down. *"That was why they were watching for you and why they attacked our main force upon your arrival. They need to kill you to stop the prophecy."*

WITH THE THREAT OF what might be chasing after us, the Captains pushed us hard. The next day and a half was a blur of putting one foot in front of the other, moving forward even though we were asleep on our feet.

As the time compressed, my thoughts ate at me. It was my decision to not only rescue the hostages but to also attack the two raiding camps. Was that just for vain glory? Was I trying to impress the Captains with my leadership abilities or was I fooling myself?

Guāng sensed my distress and bounced around me, but I was afraid that he might dismiss my concerns out of hand. He seemed to always show the most favorite side of any decision and not the hard reality of wrong decisions.

Three men had died because I thought rescuing the hostages was the main priority. And knowing what I know now of what the Kleptons were doing to them, I think it was the right thing to do. If it was, why attack the raiding parties? As mentioned, there was the idea that the enemy would have known our position.

Well, they did now. So, the blame lay with me. In a blinding instant of truth, I understood the meaning of the loneliness of leadership. You make a decision with the best information and intentions, but when everything fails, you as a leader, wear full responsibility. The buck stops here.

Step by step we closed on the distant mountains to the west. For days, they seemed to hover there above the field of grass, almost like a mirage. Never getting closer or fading further away. After nearly eighteen hours of the forced march, they appeared close enough to touch. Occasionally, when the wind was right, the scent of poplar and pine graced us with the knowledge we were close to putting this grassland behind us.

The grade changed subtlety, but our tired legs felt it immediately. We finally began climbing the foothills. Vegetation was ever changing as we moved higher off the prairie. Junipers grew in clusters while the grass and sagebrush still walked up the slope. Lodge pole pines reached for the sky in dense groupings which we circled around rather than fight our way through.

Nita, our guide pushed over a ridge and our column followed like ants on parade. It leveled off to create a shelf before plunging deep into a steep valley. A turbulent river that seemed to come straight out of the mountain base cut the valley in two. An updraft of air brought a cool mist of water, soothing us of the prairie dryness.

Nita began descending the slope on an angle towards where the river emerged from the granite. Looking back, the way we traveled, the grasslands extended as far as I could see. From on high, it looked like a barren carpet with a multitude of folds in the fabric. I noticed a dirty cloud that hung over the prairie far off to the northwest. It looked like a sandstorm, yet there were odd flashes of light inter-mixed within the cloud.

"Guāng?"

He spun towards the direction of where I was looking and immediately dropped to the ground and dulled to a mute gray. *"Kleptons! A lot of them."* Without another word, he sped along the ground towards Nita at blinding speed. It seemed he was at my side one second and bouncing around the mountain man the next. Whatever his message to the guide was, Nita quickened the pace, and the march became a run. Guāng zipped across the landscape to pass on the sighting to the other leaders who ordered us to a faster pace. I couldn't understand what the urgency was. The Kleptons were miles away. We should have lots of time to hide or find a suitable spot to make a stand. But no one was asking for my leadership advice just then.

Suddenly we were in the race of our lives.

Chapter 17
(Ian)

As we ran like demons chased us, Hattori signaled one of his soldiers a strange sign that I'd never seen. Before I could ask one of my cohorts what it meant, the one in question, motioned me to follow. Without a word, he turned and ran against the tide, back towards the lip of the summit. With no choice, I handed the reins of my horse to a fellow soldier and followed, my legs pumping like pistons against the steep grade.

As he approached summit lip, he slowed and crab walked sideways, moving across the top of it.

Not understanding, I followed suit. After about 200 yards, he came to an abrupt stop.

"I am Riku," said the Ninja in a soft voice.

"You're a girl?" I said in shock.

She pulled her facemask down to reveal a mischievous smile that was reflected in her eyes. "Women can be warriors. There are two more in our troop."

"Wow! I didn't know."

She smiled and kept walking. "Hattori-san has ordered us to watch the enemy's approach. He says you can speak to the Guāng through a mind-link so can communicate with the others what we observe."

"But I can't."

"Yes, you can, Ian," said a voice.

I started, looking frantically around for the speaker. From below, the globe that followed Adam around like a puppy slid up the hill, close to the ground towards us.

"I am not a puppy," said the voice. The orb spun in front of us.

"I am Guāng and speaking to me is like sending me your thoughts. Speak my name and then send me your thoughts. I can see through your eyes."

"O... kay," I said wondering if I was losing my mind.

A low chuckle echoed through my astounded brain. *"Give it a try."*

I looked down the ridge to the warriors jogging towards the river, and said, *"Guāng"*

"Perfect! You're a natural." It spun on the spot before saying. *"Just remember to say my name before you push the thought or image,"* said Guāng. With blistering speed, the globe sped back down the mountainside, leaving me to look at my fellow Ninja, Riku, in bewilderment. Seemed I was surrounded by surprises.

She raised her hands as if she didn't want to know what had transpired.

"We... we have been tasked with monitoring the enemy. I will show you how to build the perfect hide so we can observe without detection." Not waiting for any comment from me, she pulled out a bayonet and proceeded to slice the top layer of the grass that covered the shelf that overlooking the prairie lowlands. Putting her hands under the loam, she heaved on it and folded it back to reveal a rectangle of soil. She attacked the earth, loosening the dirt.

Satisfied with the results, she turned to me. "We must do away with the dirt so they will not recognize it. Break it with into small grains before you throw it. And ensure you leave no piles." She lowered herself into the depression and pulled the cover of sod over her so there was no sign that she was even there.

The slab of sod flipped up and Riku's face poked out. "Hurry, Ganji! The enemy will be here in minutes."

Moving closer to the edge, but keeping low, I carved out my own hide. After throwing the excess soil in all directions, I settled into the cool shallow grave in time to watch the enemy's approach. I was shocked at the speed in which they raced towards us. When Adam had first sighted them, they were twenty or thirty miles away, now they were poised at the base of the foothills, still moving forward.

To speak to the globe, I concentrated at pushing what I saw to the entity until I remembered his name. *"Guāng,"* I said inside my thoughts. *"This is what I see."*

A Comanche warrior jumped his horse over the lip of the ridge to land beside my hide. He was part of the rear guard. Looking further left and right, I saw more racing for the top of the slope, leaning forward as their sweat-covered mounts pushed themselves to Olympian efforts.

Further below, the Kleptons had arrived at the foothills. Like hard shelled wheels, they spun at a furious speed and climbed the slope like dirt bike racers, flinging dust and dirt into the air behind them. What took us over an hour to climb, they did in minutes. Just before they crested the ridge, Riku hissed a low command. "Down."

The ground rumbled and I could hear the crunching sound of rock against the exoskeleton of the Klepton army. I cringed, my eyes tightly closed fearing they would crush me under their rigid treads. Not knowing if my friends found shelter, one thing became crystal clear.

There was an entire army between them and us.

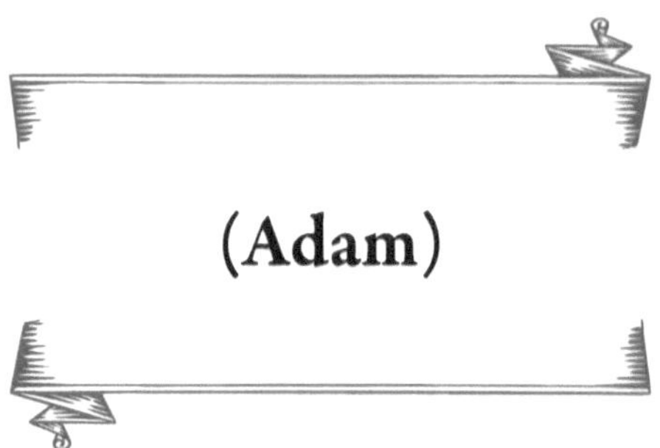

(Adam)

Running all out, my breath coming in ragged gulps, we headed towards the birthing spot of the watercourse. As we got closer, I could see that the water pulsed out of a ragged tunnel that had been carved out of the side of the mountain. The tunnel was about eight feet across and five feet high. Nita jumped off his horse into the stream, pushing against the current and ducked under the rock entrance. One after the other, the warriors followed, leading their horses by the reins.

As I entered the dark cavern, Nita put his hand on my shoulder. "Move to the left. Keep going to make room." This he repeated as each man entered the opening. Guāng turned up his brilliant glow and it pushed the darkness back to reveal a shelf that ran along the watercourse. Stepping out of the knee-deep water I wondered if the Kleptons would follow. There seemed to be nothing to deter them. With the narrow confines, we would only have to worry about fighting a few at a time.

Behind me the Comanches were guiding their horses through the entrance, speaking softly to the animals to keep them calm. I shuffled along with the others pushing deeper into the tunnel, but was relieved to see Rob steer his horse through the cave opening before the shelf turned a bend in the subterranean concourse.

Guāng's light faded deeper into the tunnel as he and Nita lead the way. The rest of us followed, each man clasping the shoulder of the man in front of him so we wouldn't stumble in the dark. Blindly, we marched on for what felt like hours before the line slowed to a shuffle. We were still moving, but at a crawl. Curious of the cause, my mind strayed as I crept on with my group.

Beside us, the river ran its course, gurgling in an almost hypnotic and relaxing way. Up ahead, Guāng's light showed what had slowed the column down. The ceiling above the water dipped to just where it hovered over the water, while above us our side of the ceiling seemed to close in. From Guāng's illumination, I could see a thick stone pillar on the edge of the shelf. It created a narrow doorway that each man had to step through. I wondered about the horses, but remembered that Nita's horse was near the front of the group so must have already squeezed through. The Kleptons might have trouble slipping through though. We stepped through the opening and kept marching, now in the dark as Guāng stayed put for the benefit of those after us. Behind us, I heard the nervous neighing and the calming voices of the Comanche or Ninja riders as they coached the frightened animals through that narrow doorway.

Time stretched in the darkness. Guāng bounced through the passage towards the front of the line. I had to squint my eyes at the brilliance of his light, but was saddened as it faded away to leave me blind again. There was something so comforting about Guāng's light.

Eventually we came to a massive cavern where we could spread out. The ceiling rose far above our heads, lost to the shadows. Stalagmites grew from the floor throughout the stone grotto and we marveled at the delicate natural sculptures. On the far side of the cavern another tunnel led deeper into the mountain.

"Adam!"

I turned to see Freddy approaching me with an open smile splitting his face.

He grabbed me a hug with real emotion. We had been so busy with our separate groups that there had been little time to spend with my friends. I noticed a bunch of lines on his arms and realized they were welts. I looked at him with concern.

"That's what happens when you let your guard down in stick fighting," he said, his eyes sparkling in mirth. "Great way to ensure you don't make the same mistake twice."

From the tunnel mouth, Rob's big form stepped into the cavern leading his horse. He waved but steered his horse away from us to where the other riders were watering their mounts. As the animal drank, Rob brushed the horse with long strokes with a coarse brush. Once done, he hung a feed bag over the horse's ears and filled it with oats. Only after taking care of the animal did he turn his attention to us.

In a surge, he grabbed both of us in a massive hug. "Damn, I missed you guys."

The big guy crushed Freddy and me in an embrace, then dumped us unceremoniously onto the cavern's hard floor with a boisterous laugh. He looked around before asking, "Where's Ian?"

Lifting ourselves off the floor we looked towards the Ninja contingent that had been the first to enter the cave system. Ian's small frame was nowhere to be seen.

"Guāng, where is Ian? I can't find him."

"He stayed behind with another to act as our eyes on the enemy," came the reply instantly. *"He will return once the Kleptons move on, or when it becomes dark."*

This did nothing to assure me. I had come close to losing him once already.

"Relax, Adam. I am in contact with him and he is safe."

But I couldn't relax. Ian had always relied on Freddy, Rob and I to protect him. He was a target at the bootcamp. Each of us had taken abuse from the three 'D's' to deflect worse treatment towards him.

Now, we couldn't be there for him.

Chapter 18
(Ian)

I heard a muffled bird call from outside my burrow. It sounded like the typical Ninja signal, so I risked lifting the sod and peaked out. Realizing I was still facing the slope and the prairie I slowly began moving I would face the river valley behind me. For the first time in my life, I thanked God for having been born short. My only hindrances were total darkness and the hilt of my sword which grabbed at every root within the damp hole.

After much grunting, hopefully muffled by the layer of sod, I raised the lip of my cover towards the tunnel where the enemy milled. They had transformed their bodies from the wheel-shape armored rolling juggernauts to the familiar beady-eyed, monster clawed, walking lobsters.

The group scattered around the river valley, looking for any sign of their prey. Repeatedly, they turned towards the deluge that erupted from the cliff face. After a few minutes of clicks and clacks of alien argument that echoed up the rock-face, a group of the anthropoids ducked under the low mouth of the tunnel.

I sent a frantic message to Guāng, and he accepted the news as if he had expected it.

Within the alien camp, they assigned the soldiers different watches, and I noted where each group of guards stood. To my horror, one such guard marched up the slope towards our position to stand not five feet away from my hide. If she walked around to stay awake, it would only be a matter of time before she stepped onto my hiding spot.

I lowered the lid of sod back in place waiting with growing angst for her to move on, but she never did. A heavy thud shook me upright.

My whole body tensed expecting one of those monsters either tromping on my hide or ripping my head off with their immense claws. Immediately, the clump of sod was ripped off of me, exposing me to the cool night air and Riku's black outline against the sky.

"Quick! Help me roll her into your hide," Riku said, her voice barely rising above the night breeze that swept from the prairie. The corpse rattled hollowly as we rolled the dead guard into its shallow grave. Even when the sod was replaced, the massive carapace created a bump in the ground. It might fool someone from a distance, but up close...

Moving in sequence, Riku and I descended towards the entrance of the tunnel where our friends had disappeared hours ago. Klepton groups spread across both mountain faces. Teams of two or three broke out, meticulously combing the valley.

We kept low and to the darkest shadows, leapfrogging over each other. Once or twice, we stayed close to a bush, trying to hide ourselves from the search parties.

Being advanced logical thinkers, the Kleptons could only search in grid-like dimensions. Sniffing the air, Riku put out a hand to hold me in my crouched position. I heard her sniffing, but detected nothing out of the ordinary. From her garments, she pulled a package wrapped in a wax skin. She opened it quickly and tossed it towards a guard who blocked our way to the tunnel. As the package left her hand, the repulsive stench of rotten meat made me gag.

With a thud, the bait hit the ground and rolled through the short alpine grass. The Klepton standing guard jumped and extended her massive claw to ward off any threat.

I slowly drew my blade, ready to silence the anthropoid should it raise the alarm. It was a wasted effort.

No sooner had my blade cleared its sheath that a low growl vibrated across the slope where we hid. The Klepton, not detecting the threat, moved toward where the package hit the ground.

The mountain lion struck the huge, armored Klepton with primal ferocity. With blurring speed, it went for the throat, knocking its prey to the ground. The chalk-board scratch of its claws against the alien carapace made me cringe. The male cat's weight and power kept the flailing Klepton pinned on its back, while tearing at the stomach, as if it were a deer. Watching the lion's claws fruitlessly scrape the creature's armor, prompted me to rise from hiding. I lunged the five feet that had been Riku and my viewing area, sliding my sword under the cat and into one of the fleshy spots beneath the Klepton's chest plates.

I backed off rapidly as the big cat turned towards me to claim the kill as his own trophy. It crouched low, muscles taut, a low hiss vibrating between its deadly jaws, daring me to challenge him. Keeping my blade in the guard position, I slowly retreated from the mountain lion to figure out how it would eat its fish-smelling trophy. It continued to snarl until the darkness swallowed me.

I almost jumped out of my skin when a hand closed over my shoulder. Riku's eyes twinkled in amusement as she pulled me towards the entrance of the tunnel. Dropping to the ground, we inched our way into the cave not knowing if any of the Kleptons were standing guard within. It was completely black inside, but there was no sound or smell of our enemy's presence, only the rush of water to our right.

"Stay to the left and follow the ledge," Guāng whispered in his head. *"It will narrow at one point which will ensure the Kleptons cannot follow."*

By feel, we found the ledge, and by keeping one hand touching the cave's rough wall; we pushed deeper into the mountain. Riku shoved a long ribbon of silk into my hand so we would stay together. I knotted it around my wrist so there was no chance of dropping it. I made a point of counting my steps as it kept me from thinking about all the rock above me. I was glad I could not see the roof of the tunnel because I'm sure it would have enhanced my feeling of being trapped.

We found the bottle-neck area six hundred and thirty-eight feet in and slid easily through the opening. Other than the stream of gurgling water, there was nothing to show our passage. Our padded shoes made no noise on the smooth stone floor and we might as well have kept our eyes closed for nothing could be seen in the Stygian darkness.

At about the thirty-four hundred count, both of us froze at a far-off sound. Faint as it was, it echoed coming from the waterway. Riku took the lead, and we moved forward with greater caution.

"Guāng, did you leave men in the tunnels?" I questioned through our mind-link.

"No, we are all gathered into a large cavern midway through the mountain. You'll be able to rest once you reach us."

"We are hearing something ahead of us. Not sure just what it is, be on your guard." I said in warning.

The sounds began to get louder as we closed on the unknown source. By feel, we knew that the wall on our right had dipped down, so the ceiling over the watercourse was mere inches from the torrent. From this crack, we could clearly hear clicking. In the darkness, I pictured a school of Kleptons as they swam upstream like salmon returning to lay their eggs. But they had a more sinister goal. It now made sense that there were so few of the enemy outside the tunnel entrance. Our people thought themselves safe after going through the narrow tunnel which blocked the massive creatures. But they hadn't thought about the Klepton's similarity to Earth's lobsters. They were probably more comfortable in water. It would also explain their awkwardness and stiffness on land.

"Guāng!" I mind-screamed. *"The Kleptons are swimming towards you and there are a lot of them."*

"Hurry, Ian. Get to the cavern. We will try to hold them off."

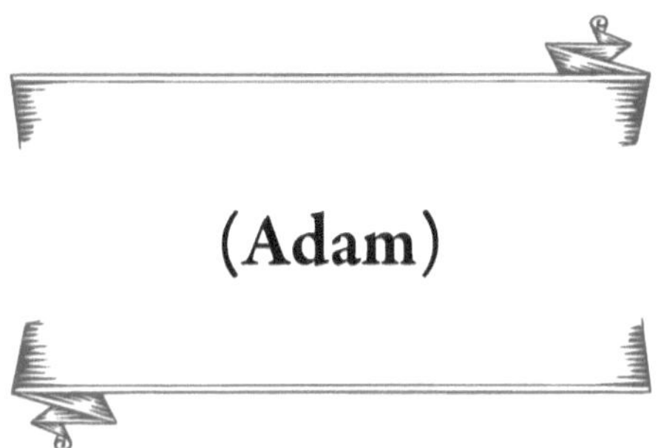

(Adam)

Guāng's voice rebounded in every warrior's head as he shouted out his warning. His light pushed back the shadows as the men jumped from an exhausted sleep to full battle readiness. Swords drawn and arrows notched, the soldiers scanning fervently for an enemy.

"They are swimming up the river," Guāng said.

As one, the entire human army turned towards the turbulent waterway, its surface black and threatening. Each man pushed their senses out to determine how far off the enemy was and how many.

"Have you seen them, Guāng?" Hattori shouted with his mind, his eyes never looking away from the fast-moving current.

"Riku and Ian have made contact with them and have sent a warning. There are many of them."

"Iron Horse. Kwegu." Hattori called out. "Gather your horses and our supplies and continue up the tunnel while we hold this position. We will follow as soon as you are clear."

The Ninja and Gurkhas closed together as the other warriors ran for the equipment and animals. Without hesitation, the two groups began filing out of the cavern. From the cooking fire that the Suri women had used to prepare a warm meal, several thick branches were quickly fashioned into makeshift torches with torn fabric dipped in rendered fat. I almost gagged at the acrid smoke that came off the over-sized candles. It reminded me of pork—way past its due date. I began to wonder if Nabala was feeding us the flesh of Kleptons. That thought had me bent over, painting the cavern floor and gaining me a lot of snickers from my fellow Gurkha soldiers.

Guāng stayed with us so that the Kleptons could not take us by surprise. I had one of the longer spears, shoved into my grasp by a Suri warrior as he left the cavern. Before he followed his brethren into the tunnel, he pulled me into a ferocious hug. Before I could recover, he let go and marched off, leaving me to stagger with the implied brotherhood. I watched more than a few similar displays of emotions, each showing the bond that had been readily growing between the groups as we marched towards the riff.

I found myself helpless to the raw emotions, unable to swallow and tears threatening to spill as I realized that for the first time in my life, I was part of something so much bigger than anything I had ever thought possible. All the hatred towards those adults who couldn't see what I had been experiencing since Grandpa's death, throwing their stupid rules and laws in my face, disappeared. This was so much bigger that the rest didn't matter anymore. I was respected and trusted to make a stand with the warriors who had adopted me into their fold. I felt the first ember of their fire ignite my soul and understood the comradery of brothers in arms. Although the fear remained, it was manageable, and I was ready—no eager—to take the fight to the enemy.

Gaje moved to my right side while his father stood at my left. I looked at both, the question unasked.

"Although I see your bravery, Adam," Gopi said, his eyes full of warmth. "You need to survive this quest. You need to learn the way of the warrior, but allow us," nodding at his son, "to ensure you live to walk in the alien's Heaven."

I nodded. "Just allow me to fight alongside the others. I need this for myself as much as for those who will follow me."

Gopi nodded, his eyes sparkling in respect. "My son has done a great job preparing you, but you have grown much in the past weeks."

The first Kleptons didn't rise from the water to attack us. Rather, they ejected from the fast-moving current to seemingly fly across the cavern to land among us, their massive claws scattering anyone in their way. One after the other, the arthropods jumped like fish, hurling themselves up a steep set of rapids to the calmer pools that waited above.

However, there was no calm pool.

The two groups of warriors met the aliens with their own ferociousness, throwing themselves and their weapons at the monsters without hesitation, knocking them onto their hard-shelled backsides and attacking the venerable undersides, aiming for the weak membrane between the armor plates.

Gopi fought with his kukri as a huge Klepton soldier landed in front of us, neatly slashing at the thing's eyes, while his father shoved his spear between the monster's legs and barreled into the hard-shelled creature. Gravity did the rest. Once the alien lay helpless on its carapaced back, it was child's play to dispatch him from a distance with the longer spear.

Even Guāng played a part as he dove in among the assailants to flash his light with a blinding effect like a mad strobe light, blinding the Kleptons, so they did not see the attacks from their human foes before we slammed into them.

But the Kleptons kept coming. As more of our small force were injured or dropped, unable to rise back up, we backed towards the far wall of the cavern leading into tunnel that snaked deeper into the mountain. Hattori pushed the injured into the tunnel and set up a wall of warriors, their steel weapons keeping the enemy at bay. It allowed us to inch towards the tunnel entrance with the most protection possible. It was like a deadly moving pincushion.

As they pushed me into the tunnel, I thought about Ian and his Ninja partner. They were separated from us with the enemy between us. Fear for my friend welled up inside me and I screamed at Hattori, pointing at my friend, "We can't leave them!"

Someone pushed me unceremoniously into the tunnel, with no care that I was the so-called-leader of this troop. Part of me understood that they considered me invaluable because of the prophecy, but it was becoming a tad annoying.

"They are Ninja! Darkness is their friend|," Hattori hissed.

As I stumbled into the tunnel, both Gopi and Gaje pulled me backwards by the crook of an arm. I saw brilliant flashes of light assaulting the Klepton's forces, disorienting them so that our warriors could duck into the confining space of the tunnel. The narrowness of the space ensured that our people could not be flanked, but Ian and Riku were stranded on the wrong side of an alien army.

With a suddenness that caught everyone off guard, the entire place was pitched in darkness.

Guāng had gone black.

They dragged me through the tunnel understanding what Hattori had orchestrated. He had given Ian and Riku their greatest chance of not only survival, but also of re-joining with our main force. Guāng had blinded the aliens, giving Ian and his companion a chance to sneak past the enemy troops.

Even as we followed the tunnel, there was a cluster of steel striking alien armor as the enemy probed the tunnel and met our rear guard's blades. In a rage, born from fear of Ian's safety, I hungered to bring the attack to the aliens and slaughter every one of them. I wanted them to fear my friends and me.

The aliens were obviously comfortable in water. What else did we need to know about our foe before we entered their domain? Such knowledge could decide the success or failure of our mission. I would have to make time to really talk with Nita once we were clear.

Chapter 19
(Ian)

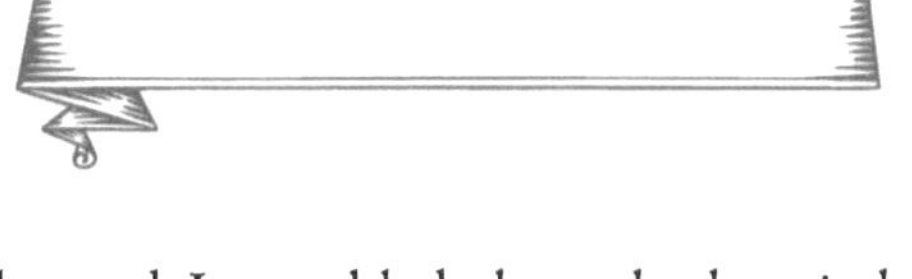

Riku and I stumbled through the pitch-black tunnel, glancing off the sharp-edged rocks. I could feel several scrapes bleeding under my garments, where the ragged stone torn skin and fabric. Other than keeping a hand on the left wall, the only guide we had was the distant crash of steel from the battle that raged in the cavern ahead of us and the familiar rush of water. Unable to see anything, we were like two blind people in a strange room. Riku, who led the way, let out a grunt as she hit something. A thud followed. Before I could call out to her, I tripped over her and slammed into a hard surface. Pain flared in my right shoulder as the wind left my lungs. I lay motionless, gasping for air like a land-locked fish.

It took what seemed forever before I could draw more air into my lungs. Riku struggled to gain her feet by roughly shoving my legs off her chest. Rolling onto my knees, I put out a hand to the jagged rock. Bracing myself against it, I rose gingerly to my fee. I would feel the pain more so later.

"Listen," Riku whispered.

I held my breath pushing my senses outward to pick up what it was she heard, but I could detect nothing other than the moving water to our right.

"The sounds of fighting have stopped," she said. "They are dead or they've escaped further into the tunnel."

"Guāng, what's happened?" I asked through the mind-link.

"Your warning gave us the time to escape, my friend. We are pressing on. It didn't take long before

the tunnel became too restrictive for the beasts and they have turned back. Be careful as you approach the cavern. The Kleptons may still be there, but they have no light so you may have a chance of getting past them."

I relayed the information to Riku in a low voice.

"There is no need for us to run blindly," she said. "It will only get us hurt."

"Slow and silent," I said.

"Hai."

Moving at this less frantic pace avoided any more mishaps and injuries. I resumed counting our steps, even though I had to start over at one. In our mad race to reach our group, I had forgotten to keep track. The counting was comforting, as it caused me to concentrate, not letting my mind wander thinking worst-case scenarios. With no way of knowing how long we had been walking, the counting also gave some indication of how far we had come. Of course, we had no way of knowing just how far we still had to go.

Twenty-five hundred steps later, the clicking of the alien chatter flowed on the water. Slowing our pace, we crept forward without making a sound. Even in the darkness, we could sense the openness of the cavern. I felt the difference in the way the sound traveled in the vastness. In the tunnel, the noise fell flat through the tight channel of the passage. Here in the cavern, the sounds rang clearer, with a bright tone. Even the gurgle of the water was crisper.

Somewhere in the dark, several Kleptons communicated in a flurry of clicks and snaps, sounding like an old fashion typewriter pounding out ninety words a minute. The conversation stopped with an abruptness that made me flinch. We froze in fear that they had detected us. As we held our breath, the silence was broken by many splashes. Some aliens were leaving, but we couldn't tell if they swam upstream or down.

I conveyed the information to Guāng through our link.

Riku moved silently, following the left wall of the cavern. We could hear the hollow clanking of the Klepton's carapaces as they moved about. It would be child's play to avoid them in the dark, as long as we kept silent and there was no sudden movement. I tried to map out the positions of those I could hear, but there were too many to keep track of.

New sounds reached us, and I had to strain to identify them. It was crunching and crackling followed by a wet slurping. In horror, I realized they were eating our dead warriors! Feeling the gore rise up my throat, I swallowed hard over and over. If I started to retch, they would find me in seconds and both Riku and I would be their dessert. Rage turned my guts at the thought of these aliens feasting on my friends. It took every ounce of willpower to keep my Ninjato sheathed. Revenge would have felt good for only seconds before they overwhelmed us. I was thankful for the darkness. It was a blessing that I couldn't witness one of my brothers-in-arms being devoured, but I had to force my imagination to more pleasant subjects.

It felt like hours had passed before we reached the far side of the cavern. Two of the creatures stood guard where the cave reduced into another tunnel. We heard them shuffling from foot to foot, low clicks passing between them. Riku tugged the silk ribbon taut and lightly chopped my leg below the knee. I reached out and gave her my hand so she could feel my thumbs up signal of understanding.

We moved forward with minute movements, feeling ahead for anything that might make trip us up. Her hand reached out and touched my chest when the smell of the guards became overwhelming. I crouched in place as she continued to crawl away for the full length of the ribbon. She raised her end and I tried to match it.

I wasn't sure what else she had planned, but the wait wasn't long. A rock clattered across the cavern's floor; the noise magnified by the darkness. With a surprised click, one guard rushed towards us, and

I pulled my end of the ribbon as hard as I could. When the guard's leg hit the trip line, it almost pulled me off my feet. She went down hard; a grunt mixed with a squeal spoke of her surprise and fear.

I felt the ribbon being tugged forward and struggled to keep up. The second guard, not sure what had happened to her partner, rushed forward in a stuttering series of clicks and clacks.

This one also hit the ribbon and went down, but she didn't fall straight. Because of the primal darkness, I never saw it coming. Her body crashed into me, the ribbon ripping off my wrist as the Klepton's full weight fell across it. For the second time today, the wind was knocked out of me. To make matters worse the creature was thrashing on the ground and her armor repeatedly hit me.

I rolled away from the beast, finally gasping for much-needed air. There were multiple crashes, before a high piercing squeal cut through the cavern and the creature stopped floundering. I pulled back as hands patted my chest and Riku grabbed the rough linen of my shozoko and pulled me to my feet. She pushed the ribbon back into my hand and tugged me forward.

We moved blindly forward, searching for the entrance of the tunnel. Unyielding stone clipped my right shoulder, and I stifled a cry as I felt more skin tear. As I bounced off the jagged rock, I staggered and banged into the left wall. We were in the tunnel!

Behind us, there was a chorus of clacks, clicks, and the thunder of running Kleptons following the commotion.

"We're through the cavern, Guāng,"
Suddenly, ahead of us, light flared, exposing the tunnel and another bottleneck. Now able to see the surrounding hazards, we ran full speed for the exit. The stomping of the Kleptons echoed off the tunnel walls like thunder, as they too ran to catch us before we could safely get through the narrow passageway. Fortunately for us, our lead was enough and we dove through the narrowed passageway. The opening was too small for the aliens and we heard the clatter of

carapaces colliding with the stone blockage and each other.

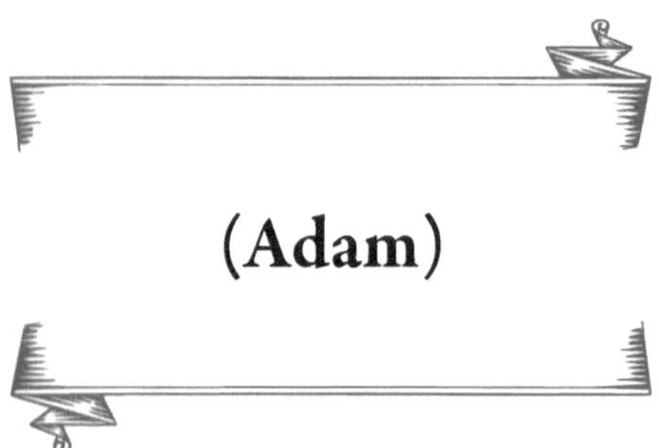

(Adam)

As Guāng's light left us, everyone settled down to rest. He raced back through the tunnel to guide Ian and his ninja partner to us. The relief of knowing my friend was alive and would soon join us was a huge burden lifted from me and I felt elated. But in the pitch darkness, it was not enough to keep me awake. My head dipped onto my chest and I knew nothing until a firm hand shook me awake.

"They come," Gopi said holding out his hand to help me up. I took it eagerly and stood to see Guāng leading two black clad fighters back to our band of warriors.

Striding forward, I met Ian and his companion, pulling them into a huge hug. "I'm so relieved to see you alive."

"It was a close thing, but thanks to the darkness and finally Guāng's light we were able stay ahead of the Kleptons," Ian said with a tired smile.

"Get some rest. We're safe here in the tunnel."

With no other words the two limped and staggered to find their bedrolls.

"Can we sit tight to allow them some sleep?" I asked Gopi.

"A few hours at least," he said rubbing at a scar that ran along the underside of his jaw. "We need to know how much farther this tunnel goes and what might be at its end. If the Kleptons have swum ahead, we need to know where we might encounter them."

I nodded, knowing I had other questions for our mountain man guide.

We found Nita near the head of the tunnel wall line, buried under a trading blanket, his head propped up on his backpack.

His eyes popped open at our approach and he sat up. "What did I miss?" he said with a yawn.

"Our men made it back," Gopi said, "and think the Kleptons may try to get ahead of us by swimming further upstream. We need to know what waits ahead."

"Well then, you'll be happy to hear we won't be seeing them anytime soon," he said stretching his back till it gave an audible click. "The river and this tunnel go in different directions after the cavern. Have you not noticed we can no longer hear the moving water?"

Until he mentioned it, I had not noticed, that there was no splashing or gurgling to be heard.

"When I first explored these mountains, I never found a source for that river. Might come from within the mountain. There are some water holes on the far side of the tunnel, but nothing seemed to feed this river. As for the tunnel, we have about half a day traveling before we reach the other side."

Gopi and I exchanged a glance. Everyone would be happy to have the sun on their face after all the darkness. I couldn't help wonder how Ian and Riku made it through the first part with no light to guide them. The horses would be happy as well. Rob had told me that what oats they carried were quickly dwindling and fresh grass would be welcomed.

I squatted beside the grizzled explorer. "What kind of world do the Kleptons come from? They are clearly amphibian."

Nita considered his words before saying, "Hot and humid. There's more water than land, so they probably originated from the depths. When you go through the riff, you'll emerge on one of the inter-locking islands that stretches right up to the Klepton's Citadel." He ran a trembling hand across his face as he recalled the time he spent there. "Unless you plan to do a lot of swimming, you won't have to worry about getting lost. Just stay on dry land and it'll lead you to where you want to go."

"Try to travel at night, because the fliers hunt during the day. If they spot you, you're as good as caught. And you can see the Scavengers better at night because of their glow."

"Tell me about their Citadel," I said calmly as I could see Nita didn't even want to think about the place.

"It's huge. From a distance it looks like a mountain, but as you get closer, you can see that it's a huge mound, similar to an anthill. There are hundreds of entrances but each one takes you somewhere different. If you can find your way to the top, you'll find the bastard Queen who ordered my torture after she could not communicate with me. If the staff is anywhere, it would be in her chamber."

He was sweating profusely, and it scared me to push him further. What he had endured would have broken a weaker man. Of course, he also had to live with the thought that he had led the Kleptons to the riff and into our part of Heaven.

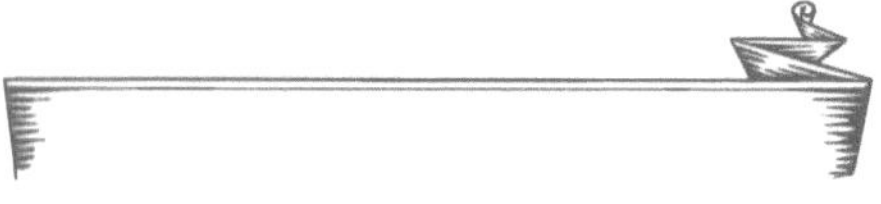

Chapter 20
(Adam)

True to his word, Nita led us out through the last of the tunnel the next day. The rest had helped everyone, and we made good time. Even before we caught the first sign of light, the horses picked up the scent of fresh air and had to be controlled so they wouldn't rush the opening. Not knowing what lay ahead, we needed to be cautious. A few of the Comanche scouted ahead and sent back the all clear. Eagerly, each group moved forward.

We emerged in a giant quarry with stones ranging from as big as a house to the size of my fist. It resembled an ancient riverbed. The tunnel we passed through may have served as a subterranean river in the past. The sun had already descended behind the mountains ahead, which helped to ease the transition from absolute darkness to light. Even the early evening gloom felt harsh after two days of constant blackness.

After discussing our route through the mountains with Nita, the Comanches mounted and rode off in pairs.

As the light faded from the sky, the stars lit our way. A breeze followed us, driving the cooler air from higher up the mountain into the valleys. It didn't take long before we all pulled out a blanket to wrap around our shoulders to ward off the cold.

Hours later, Nita led us to a clump of wind-shaped junipers beside a still pond. The remnants of a fireplace showed that someone had used this camp in the past.

"Lived here for over a month, while I mapped out each of the valleys throughout this whole range.

Trees supplied a windbreak and fuel, the pond supplied clean water and when they're inclined to bite, a trout dinner."

Nita's demeanor had changed. He was in his element out here in the rugged wilds. I hoped it gave him peace, especially after all he suffered. Once he led us to the riff, Nita could return to the solitary life he loved.

OVER THE NEXT FEW DAYS, we eased the pace to allow everyone to recuperate from the race to the foothills and journey through the mountain tunnel. The breaks were longer, and the training was only to keep everyone limber.

Nita steered us through the maze of valleys with no hesitation. I would have been lost within a day.

"On your way back," he told me, "watch for stone cairns to mark the way. They are stones set upright which the Inuit called inuksuk used to guide travelers. I will mark your way through the mountains."

On the third day, one scout rode towards us in a hurry. Gopi waved me forward, and we jogged to meet him. He hopped off his horse to run the last couple yards to where the four Captains, Nita and I waited.

"Iron Horse sends greetings. We have spotted a lot of troop movement about an hours' ride from here. The Kleptons are both coming and going from one particular valley."

"That sounds like the entrance to the riff," said Nita. His complexion had gone pale knowing that the monsters were that close. I could see he was fighting the urge to flee.

I turned to Nita and asked, "Is there somewhere you can hide our men, while we try to get a better view of what is happening?"

His head bobbed in relief that he would not have to face his former captors. Three horses used for carrying supplies were unloaded so that Gopi, Hattori, Kwegu and I could follow the scout back to his observation post. Looking over my shoulder, I saw Nita wheeling the remaining men towards another cut in the mountains where they would remain out of sight and for his sake, safe.

The scout set a mile-eating pace so as not to exhaust the horses. We stayed close to the tree-line in case we had to duck out of sight at the first sign of the enemy.

My heart was racing as the point of no return was almost on me. Up to this moment, reaching and passing through the riff was indefinite, in the future. Being so close now, the riff and all it meant was palpable.

Faster than I wanted, we arrived at the base of another mountain. It didn't look any different from the countless ones we had been traveling around, but the scout jumped off his mount and guided us through a stand of trees that opened up to a small meadow. We picketed the horses so they could feed on the rich alpine grasses and followed our guide on foot. As the slope increased, we were sweating freely from having to use trees to help haul ourselves up the mountainside. Even after marching and training, my breath was coming in ragged heaves as I pushed up-wards.

Just when I thought I could go no farther we reached a saddle in the mountain that cut a narrow break across the face. With rock towering above us on either side, I relished the coolness of the deep shadows as it relieved my exhaustion. After walking through the cut, our scout motioned us to crouch as he crept towards the lip of the cliff. Iron Horse and Rob lay watching the activity in the next valley. Rob shot me a wink as I crawled towards his position. We lay on our stomachs and peeked over the edge.

Far below, we could see a huge contingent of Kleptons camped in a large meadow at the base of a box canyon. To one side, a large corral had been erected and we could see the listless movement of men and women walking back and forth like cattle waiting for the slaughter. In the pit of my gut, a slow burn of anger was lit. I wanted to help them escape their fate, but with the army below, I knew it would sacrifice the main mission. It would be like spitting in the wind. I couldn't do both.

I pulled my eyes off the prisoners and studied the rest of the camp. They had erected large swaths of fabric to create shade for the army. Guards surrounded the entire camp while others patrolled the perimeter in both directions.

At the very back of the canyon, I spied two massive Stonehenge-like slabs of smooth stone, a deep shadow hung between them. To my astonishment, from that darkness, a line of Kleptons emerged and stepped into the light of this world.

We had reached the riff.

Chapter 21
(Adam)

After watching the enemy camp for an hour, we crawled back away from the lip before standing for a much-needed stretch. I said very little as we marched back across the cut between the two cliffs. I couldn't hazard a guess at what the Captains were thinking, but I was close to panic as I realized that I was at the pinnacle point in my journey.

This wasn't a computer game alien world, there were real lives and consequences at stake. Whomever I choose to take in might not make it back out.

Man, I desperately wanted my regular fifteen-year-old life back.

Is this what being an adult was about? Did my parents ever have these moments of indecision or anxiety? They seemed to have all the answers. So did Judge O'Brien. They dropped decisions with little thought or reflection. Of course, they weren't life or death decisions—not from their point of view. I wish they were here to help me make these choices.

The trip down the side of the mountain was much easier than going up. We hopped like skiers from tree to tree, our feet held together for braking power against the grade. It took all of my concentration to avoid tumbling face first down the steep slope. Thankfully this gave me a bit of a reprieve of my dread.

Once we reached the small meadow at the base of the mountain, we gathered our horses and led them through the trees. In a single line, we traced our steps back to the main force. I allowed the others to take the lead, happy to follow, so I didn't have to talk to anyone. The worry was eating away at me and I was in no mood for small talk. I occasionally caught one of the Captains glancing back at me, concern written on their faces.

"I feel your heavy thoughts, Adam," came through our link.

"I'm scared, Guāng," I took a shuddering breath to push my panic away. *"I'm scared to pick the other four warriors. I'm scared of failing. I'm scared of getting my friends killed."* I swiped at the stinging in my eyes. *"I don't care about myself, but everyone is relying on me; the Prophets, Grandpa, the Captains and my friends and I don't know if I can do it. I'd rather go through the riff alone. That way if I fail, they would still be safe."*

"That's where you are wrong. The prophecy did not mention just you. It included your friends and four others. This isn't up to you. That decision was made eons ago by God. He who knows everything, must know that you do have what it takes to complete this task, otherwise He would never have chosen you."

I reflected on what Guāng said and felt some fear and oppression fall away.

"Remember, Adam," he said, imagining his warm comforting light, even though he had stayed with the main force. *"You are not alone. Your friends can help you decide whom to choose. They have worked more closely with the different warrior groups and will have seen those who have stood out. And the Captains know the true qualities of their people. They will be happy to advise."*

"So, I don't have to be the one to decide?"

"A leader doesn't do everything. He delegates tasks fairly, with regard to the individual's strengths. He also encourages ideas from the team. Eight heads can bring more to a plan than just one. Rely on your people. They want to succeed, as well."

"Thank you, Guāng. I feel better, now that you've put things into perspective."

I swear I felt his warmth through our link.

BY THE TIME WE FOUND the new camp, the shadows of the mountains spread across yet another lonesome valley. This one stretched south-west before disappearing behind the knob of rock. Nita had once again found a sheltered camp with fresh water and good grazing for the horses. A Comanche led mine away as I strode to the main campfire that was built up against a flat slab of granite. It was built to reflect both the heat and light on our group.

As we settled, Nabala and her companion passed steaming plates of hot stew to each of us. Hunger hit with the delicious smell of the food, and I dove into it without hesitation, even burning my mouth as I devoured it. The two women laughed at my appetite and were happy to reload my plate with a second helping. As I ate at a more leisurely pace, I asked one of the men to have my friends join us at the fire.

I finished my supper and had carried the plate back to the ladies when Freddy and Ian showed up. We exchanged back slaps and high-fives each conveying an excitement of being together again.

Ian was in the traditional ninja outfit, his sword rising between his shoulders and I could see he moved with a grace he didn't have before. He also was comfortable and confident in himself; no longer timid and scared. The '3Ds' would find a totally different reaction if they picked on my small friend now.

Freddy wore the loose fitting dark blue shawl, his fighting sticks tied to his waist, and he carried an extra-long spear with a wicked-looking blade. Swinging from a chain that hung down his chest, were two sharp looking, curved tusks. When I lifted them, he said, "They're the mandibles of the first Klepton I killed. Kwegu had Nabala made them to honor my first kill." The pride shone in his face and I could see he had changed much as well. Although he feared nothing and would fight at the drop of a hat, he now held himself in a calmer state, not having to puff his chest to show everyone how tough he was. He knew what he was capable of, and that was enough.

Rob and another Comanche warrior rode into camp and he dropped from his horse Moonbeam as she was mid-stride. His dexterity shocked me. He had lost weight, his body tighter, but no less powerful. His face and bare chest were darkly tanned from both the wind and the sun. The familiar, bright white smile flashed across his face as he approached. As always, he crushed us in his bear hug like we hadn't seen each other in years.

"Come my friends, we need to talk," I said pointing at the pit. "Rob, get yourself some food."

The Captains had watched our reunion in silence and waited patiently for us to settle in place. As everyone found a spot around the fire, Hattori passed his famous rice wine around the gathering. He raised his wooden cup in salute, "To our young warriors who have come so far in such a short time. Kanpai!"

"Kanpai," we echoed and threw back the saki. I was ready for it this time, but it still burnt all the way down.

I bowed towards these ferocious fighters. "Captains, I thank you for your teachings and guidance. We come close to the next stage of our mission and there is much we must discuss. Before we talk about how we are to get past the Klepton presence to enter the riff, we have to decide who is to join my friends and I on our journey to the Klepton world." I looked around the circle and each nodded at me to continue. "I would like to hear each friend's preference as they have worked with your people and are better suited to make that selection. I ask you Captains to determine if the choice is wise, as no one knows your soldiers better than you."

The four leaders exchanged glances, and each nodded in agreement. Hattori gave me a curt bow of respect at my decision to ask what the others thought.

I turned to Gopi. "You assigned your son, Gaje to teach me the fighting skills of the Gurkhas. Since that time, we have become friends and have fought side by side. It would do me great honor to fight alongside him moving forward."

He cleared his throat before replying. "I admit, I thought this a fool's errand, but you have met every challenge we have put in front of you with stubborn courage. To choose my son, who I have trained to be my equal, honors both him and me. Thank you."

I nodded to Gopi. I had proven myself worthy. I was one of his warriors and my heart soared in pride.

Looking over at Ian, I raised an open palm to show his choice.

Without hesitation he said, "Riku."

We both swiveled to see what Hattori thought. "Any of my soldiers would be suitable, but you and she have worked well together. It would be a good fit." He gave a sharp nod to indicate his agreement.

"Chief Iron Horse," Rob said standing in respect for the ancient warrior. "You have entrusted my training to your son Peta. He has taught me much, but I feel I still have much to learn from him if he will join with your blessings."

The old chief, eyes narrowed, his arms crossed over his massive chest. With no emotion, he nodded.

All eyes turned to Freddy, who rose gracefully to his feet. "I would follow Kwegu into battle without hesitation, but I might have to fight Nabala first and that is not a fight I would want to face."

Laughter erupted around the fire, none louder than the Suri chief who was reduced to tears. "You are wise beyond your years, Freddy."

"Therefore," Freddy said, "I would ask for your recommendation."

"As Tumu is my witness," he said swearing on his sun god. "I think the best of my people is Ganjo. He is our champion stick fighter and knows no fear."

The man, who stood just outside the firelight stepped forward, a royal blue shawl tied at the shoulder, his arms marked with ritual scaring. He flashed a fearsome smile at Freddy. "This warrior has proved himself a killer of our enemy not once, but twice. He honored me by using my spear to dispatch his second Klepton, which he took down with just the fighting sticks. Thank you mighty Kwegu for allowing me to fight beside Freddy, a true brother of the Suri."

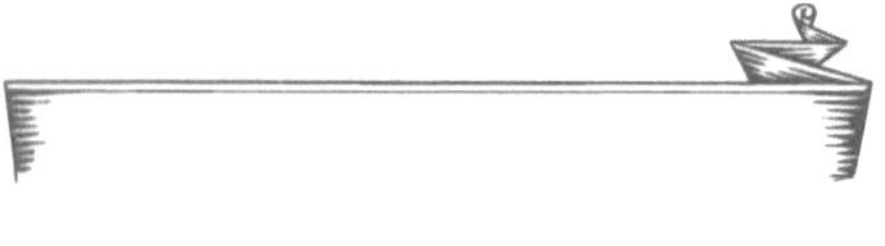

Chapter 22
(Adam)

I woke in panic as I heard the warning.

"Scavenger!"

Guāng's light ignited the entire box canyon, exposing the floating skull that emanated darkness rather than light. The jaws opened as it screamed in either surprise or pain; maybe both.

Everyone in the camp was up, weapons poised as they searched for an enemy to strike at. Arrows were shot at the Scavenger only to be lost in the night as it dodged in every direction.

It was Guāng who was most suited to take chase and chase he did. With an elastic snap, he surged directly at the evil thing and would have crashed right through the dark being, but it slipped clear at the last second. The two zipped and zapped back and forth between the mountains with blinding speed. The residue of their tracks hung in the sky, dazzling the eyes and minds that watched.

"Gather your gear," Gopi yelled, breaking the spell of our amazement at the aerial battle. "Be ready to march in five minutes."

We stored bedrolls and blankets in record time as everyone prepared to leave before the entire Klepton army made their appearance. Hurriedly, I broke through thin ice on the mountain spring, filling a dozen water skins at once. In spite of the turmoil, this regular duty was paramount. My hands were numb when I handed the skins to the other soldiers who were policing our campsite. Nothing could hide the crushed grass where we had laid nor the campfire's hot coals, but all other evidence that might help the enemy was eradicated.

The soldiers formed up in their regular marching column but Gopi ordered our team of eight to form up together in the center where we would be most protected. Rob and Peta had surrendered their horses to Iron Horse earlier as they would not be crossing the riff with us. From our discussions with Nita, the lack of solid land where we were going meant the animals would hinder the party. The two men carried their bows, and two quivers of arrows. On each hip sat a savage-looking war axe. They would act as our scouts and trackers, finding the safest way to the Klepton Citadel, hopefully without being spotted.

By the time we were ready to move out, Guāng and the Scavenger had cleared the mouth of the box canyon. We knew that the dark skull would be making a run to tell his masters what he had uncovered. We would have the entire Klepton army after us.

"Nita, where can we hide?" Hattori asked. "We need to go to the ground until the hive we just kicked over calms down again."

Even in the darkness I could tell the mountain man was having trouble thinking, and I guessed his fear of being recaptured was playing heavily on him.

"Ah... there is one place if we can get to it before first light that should be able to conceal us, but we must move fast." Looking up at the sky he said, "We have less than two more hours of darkness."

"Then let's move," Hattori said and let out a sharp whistle that announced the beginning of our race against the sun. Our seasoned taskmaster started us at a steady jog and kept it there. Before long, I was sweating freely. my breath was easy, and it became easier as my muscles warmed up. This was a lot different from the forced marching we had used to date.

At the mouth of the canyon, Nita turned us back towards the tunnel we had recently emerged from and I wondered if we were to return to that black hole in the ground. How he could find his way through the alpine meadows in the darkness was a mystery. The night was overcast, so he didn't even have the stars to guide him. After an hour of running, we came to a fast-moving creek that flowed out of a deep, dark canyon.

We entered the almost freezing waters and Nita pushed us upriver. "Stay in the middle of the current," he said in a tight whisper. He repeated the direction to each man that passed him. There was no running now. We slogged against the current as it pummeled our burning thighs. It was a struggle in the dark and the uneven gravel creek bed did little to help. I staggered and fell completely soaked more than once. Later I would find out that the fast-moving water washed away all signs of our passing. Nita had the Comanches lay a false trail running further east towards the tunnel and then return to follow the river as we did. The old mountain man was mighty canny.

Once he had the entire column moving deeper into this new canyon, the old man showed us all up by pushing past us, tugging his mule by its bridle. By now, I could barely feel my legs and had to consciously force myself to keep moving forward. With arms apart for balance, we must have looked like a zombie horde from a low-rated flick. The grade was gentle rising with the odd step-up which caught most by surprise with a plunge under the surface before they could get their feet steadily under them.

A low rumble far ahead rose steadily over the splashing line of quiet men. It sounded like thunder and for a moment I remembered Nita warning us about the dangers of flash floods in the creek beds that crisscrossed the prairies from storms in the mountains. It didn't seem to worry the grizzled explorer as he kept pushing ahead.

We were all soaked and freezing, feeling the cold breeze that followed the contours of the valley. It sucked body heat from me until I could barely make a fist and I thought my teeth might shatter as they chattered uncontrollably. If the Kleptons came out of the darkness, I don't think my hands could draw my knife, let alone use my bow. We would die were we stood.

The old man, experiencing the same distress said in a low voice over his shoulder, "Almost there fel...lows. Not fa... far now."

The creek bent around a shoulder of the mountain and that thunder became a roar. Waves of mist washed over us as the wind played with the water of the falls, pulling what was left of my body heat.

I could see where the water crashed into a pool that was about sixty feet across and realized that the sky was lightening. We had to get under cover, but I could see nothing that would hide us from enemy scouts or the Scavengers.

"One last plunge, boys," Nita called out, almost shouting over the roar of the crashing falls. He pointed our way through the curtain of water. "Hurry, the dawn is almost here!"

He was right; I could see the bewildered expressions on my fellow warriors. Taking the lead, I pushed through the wall of hard pounding water. The weight of the Niagaran curtain almost crushed me to my knees, but then I was through. The pale light revealed a wide underscored cave, almost twenty feet deep in a shallow graded slope. I could not see the end of the cavern because of the limited light. I staggered forward as more of my brothers pushed through, following my example.

Nita entered the hidden cave with a maniacal laugh as his mule kicked and pulled at his leash. "He hates when we come here," he laughed, his voice almost drowned by the crashing water. "Surprised he didn't start fighting long before we turned off." The animal's nostrils were wide in a mild panic and its eyes rolled, showing white in the dim light.

He slapped me across the shoulders and yelled, "Well come on boy, don't you know enough to get out of the rain?"

My team followed the old man as he coughed and laughed like a lunatic, making way for the others following. He walked towards a solid back wall of climbing branches, its foliage rich from the steady supply of water and the fertile soil being washed down the mountain. I was shocked as Nita did something and the black maw of a tunnel opened up before us. Without hesitation, he entered the dark hallway. Having no choice, I followed the mountain man, surprise warming my limbs enough that I at least wasn't thinking about them for the moment.

"It rises and curves to the left," he yelled out, loud now that we left the waterfall behind. The mule's unshod hooves echoed through the tunnel and I used the sound to guide me as the tunnel slowly rose. I lifted one hand and traced the smooth tunnel wall as an extra guide through the dark.

"Keep following my voice," Nita said. "We have to make room for everyone and I will get us some light." Not sure what I would encounter in the dark, I moved forward, both hands held out in front of me so I wouldn't end up running into a wall. Sudden movement to my right spooked me. My imagination jumped to cave bears and I had to choke back my scream.

A flash of spark being struck on flint showed me that there was no menace. After repeated strikes, a flame ignited and Nita raised a torch above his head. "Fear not, you'll be safe here from the monsters."

He lit several torches and jammed them into holes that had been hacked into the living rock for that purpose. As the light spread, we could see the remains of a fire pit with a drying rack and piles of firewood leaning up against the back walls, safely away from its source.

"Adam, have a couple of fires lit so we can warm our bones and dry our clothes. Hope everyone used oilskin to pack their spare clothes, otherwise you'll be sitting in the raw for a while," he said, laughing at his own joke.

I didn't have to issue any orders; everyone jumped forward to gather wood from the piles and set about preparing the campfires. Moving helped generate heat, but the promise of a fire was inspiring. Using the torches to ignite the campfires, light and heat spread across the extensive cavern. The ceiling was lost to the shadows, but the grotto showed itself to be large enough to house three times our numbers with ease.

I stripped out of my wet clothes, my entire body covered in goose bumps and aching from the chill. After all the weeks fighting, training and living with these men, I was no longer shy at removing my cloth-ing. After all, we all had the same equipment and it's what God had supplied. I stood as close to the fire as I could without fear of being burnt, allowing the heat to slowly enter my body. As the blood began to flow in my fingers and toes, I bit back a cry of pain. It reminded me of the winters of my childhood; where we would slide down a snowy slope over and over again with no regard to the cold. When we returned home to hot chocolate and warm clothes, pain racked us as the feeling came back to our extremities.

We would swear off tobogganing forever because of the pain. That would last until the next snowfall. My skin tingling from the heat yanked me back to the present, and I turned to warm my backside.

Once dry and almost warmed, I dug through my bag thanking the training and equipment the Gurkhas had given me. The oilskin wrappings had kept my other clothing dry even after repeated falls in the creek. Once changed, I warmed up quickly, which is when sheer exhaustion swept through me.

As much as I wanted nothing more than to curl up in my bedroll as many soldiers around me were doing. I staggered to where Nita and the other Captains stood conversing in quiet tones.

"Warmed up, Adam?" Nita asked, passing me a ragged cut of dried venison.

I nodded, ripping off a bite of the meat and tucking it into my cheek to soften up, the flavor already flowing out of the rich protein.

"The last of the Comanches are arriving," he said, pointing at a line of horses that stood along one length of rock wall, dripping with steam rising from their warm bodies. Their riders were wiping them down with damp cloths and adding oats to their feed bags. "Once they are all back, I'll close the entrance to the cave and we'll be safe."

"Now they know we're in the area, how are we ever going to get near the entrance to the riff?" I asked the group of leaders. "I mean, if I was the Klepton's general in charge of securing the entrance, I wouldn't move from in front of the opening."

"We'll have to give them a target they cannot resist," Hattori said his tone flat, almost hostile. He wasn't upset with me, I could see that right away, but he wasn't mincing words either. There was no avoidance of the dangers we faced. My team had to get through the riff if we were to have a chance of stopping this invasion, but the cost might be high. He made that point, and he directed it at me. He knew that I had almost balked at killing innocent people who had been infected by the alien seed. He and the others were willing to die to give us a half chance of entering the alien version of Heaven and he did not want me to waver. He was telling me I had no say in that course of action.

He held my eyes as if he was ready to crawl into my skull, until I nodded my understanding.

Once satisfied, he turned on the old scout. "Is there any place we can watch the valley without being spotted?"

Nita nodded. "There is one, built by whoever excavated this shelter; it is man-made," he said throwing his arms around the cavern. "The markings and tools I found, point to an earlier group of settlers or explorers who built this sanctuary and a few others in these mountains I have managed to find over the years." Pointing near the staircase, he said, "There is a vertical shaft that climbs near the lip of the waterfall and from there you can see the entire area before it turns with the mountain. If we post a guard, there is no way they can sneak up on us, but I don't think they'll find us once the cavern door is closed."

"You found it," Gopi said in a stern voice.

"Yes, I did," said the old man, puffing out his chest. "But I had heard about it from a fellow explorer and it still took me a month to figure out how to open it."

Chapter 23
(Adam)

The familiar fluttering of Guāng's presence in my mind pulled me from my sleep.

"I've woken you," his soft voice said. *"I am sorry, that wasn't my intention, Adam."*

I opened my eyes to the soft glow from one of the torches that had been left lit in the dark cave. With no external light I couldn't guess how long I had slept.

"It's okay. Where are you?" I asked.

"I'm in the mountains trying to find my way back to the group, but I cannot pinpoint your position. Can you share your thoughts so I can see what you see?"

"It wouldn't help, we're in a dark cave."

"Another cave?"

I chuckled at his disbelief. As I sat up, a sudden thought rushed out of the sleep-deprived fog. *"The Scavenger. What happened?"*

"He is no more," he said in a disquieting way that stopped me from asking more. After a minute he continued. *"He never got his message to his Masters, but they heard his death scream and have search parties out in every direction. It is a good thing you found a hole to hide in because they are marching through every valley for miles around."*

"It was dark while we marched," I said racking my mind on a way to describe where we were. *"The sky was just starting to lighten up when we came to a high waterfall. Are you able to access my memories if open them to you? Perhaps it will help you find us."*

"I'll try."

Light fingers seemed to touch my consciousness as I remembered the column of falling water, sensed more than seen in the gloom.

"There is a little here that might help guide me to the group. It will be slow going as I dare not let the alien search parties detect me. I would end up leading them straight to you."

Remembering the lookout post Nita had told us about I said, *"There is a spot from within the mountain where we can spy the surrounding area. If I see you enter our valley, I will let you know."*

"That would be helpful."

ARMED WITH A WATER skin, a chunk of jerky and a round piece of course bread the Suri women made for us, I found the shaft and began my climb. Someone had hacked the tunnel out of the rock at an angle with foot holes. I counted 150 steps as I ascended the chute. The shaft opened to a room with light defusing from around a bend in the rock. I moved carefully and eased around the wall to find a window carved out the face of the cliff.

The roar of the waterfall rose from where it met the pool far below me. Looking out the opening, I saw that an overhanging piece of the cliff stretched out and cut the falling water in two. The gap in the curtain of the falls allowed the watcher to see the entrance to the valley without being visible from below.

Who had built this fortress? And why? Was it to protect against enemies or was it as a blind to watch for approaching animals that some ancient tribe hunted? Of course, this was Heaven, so the dwellers were people who had once lived on Earth. Technically, they should still be around unless the Kleptons got to them first. I couldn't help wonder what they might think of our squatting on their property.

Movement caught my eye, and I watched as a group of Kleptons marched out from behind the rock face across the bowl-shaped valley. I stopped counting after twenty realizing that they had sent a sizable force in search of us or whatever had killed their scout.

"Guāng," I said. *"The enemy is in our valley."*

I eased back from the window slowly so my movement wouldn't be noticeable. Once clear, I ran to the chute and almost slid down the entire way to warn the others. Most were still sleeping. I ran towards where Gopi and the others had put down their bedrolls. He was already rising in a rush having heard my running feet.

"A strong force of Kleptons have entered the valley," I said.

"Rise and prepare for battle," he said in a loud voice that reached across the cavern. With no hesitation, every warrior jumped up, weapons at the ready. He strode towards the entrance, with me at his heels. The other Captains came forward, and I explained what I had seen.

"Adam, take Gaje with you and return to the observation window. Make sure they do not see you, but we need to know what they are doing."

I waved Gaje forward and the two of us scurried back up the shaft. He stayed at the top of the ladder, ready to convey any message back to his father. Moving cautiously, I peered out the opening. A small army of the aliens milled about the base of the pool. To my surprise, several of them were swimming in the water like kids on a trip to the beach. From here it looked like they were playing, moving alarming fast in the shallows, chasing each other.

I couldn't believe it. Here they were hunting us so they could either eat or impregnate us, and yet they could take time out to enjoy a little fun. For the first time, I was seeing them as more than monsters. In their own way they were a little like us.

I eased further out the window so I could see straight down behind the curtain of water to where the entrance of our cave was located. There were a few of the creatures moving about, but they showed no real interest in the vegetation on the back wall. I stepped back before turning and rounding the wall. I briefed Gaje whose look of disbelief must have been a mirror of my own a few minutes before. With a shrug, he descended to fill in the others. I returned to my post only to find the first group leaving the water while another entered.

This routine continued for almost an hour until they formed up and marched away from the wading pool. Being an aquatic species, it made sense that they would enjoy the opportunity to spend time in the cold mountain pool, where all water raced downhill away from the entrance of the riff.

"The Kleptons are finally leaving, Guāng," I said through our mind link. *"Maybe you'll see them when they return to the main valley."*

"I'll watch for them, Adam. Thank you."

Gaje brought the news of the alien's exodus to those below while I remained at my post waiting to guide Guāng to our sanctuary.

An hour went by before the now familiar globe of light zoomed into the clearing to hover in front of the waterfall.

"*Guāng,*" I shouted out loud and in my head. "*Do you see where the water is split? There is a window under the overhanging rock. You can enter the cave though the opening.*" I stood waving at him until he saw me. He rose so fast that I threw myself out of the way, instinctively thinking he would hit me, as if from a line-drive foul ball into the stands. But Guāng slowed and spun in place, once again destroying the laws of physics.

His light was a warm glow that pulsed happiness. I led him to the chute, and he dropped down it like a stone. A cheer chased up the ladder seconds later that expressed the men's excitement that one of their own was safe and back with the group. As I emerged from the shaft, the men were all standing in a circle around Guāng's glowing spirit and it wasn't hard to see the love they had for the guiding light.

"Thanks to Adam's warning and guidance, we are once again united," Guāng said to the assembly. *"The aliens left this valley and headed back towards their main camp at the riff. It seems they've given up their search."*

Chapter 24
(Adam)

Three nights later, my small party of blooded and tested warriors, crouched overlooking the alien camp. We were once again in the saddle between two mountains, having traveled under the cover of darkness and camped out among the trees till it was light enough to climb the slope to the saddle.

For the first time, we were on our own. The main group had left us to prepare the main tactic of strategic envelopment. Usually it was a small group who distracted the enemy so a larger unit could get behind the enemy force and attack it from the rear. Napoleon had perfected this strategy, outwitting and annihilating his enemies in a quick and brutal move. Here, the larger group would create an irresistible target that would force the aliens to throw everything at our friends so we could slip behind and enter the riff.

I tried not to think of my friends as bait to offer us a chance to enter the riff.

Earlier this morning we ate a meager breakfast of cold jerky and a hard, starchy cat tail potato-like root. We did not dare tempt a fire as the enemy or their scouts might see the smoke.

I sat under the cover of the pine trees which clung to the steep slope and could not but marvel at how I had changed in these past months. Unable to face Grandpa's death and becoming a defiant punk, I had been transformed into a warrior leader entering an alien world to save Heaven. I shook my head at the absurdity of the entire situation.

Weeks ago, I would not have believed that there was a God, or a place called Heaven. No way would I have accepted the idea of destiny, or that everyone in this crazy realm thought this was the way it should be. Because of a prophecy left behind by the top dog himself, God.

I was living the experience, but still felt the need to pinch myself to prove it was real. How can any of this be real? But there was no disputing that my friends and I had changed. Rob moved with grace and purpose.

Ian would never be bullied again.

Freddy had gone totally native. He was a real force to be reckoned with. His knack for killing surprised his warrior brothers, but he had also begun scarring his arms in the Suri tradition.

"Adam," said Guāng in my head. *"Are you in position?"*

"Yes. Waiting for you."

"The Comanches will attack the camp and attempt to free the prisoners. The Gurkhas and Ninja will sup-

ply archery support while Kwegu's men will help guide the prisoners to a safe location. Hopefully, this will motivate the Kleptons to give chase and open the way for you and your team."

"We're ready," I said.

"God's speed, Adam. I will be here when you return."

"I thought you were heading back to the Prophets to let them know we made it through the riff?"

"And I'll be returning right after I deliver that message."

I swallowed hard to keep my emotions in place. Guāng had become a confident. He was also like having my very own guardian angel.

"I'll watch for you, my friend." I said tearing up despite myself.

"Believe in yourself and your team. They chose you for a reason. Get in, find the Staff of Moses and get back."

And then he was gone. I lay there with the sun beating down on my back thinking about his words.

Even though I was terrified of failing everyone, I felt more confident because of the skills the others had taught me. The entire trip had helped harden me and with the others of this small group to support me, I was anxious to begin the next stage of this adventure.

I might not be the ultimate leader; I wasn't sure I wanted to be as ruthless as Hattori or Gopi, but I had never lived in their times. They may not have had a choice. Knowing I had these seven others to lean on took a lot of pressure off me.

"Prepare yourselves," I said to the others. "The show is about to start."

We had gone over our plan many times, but the reality was that our successful entry depended on how the Kleptons reacted to our soldiers.

"There," Ian hissed pointing towards the canyon's entrance.

Running at a full gallop, the Comanche horse soldiers raced towards the Klepton camp. We could hear their whooping war cries echoing off the cliff walls. A dark cloud rose up from behind the horsemen. It overtook and surpassed the racing cavalry, arcing down on the alien soldiers who stood in shock at the approaching warriors. A vail of arrows fell on the surprised enemy, most bouncing off their hard shells, but a descent number of arthropods collapsed as the broad-heads found soft spots. More than anything, it caused the Kleptons to scatter in panic. Running in a frenzy caused many to bounce off each other into a staggering dance that left many helpless on their backs.

The native cavalry pushed towards these foes, allowing the hard hooves of the horses to trample the prostrated Kleptons. But the alien warriors were not helpless. The screams of pain-maddened horses echoed the valley's walls as razor sharp claws cut into delicate horse limbs. Legless animals collapsed in midstride, their riders catapulted forward. Few rose from where they landed in a heap.

Those who managed to get past this snapping trap pushed through and lassoed one railing that made the framework of the prisoner stockade. Digging their heels into their horse's flanks caused the animals to bolt back into the chaos of the stumbling Kleptons. The alien soldiers were trying to assemble themselves into an organized defensive position. The Comanches rode right through the bunch with the railings bouncing behind. The force of the horses bashed through the enemy troops and the railings followed through tripping those who remained standing.

The other Comanches helped the prisoners and a few horseless riders onto the rear of their mounts and ran for the valley's mouth, yelling and hollering, causing more panic in the enemy.

While all this happened, volley after volley of the deadly arrows landed among the Kleptons, not allowing them a moment to gain the initiative.

As the horsemen left the camp, the dark-skinned Suri stepped forward, and using their long spears, killed several exposed arthropods before turning and following their comrades on foot. They leaped and ran like gazelles in the tall grass towards the valley's entrance.

As fast as the attack had happened, it was over and silence descended over the canyon. We watched as the Kleptons helped those upended or wounded. Some of the injured were put out of their misery. I don't even know if they understood the concept.

Not all the prisoners escaped and, in a rage, two aliens went through the pen killing the survivors with vengeance. I had to grit my teeth and remind myself what was at stake. With no one to watch the captured humans, all the Kleptons soldiers formed up into two large marching squares, the walking wounded placed in the protective centers of the square. It was eerie to watch as no sound reached us because of the distance. They formed as if a hive mind where each soldier knew his place in the group controlled them.

The lead alien must have been an officer, as her carapace glowed a deep crimson and she stood taller than the average beast. With a wave of her huge claw, she ordered her troops forward, giving chase to our friends.

Within minutes nothing stirred in the canyon below us except the grass which bent to the gentle breeze. Without a word, we rose as one and started the steep descent towards the riff. Once we entered the trees, the branches and foliage choked the view. An army could be waiting for us and there would be no way to know until we were upon them. We used the trees for support and to break our progress so we didn't slide down uncontrollably.

Once we reached the bottom, Rob and Peta moved forward to scout the area past the tree line. A low songbird signaled that the way was clear, and we followed in silence. To ensure we were not caught by surprise, we kept inside the trees and circled the box canyon under cover.

Approaching the two leaning slabs of stone that hid the entrance to the riff, we could look down the throat of the valley to the mouth and saw no troop movement at all, theirs or ours. There was an electric hum and a strong smell of ozone that emanated from the riff. It was like after a lightning strike has hit a little too close for comfort. We approached the portal and looked in between the huge boulders.

Like the first riff that Guāng had dragged us through, the portal glowed a milky white. It snapped and bulged with a life force of its own.

Exchanging glances with the others, I stepped forward ready to enter the riff. With no warning a large, squat figure emerged from the riff. It stopped moving in surprise.

The newcomer was a Wizard.

Moving faster than I could even process the danger, Riku's Ninjato flashed in a downward slash that cut through the creature's neck. The head rolled aside and green goo pulsed out of the twitching corpse.

Gaje pointed to the corpse and said, "We must hide the body. Help me move it into the trees."

I ran to the opposite side and reached down to grab one of the creature's legs, ignoring the course hair that pricked my skin. The beast was about twelve feet long and it took all of us to move it far enough into the bush so it wasn't visible. Rob made the return trip with the thing's head, its beady eyes glazed as Peta threw handfuls of soil to hide the green blood. Within minutes there was no evidence of the kill.

"We best hurry before another comes through," I said not knowing what would happen if we met one as we traveled through the portal.

Drawing my Kukri, I stepped forward and led the way into the riff.

As with the gateway to Heaven, it was like walking into a bright void. I existed, but I felt no time or movement. I no longer felt my footsteps. It was like I was floating in space, until with a sudden pop; I staggered into a new world.

Chapter 25
(Adam)

Sweltering heat hit me like a physical blow. Nita had said it was hot and humid, but this was like nothing I could compare that to. As the others broke through the gateway behind me, my clothes clung to me because of the sweat that gushed out of every pore. Even to draw a breath was a struggle.

The air was saturated with moisture. You could almost drink from the mist that exuded from the canopy of trees which blocked out the sky.

A path disappeared into the jungle, its surface criss-crossed with roots and round damp stones.

Ganjo pointed with his spear to the deep cover of the trees and we slid between the heavy, broad-leafed curtain to a darker gloom. We settled in to wait for the darkness, taking in the strange noises of this new world. Unseen creatures slithered or crawled around our small camp as if sensing our readiness to attack anything that came too close. We knew nothing of the other life forms of this world and assumed all were hostile.

The place was alive with a dance of survival; muffled struggles with high-pitched whimpers of pain and hisses of warning. It was most unsettling to be right in the midst of it, yet never catching sight of the creatures attacking and devouring each other.

Above us came the drone of fast fluttering wings moving through the trees in a zigzag pattern as if searching for prey. I remembered both Guāng and Nita warning about a dragonfly monster that hunted the forest through the day, and wondered if this was one. It moved with tremendous speed and I understood the warning about being as good as caught if spotted by one of these fliers.

As daylight faded, we ate a simple meal and gathered our equipment. Peta and Rob took the lead, scouting ahead. Once the leaves closed them from view, I heard nothing, marveling that someone as large as Rob could move so quietly. Minutes later, one of them gave a low whistle that told us it was safe to move. One by one, we left the small natural hiding place moving from cover to cover to avoid being spotted if an enemy was present.

Even though it had grown dark, we could see well enough by blue-green light emanating from the surrounding water. Wherever the water pooled, it gave off a soft light that lit up the entire forest. It was like the water was filled with luminescent sea creatures that give off light when alarmed, but this was in puddles and in the droplets on leaves. It was beautiful, and I had to remind myself to look beyond it for the dangers we knew were out there.

The landmass we followed narrowed to a sand beach that extended to the next island. We walked through ankle deep water to reach the other side; the path cutting through the thick jungle like a knife.

Ahead of me, an animal lunged onto the path just as Riku passed by. It drew its mouth back in a menacing snarl, a double set of incisors that foretold what he was after. He crouched lower, building the tension in his hind legs, ready to attack me, when a larger creature slammed into it with a roar. The two went crashing through the undergrowth, screaming wild cat-like whines that caused other creatures to flee the battle. Not waiting to discover the victor, we ran past the thrashing pair, hoping they were too busy to notice us. We reached a steep embankment overlooking the next island in the chain when the final death-cry reached us, sounding like the animal was choking on its own blood.

We silently exchanged glances, knowing how lucky we had been not to be the dinner of either of those alien animals. Even with all of our stealth training and tracking, we had no clue that they were right next to us as we walked.

Peta made the crossing, followed by Rob. Far off, Ian spied a moving object and pointed towards it. It was the glowing skull of a Scavenger. Freddy gave a sharp whistle to warn Rob who was climbing up the opposite slope of the island, before diving into the foliage alongside the trail. I moved into the trees but kept watch as Rob hustled up an embankment unaware of the danger. He threw himself under the leaves of a large bush that overhung the hillside. Knowing he was safe, I lowered myself to one knee to ensure the foliage hid me. Through the leaves, I watched that glowing menace slide across the distance as it followed the trail but towards the riff. Its light pushed back the shadows slightly before fading as it left us behind. With the Scavenger behind us, we would have to be doubly wary of being spotted by the aliens.

We wasted no more time and continued with the crossing, Freddy and Ganjo bringing up the rear with continuous glances down our back-trail. We were all on edge which was to be expected. It was one thing to know we were marching towards the enemy, but the hidden dangers exhausted all of us, never knowing when something would explode out of the jungle at us.

Two tense hours and three islands later, we broke from the cover of the trees to see the Citadel across an open section of beach that stretched from the last island to the base of the mountain. Stepping back into the foliage, in case they had sentries, we examined the massive structure.

Nita had described it as an anthill and I could see why. The mound grew upwards as much as it did outward. The structure was multi-tiered, rising eighteen levels. They scattered balls of lights across each tier and I wondered if they made them from the luminescence water that had lit our way through the jungle. I could see many openings on each tier and I remembered Nita's warning that each goes to a different location. It would be a maze inside and we might never find our way out, even if we could enter undetected.

We pulled back to the last island we crossed and went to ground to wait out the day. Everyone was exhausted and needed to be fresh for the final push to reach the throne room. Peta and Rob found a suitable camp far enough from the trail that anything flying or tracking should be blind to our position.

Gaje and I took first watch as the others dropped into their bedrolls, fatigue winning them over. We spoke in whispers of what we had seen, more to help keep each other awake while watching for any danger. The time dragged as we fought to stay alert. Finally, Ian and Riku replaced us. Exhaustion took me so quickly; I cannot even remember lying down.

Chapter 26
(Adam)

I woke as the light was fading, feeling stiff but re-freshed. After a chunk of stale bread, more jerky and lukewarm water, I felt better but wished I had a hamburger to sink my teeth into. The steady diet of jerky was getting old. A cup of coffee would also be a welcome change to my mornings; or in this case, nights.

Our plan was simple enough and had been de-cided days before we entered the riff. With Nita's de-scription of the Citadel and the Captains' input, we decided that only four of us would attempt to infiltrate the Klepton city. Because of our training in stealth, Riku, Ian, Gaje and I would make for the throne room at the top of the structure. The others would guard our backs. If we failed, they would return with the news.

In the dead of night, we hit the trail. Once again, we crossed to the island that stood between us and our goal. Moving silently, we navigated the landmass to reach the long sandbar that stretched toward the city. Our position overlooked the landscape, so we settled in a thicket to observe.

Although we didn't see movement on any of the tiers, the Citadel was likely under constant surveillance. If it was, then all the stealth training in the world would not help us. They would see us the minute we stepped out on the pale strip of sand that served as a roadway to the structure. But we had no choice, as Nita said that there were large aquatic predators that guarded the water approach. We would be helpless against such a menace.

Having said our goodbyes at the camp, I nodded to the others and left the cover of the bush for the stark open shoreline at a jog. Gaje, Ian, and Riku followed at my heels. We hoped to cross as fast as possible and pray that the aliens were arrogant enough to think no one would ever attack them.

Within seconds, I was soaked from the exertion of running. My lungs struggled in the heavy damp air, panting heavily with each step. I was anxious that even if we survived this run, the four sets of deep tracks might mark our doom.

The distance had disguised the real size of the Citadel as it towered above the water. I wondered how we would ever find the Staff in its huge expanse, especially without a guide. If it wasn't in the throne room like Nita told us, we might never find it. But we still had to reach the top of this massive mound just to make to the Queen's Quarters.

Gasping for air, we reached cover at the lower part of the structure. Bent over as if in a football huddle, we gulped breathlessly for several minutes. It was like breathing through a mask and I had to fight the panic of passing out from lack of air. With no choice, we waited to recuperate even though it was eating away at the time we had to act.

We were planning to climb the exterior as we might never find our way through the multiple, intertwining tunnels.

Using a pair of cupped hands allowed Riku to scale the first tier. Seconds later, a knotted rope dropped to us and we quickly climbed up to him. As I pulled myself over the lip of the wall, I saw that we had come up right in front of a large tunnel opening. Had anyone come from the opening, we would have been caught immediately. As the others climbed up, I walked to the entrance and cautiously stuck my head in. Luminescent lights were mounted on the tunnel walls in a downward spiral that disappeared with the curvature of the tunnel. I felt airflow on my face and my stomach turned at the foul stench. The familiar clicking and clacking echoed off the tunnel walls. It was a constant chatter, as if hundreds were

speaking. It sounded like eggshells being crushed together.

Riku kept us in between the exterior lights so
shadows could best hide our movements. She would
look for the telltale glow before climbing to the next
level. Ian was like a monkey as he scampered up the
rope ladder, not making a sound.

I could not believe they had no guards posted
and was constantly waiting for an alarm to go off,
but none came as we reached higher and higher levels.

Halfway up, we took a break again to bring our
breathing under control. We crouched behind something that resembled a park bench but on a massive
scale. It was made of the same smooth material as
the Citadel. Part of me wondered if the Kleptons sat
in these frameworks as they looked over their kingdom. Looking back the way we came was breathtak-
ing. The waters stretched as far as the eye could see,
all lit up with the luminescence we were used to seeing. It was vast and beautiful. The sandbar almost

glowed in the darkness and the islands looked like dark stones protruding from the water.

But that loveliness was deceptive, because from what we had encountered, everything in this world was trying to kill and eat each other. It was a savage land and a savage beauty.

As I watched, a light moved across the darkened islands and I pointed it out to the others. A Scavenger. Possibly the one that had passed us last night. It spanned the sandbar at a speed that made our crossing laughable and began rising towards the Citadel summit. We ducked down in the shadows of the strange alien furniture and the Scavenger sailed over us to the top level and disappeared inside.

Not sure if it would re-emerge, we halted our climb, but after a stretch of nervous minutes, we set off again with one eye watching for its strange glow. Our time was growing short, and we hadn't even located the Staff.

At the second to last level, we paused to ensure our weapons were ready. Swords were pulled from scabbards to ensure nothing would stick and I selected arrows for the perfect shaft and feathering. I could leave nothing to chance. Surely, we would find some aliens in the top tier. This was the throne room and the queen would have many attending her. With an entire city of aliens, there would be no way we could fight our way back to our people. Only by sneaking in and finding what we had come for undetected did we have a chance to return. But we had to be ready for anything.

We all acknowledged our commitment by clasping arms. No one dared look the other in the eye, because that show of affection would be unmanly, but internally, I wanted to bawl like a school kid. These were some of the best friends I could ask for. That any of them could die in the next few minutes weighed heavily on me, especially as the leader. I never had this class of friends in the real world. I would die for each and every one of them and I know they would do so for me. I just had to find a way forward without going to those extremes.

With no more excuses for waiting, in silence and shadow we ascended the final tier—only to find an empty room.

Chapter 27
(Adam)

Was the entire Citadel empty? No, I had heard the chattering of many Kleptons talking at once down in the bowels of the tunnels. Although we had seen none, they were somewhere in this vast complex.

Looking across the Throne Room, although empty, it consisted of open windows in all directions as if the Queen needed to see for herself her entire Kingdom. More scattered islands laced the oceans on the backside of the Citadel and they seemed to extend far beyond the horizon.

The throne itself was a massive array of cushions lying across a central platform. The Queen must be huge judging from the size of the dais. There must be a hundred of pillows and cushions waiting to receive her expansive form. From the throne, a trail of slime trailed across the room towards another entrance that seemed to fall to another level. The entire room was cast in shadows but light rose from the one tunnel.

Silently with our blades at the ready and bows notched and ready to let loose, we crossed the empty room towards the only other entrance offered.

Riku dropped to all fours as she approached the descending tunnel and crawled towards the opening so she would not give herself away. Peering into the passageway, she gave us the signal to indicate the all clear, and we followed her into the throat of the hole. It was the only opening off the room, so it made sense that it would lead to the Queen and her chambers.

The tunnel curved gently to the left as it sloped downward. We hugged the wall as we padded down the hallway to help keep out of sight, and to avoid stepping in the trail of slime that ran down the center of the passageway. In the low light it looked like there were layers of the stuff as if someone renewed it each day.

The light grew stronger, and we came to another opening. Peering in the room, Riku motioned us to follow her, but then froze in place. We watched her tense form, hoping we hadn't been exposed. Finally, her shoulders relaxed, and she crept forward. Carefully, I followed her around the corner to see into a cavernous room. The trail of slime ended at what I could only think of as a bed. On it was a massive beast that must have been the Queen. Unlike her soldiers, she bore no carapace armor, but looked more like a bloated slug. Pale yellowish-green skin rose and fell in a steady rhythm that indicated sleep. Above her a fine mist fell from the ceiling in a continuous drizzle onto her entire body as if it needed to stay moist. I could see no eyes or facial features but considered that she might face away from the entrance to her chambers.

Then I saw it; the Shaft. Mounted as a trophy, like a tribute to the conquering menace. In such an opulent setting, the Shaft of God looked out of place because of its simplicity.

This may hold the power of the God of gods, but it resembled a simple, dried out walking stick. The wood showed wear and had aged to a light gray, the lines of the annual rings blending with the darker heartwood.

I glanced at the Queen to determine if she sensed our presence. Seeing no sign, I padded over to the shaft. I lifted both hands to cradle the Shaft but hesitated when I felt warmth emanating from the wood. It felt alive! To think, that I stood before an object that God himself had touched. With caution, I raised the Shaft from its resting place and nodded to the others that we should go.

On a ledge by the Queen's head, two small globes sat quietly, also being sprayed by some kind of fluid from the ceiling. Ian was bent over and was oblivious that we had recovered the Shaft, so intent he was staring at the pair. I handed the wooden shaft to Gaje and stepped towards my friend. He looked up as I put my hand on his shoulder, wonderment in his expression. He nodded towards the two globes, forcing me to turn my focus. Right away I saw what had mesmerized Ian. Within the organic circles were two shapes that moved showing that they were alive. They swam within the globes with a life of their own.

I realized at once we were looking at eggs, possibly future Queens, which would explain their presence in the Queen's chamber. Peeling my eyes from the un-hatched aliens, I tilted my head towards the entrance of the room silently telling him it was time to leave. He nodded immediately but glanced back at the egg for one last look, when one of the embryos slammed itself against the inside of its aquatic cell in either anger or fear.

The Queen lurched on her bed in frenzy, turning herself far too quickly for a monster her size. If she was surprised at seeing four infiltrators in her chambers, it didn't cause her to hesitate. With a scream, she threw a lone bony arm towards us, slamming into Ian's back and driving straight through his chest, blood and gore trailing behind.

Ian's eyes were wide and unseeing, his mouth gasping as blood dripped to the floor. His limbs wobbled as she tried to retract her arm, shaking him like a ragged doll.

My mind had gone blank at the brutal attack of my friend, but when his broken body was flung across the room, like an unwanted toy, I saw red. For the first time in my life, I felt the dark desire to kill and maim. I wanted to hurt her as much as she had Ian.

Yanking my Kukri from its holster, I rammed it into the center of the nearest egg, embryonic fluid covering my hand. The tiny creature squirmed on the floor at my feet. The Queen roared and lurched towards me, but I grabbed the other egg, my knife at the ready. Her arm drew back ready to impale me, dark beady eyes glaring at me with hatred and rage. Seeing her last egg at my mercy froze her in place.

At my feet, Ian laid still, his eyes unseeing. As I watched, his body glowed an icy-blue. The shimmering rose and separated from Ian to float over his corpse. Was this his spirit? His soul? It slowly dissipated into nothingness.

Behind us, coming up the hallway from below us, a stampede of Kleptons raced to the Queen's rescue aroused by her battle cry. The first ranks were almost upon us, before the Queen hissed a vicious command halting them. So quickly did they comply that many in the ranks behind ran into their comrades in a clatter of carapace.

"Back up very slowly, Adam." Gaje said, the tension tightening his voice.

"But, Ian-" I said blinking back tears at my friend's death.

"It's too late for Ian, but we must get back or these animals will do this to all our friends and families. There's too much riding on this."

He was right, but I didn't have to like it. Images of these monsters feeding on my little buddy came without warning and I came close to killing the last egg right then and there, but then he would have died for nothing.

Riku led the way, her sword at the ready, while Gaje kept a hand at my back, guiding me so I didn't have to take my eyes of the Queen who began a deluge of clicks and clacks. She made a move to follow, but I raised the knife closer to the egg and she stopped, quivering in kinetic rage.

At the corner, Riku had us retrace our footsteps to the main throne room. It was our only safe bet of getting out of this alive. There was no way would chance wandering the inner maze of tunnels. As far as the hallway's curve allowed, we saw no pursuit, but we all knew that the Queen would never give up. I had killed one of her offspring and threatened the other. She would do whatever it took to retrieve her egg before turning her hatred on the rest of us.

I wasn't planning on giving her the chance.

We crossed the throne room out the massive opening overlooking the sandbar so far below us. Even though I knew they were too far to see, I looked for the others on the tip of the first island. I shuddered at the thought of breaking the news about Ian and I bit my lip to keep from losing it right there on the spot.

Gaje grabbed one of the many pillows from the Queen's throne and rigged a simple bag that we could slip the egg into. I carried it like a sling, across my back leaving my hands free to carry the Staff and for the long climb off the Citadel.

Going down was a lot faster and easier than our ascent. Where Riku and Gaje just leapt down, I didn't want to risk crushing the egg and our only hope of escaping. I sat on the ledge, swiveled and lower myself with my arms before dropping the few feet to the next tier. Once I got use to the maneuver, our descent quickened.

As the pale sandbar became sharper, we could see an army of Kleptons lining across the last two tiers. There was no sign of the Queen but a huge number of Wizards lined the higher of the two tiers. Remembering Guāng's explanation that these served as the army's officers, I eyed the low riding creatures for any sign that they planned to attack. One of their sonic attacks might knock us unconscious leaving them a chance to grab first the hostage and the Queen's revenge. From another opening came the fliers by the hundreds, their multi-numbered wings sounding like a hive of bees on a rampage, but they kept their distance. The substance that glued their victims to the ground would not break the standoff, only prolong it.

Each time I turned myself towards the wall, I checked above to see if there was any pursuit from that direction. I saw nothing until we were near the two tiers with the waiting army. This time when I looked, I saw the Queen on the top tier, on the edge of her throne room looking down. I could feel her cold dark hatred even at this distance.

With a wave from the Queen, the alien troops moved apart to allow us passage. As soon as our feet hit the soft sand, we began our jog across to the first island. There would be no breaks or camping this time. This was a race to the riff and a return to our own Heaven. I knew the Kleptons would follow, especially to ensure the safety of their unborn princess.

"Hold up," I panted to the other two. They stopped and watched me pull the sling off my back.

"It's too soon, Adam. They'll be on us in seconds." Gaje said the terror in his voice reflecting the stunned look in Riku's eyes.

"Don't worry; I'm not giving our ace away." I lifted the small bag and held it over my head so the entire horde could see. Walking to the waterline, I dipped the bag into the life-giving water soaking the bag. If the spray that had been up in the Queen's chamber was so the egg did not dry out, this small concession might express to the Queen that I meant no real harm to her offspring. Re-slinging the bag, I nodded to the other two, and we began the long run to our companions on the island. As expected, the flock of fliers followed from a distance.

Chapter 28
(Adam)

We hadn't reached the island before I spotted Freddy and Rob standing among the brush rather than in cover like their counterparts. They knew how to count, and Ian's small frame wasn't part of our party, so they knew something had happened. My tears ran painfully blurring the landscape, but I did nothing to wipe them away. It was the only way I could grieve with an army at our back.

Freddy jumped off the steep bank as we came close, his long spear at his side. "Where is he, Adam?" he said in a shaky voice.

I shook my head not trusting my voice.

Gaje came to my rescue. "The Queen killed Ian. There was nothing any of us could have done to prevent it. It was over too quickly."

"Tell me you killed the bitch?" Freddy was shaking, his expression as dark as I had ever seen it.

"No, but Adam killed one of her eggs and he has the other. It was the only reason we were able to leave."

"Then let me kill it."

"No," I said finally finding my voice. "It's our only ticket home. If they see us even threatening the Queen's child, they'll attack and we'll all be dead." I reached out and pulled him into an embrace. "We found the Staff and we need to make it back to figure out how to close the riff or Ian will have died for nothing. I'm hurting too, trust me. I was there and can never erase what I saw."

All seven of us, even the hardened warriors silently wept for our friend and brother-in-arms. After a few moments, I said, "Let's finish this. Rob,

Peta take the lead. Let's keep close. We only stop for breaks and water. I want to be through the riff before the end of the day."

My words seem to galvanize everyone. Although we were all hurting from Ian's death, it gave us something to concentrate on. A goal. Rob and Peta jumped to the position of scout, pushing outward to ensure we were not flanked, while Freddy still raw with emotions, moved forwards allowing Gaje and I to take the rear. Riku fell solo behind Freddy and in front of me, having lost her partner. She was the strongest amongst us in stealth, but now we needed speed.

I emptied my last water bag on the run, the lukewarm water easing my parched throat. I would have to fill it at our next break. The humidity and constant running wore on all of us and it was vital that we stay hydrated.

We were halfway across the third island when a monstrous beast that resembled a lion the size of a small house crashed out of the jungle ahead of us.

Rob and Peta let loose a pair of arrows at the creature that elicited a roar of anger from its snapping mandibles. The creature charged towards Rob in a bluish blur, only to be slammed by four or five blasts from above. Turning I witnessed two more dragonfly like fliers launch their orange tinged mucus at the animal. The slime covered the beast, pinning him to the ground. It struggled to pull away from the sticky mess, but gave up to exhaustion.

"Why are they protecting us?" Rob said shaken.

"They're not," Peta said pointing at me. "They're protecting the egg."

With care, we gave the snarling animal plenty of space as we passed before resuming our run. At the next crossing, we filled our water bags, and I dipped the egg sack into the water as well, the droning fliers watching intently as I did this. I splashed water over my head and across my neck to help cool me off but the relief was fleeting.

By now, the night had dissipated and the day's heat became more intense. We found our progress slowing and the need for more breaks growing.

It was Peta that showed us why so many of his people wore headbands. "Our lands go from the plains to the deserts. A simple band will stop the salt from getting into your eyes. It'll save you a lot of pain later in the day."

Ganjo laughed as Freddy followed the rest of us in tying the rags around our foreheads. "Come to Ethiopia if you want to feel heat. Pain strengthens you."

The Comanche shrugged at the comment and didn't bother arguing. I didn't think there was much point. The Heaven we were racing back towards never got that hot.

Unable to see the sun because of the jungle canopy and the overcast sky, it was difficult to determine how long we ran. We were all near the limits of our stamina. My throat was raw from panting and fighting the heavy moist air. Without warning we reached the riff and slowed to a staggering walk.

"What are you waiting for, Adam?" Rob said, his face red from exertion.

"We need to catch our breath before going through. There's no telling what kind of reception we'll find on the other side. We might walk into a fully armed camp."

He nodded his understanding.

"Before we go through," Freddy said pointing at the egg sack on my back. "I want to kill it."

Gaje shook his head. "I don't think that's wise."

Freddy spun towards the eastern warrior his eyes glaring. "Why? They wouldn't hesitate to do the same to us. Ian was my friend, and those animals killed him. I want a piece of them."

I stepped between the two fearing that Freddy might take a swing at him. "Easy, bud."

His eyes flashed at mine but he backed down although his chest was rising and falling as he reined in his anger.

I turned to Gaje, "Tell me your thoughts, brother."

"First, Ian was a friend to all of us. Everyone loved him. He will be missed. But consider this; if we kill the only offspring the Queen and her people have, there will be nothing holding her back from sending her entire nation against ours. With one knife strike, we could end up losing our world before we have a chance to figure out how to use the Staff to close the riff."

"She might still send her troops after us," Freddy said. He was calmer but still thirsty for his revenge.

Gaje nodded, "But first she'll tend to her unborn child. Ensure its safety. And that will take time. Time we really need right now."

I considered his words and realized he was right. I hadn't even had a chance to examine the Staff other than to feel the power course through it. How it worked was a question for the prophets, not me.

I turned to Freddy and the others. "I think Gaje is right. You'll still have a chance to hurt the Kleptons, Freddy. Even if we manage to close the riff, we still must deal with the aliens that are trapped in our Heaven."

He wasn't happy with my decision, but didn't argue anymore.

I pulled the egg sack off my back and dipped once again in the water, looking at the hovering insects that held a healthy distance between us. "Rob, let's move. Remember, we don't know what's waiting for us so try to keep under cover of the trees and we'll circle back and climb the saddle. I don't think the Kleptons can climb that well with their armor. Once everyone has entered, I drop the egg and follow."

Without a word, the others filed through the glimmering nothingness of the riff and through the void. I backed up to within a couple of feet of the shimmering light and gently set the egg sack onto the ground. As I entered the inter-dimensional tunnel, I saw a glob of orange glue hurtling towards me, but the white light enclosed over me before it landed. Seconds later, I walked in a much cooler atmosphere and realized it was night. Without warning, I was grabbed and yanked forward.

Chapter 29
(Adam)

A small, callused hand clamped over my mouth and a whispered voice I recognized as Riku said, "The camp is occupied. Follow me."

There was a wet splat on the ground when I had stepped from the riff and even in the dark; I realized it was the mucus from the flier that had fired at me as I entered the tunnel.

Without waiting to see if the flying insect would follow, she and I both dropped to the ground and crawled towards the trees. Behind us came the ominous drone of the flier as it flew out of the riff. It seemed to hover in place and I realized it was blind without daylight. A small blessing for my team as we made for cover. Once I had a few pine trees between it and us, I relaxed and pushed my senses out into the night. We caught up to the others and followed the natural curve of the canyon, always staying within the tree line.

The cool mountain air felt as if I had dove into a deep mountain lake, my skin relishing the freshness of the breeze. This wasn't my earth, but it felt more like home than the Klepton's world did.

As we moved, I tried not to speculate about the wellbeing of our brothers-in-arms if the Klepton's were once again camped in front of the riff. Had they escaped or been slaughtered? Rather than torture myself needlessly, I reached out for a friend.

"Guāng? Are you there?"

"Adam! You've returned. Where are you?"

"We've just returned and are moving to begin the climb to the saddle. The others?"

"They wait back at the cave behind the waterfall. There was no point leaving the area until you returned."

"We found the Staff, Guāng, but...," I said tripping on my grief. The memory of the Queen's arm cutting through Ian's chest came to me and I felt Guāng gasp. He had seen my thoughts

"No-" I felt a mixture of warmth and pain cross from my spectral friend as he dealt with the news. A calm came over me, *Guāng's* presence comforting me like a loving hug. Tears fell silently as I grieved with his kind shoulder to lean on. All this unfolded while I continued to creep through the trees.

"We're at the base of the saddle and must cross before daylight. Some fliers have followed us from Klepton's world. We'll camp under the cover of the forest during the day and then make the march to the cave tomorrow night. Please inform the Captains."

"I will, Adam. Call if you need me."

Climbing by feel alone, we made the ascent, but it took a long time. Staying together as a group and assisting each other to find purchase and balance. Exhausted and drenched in soil-caked clothes, we finally reached the top of the saddle. I could not wait to wash and change into dry clothes. At this point I think the enemy could track us from our rank scent.

The night began losing its battle against the sun as we started down to our former camp in the trees. Every minute made a difference, we moved safely and faster. It helps when you can see the hazards before you've tripped over them.

The sun was full over the mountain's edge as we reached the base. Each of us crawled into our bedrolls under the thick, dark pine boughs, too tired to even post a guard. Even if the aliens had found us, we wouldn't have been able to fight back.

I WOKE TO THE SCENT of pine resin. It was still light, but the shadows were long. I shook my head to rid it of the groggy residue of sleep. I rolled out from under the trees shelter to find a dancing ball of light that dazzled my sleep starved eyes.

"Guāng," I said aloud.

The others each rose from their slumber at my voice and of hearing the familiar name.

"May peace be upon you brave warriors," Guāng said to the seven of us in a linked thought.

All welcomed him as he was trusted and much loved by all.

"I know of your loss. Allow me to spare you the bluntness of your grief. You will still grieve your friend as is fitting, but it need not consume you." A wave of love and peace infused my heart, easing the ache that haunted me. I saw the others shed the tension that they seemed not to have known they wore.

"While you have rested, we have discussed many plans. They have asked me to convey these to you."

"I hope one of them talks about a bath and a change of clothes," I said.

The others chuckled but I could tell they felt the same.

"I'm sure we can take the time for that, Adam." Guāng said as he spun in place as if studying us. *"Guess I should be grateful I have no sense of smell."*

This time the laughter was genuine.

"Iron Fist should be here soon with horses. Thanks to Nita's recollection of his time in the Klepton's world, he suggested you might need to clean up so there will be fresh clothes and some food."

"Both are welcomed," Peta said his gratitude warming his quiet voice.

"Once you're cleaned, Adam, you and I must part with your friends to return the Shaft to the Holy Ones."

"But I thought we couldn't travel that way because the aliens could track you," I said surprised.

"I've made many crossings while you were in the other Heaven and in this case, time is of the essence. There is no time to march all the way back and then return to deal with the riff which must be closed to put an end to this blight."

"But I thought my job was to find and retrieve the Staff. What else do they expect from us? We've al-

ready lost Ian." I couldn't believe that it wasn't over. We had done our duty, not that we had much choice with the Kleptons attacking soon after we learned about what they wanted from me and my friends.

"Gaining the Staff was the first step. The prophecy said that you would bring back the balance. I'm afraid there is more to be done."

"Yes!" Freddy said aloud. "There's still a chance to avenge Ian and kill the Queen and her evil spawn."

"Revenge will not bring Ian back, Freddy," Guāng said with sympathy.

"Maybe not, but it'll make me feel better knowing she'll never hurt another soul." With that he picked up his spear and stomped across the clearing as if to close the subject.

Guāng had blunted the razor-sharp pain of Ian's passing, but not enough for Freddy's anger. I could see the knuckles of his fist were white as he clenched the weapon. He would need to find some way to release that pent-up emotion or it would eat right through him.

The others all looked away, partially embarrassed but also, I think afraid they might end up being the vent that Freddy might use without thought.

As promised, it wasn't long before we heard the pounding of hooves echoing off the mountain walls. Leaving the shelter of the trees, we stepped out as Iron Horse dropped to the ground, before his horse came to a stop. Without expression on his usual somber face, he grabbed the forearm of Peta, and then pulled the younger man in a fierce hug. To my utter surprise he then repeated the gesture with each of us.

"You are great warriors who have counted coup on an alien enemy in their own camp and escaped to tell the tale. Welcome home."

Considering he usually said nothing, this was high praise indeed from the legendary Chief.

His other men had spare horses trailing behind them and we wasted no time mounting up and turning back towards the canyon where the others were waiting our return.

Thankfully the wind direction was in our favor, leaving our body odor at our backs. The ride also gave me time to wrap my head around my continued participation in this adventure. As daunting as the quest for the Staff had been, we had accomplished it and I knew I should be proud of our success, but losing Ian dampened any sense of triumph. We had entered an alien world against unbelievable odds and brought back possibly the only item that might save everyone.

I shook my head with wonder at the fact I was thinking how absurd it seemed to talk about alien worlds when I was standing in Heaven with mortal people rather than my home planet of Earth. Here, we are surrounded by people who had died, some centuries ago. They are spirits, and I am friends with them. And the fact that an alien spirit had killed Ian made it the weirdest horror story any fiction fan could encounter.

When we reached the mouth of the canyon where the river flowed, Riku moved to an area that lent her privacy. Once she was out of sight, the rest of us dismounted and stripped off our soiled clothing. I was half ready to leave them behind, but Ganjo said that the Suri women could salvage them.

Dropping into the freezing mountain water took my breath away, but I scrubbed with the hard, abrasive bar of saponin that the Ethiopian women had created from a wildflower called soapwort. It was a little rough on the skin until it lathered up. Nabala had told me that the soap was extra special as it did not harm the environment. This might be important in our own world but I figured it wouldn't matter in this one. I was glad to have it just the same because it did wonders and I could see my companions felt the same. My body was numb from the waist down as I struggled up the bank.

The new crisp clothes finished the transformation and as my body began to warm up, I felt like a new person.

Fortunately, the horses would carry us through the stream and saved us from getting both wet and cold. Before long, we turned around a rock shelf and spied the falls crashing into the pool below. There must have been a lookout in the hidden window, because as we rode around to the back side of the waterfall, Hattori and the others waited at the opened cave door.

Once the backslapping and bids of welcome finished, Nabala served us our first hot meal in almost a week. Chunks of venison floated in a thick broth with wild leeks and cubes of cattail root. After my third serving, which had the two women grinning with pride, I gracefully surrendered my bowl after wiping it with the last piece of bread.

Satisfied, I walked over to where Freddy had sat apart from us, the anger still gripping him.

"Freddy, I have to go. Are you going to be okay?" I said couched in front of him so we were eye to eye.

"Gonna have to be, until we get another chance at killing those evil bugs."

"And I'll be there to have your back, buddy."

A lone tear slid down his face. He bit his lip and nodded but refused to say anymore.

Rising I went to Rob and said my goodbyes. "Back as fast I can. Do me a favor and keep an eye on him? He's mad enough and crazy enough to take off after them by himself"

"I'll watch him, Adam. Don't you worry." The big gentle giant put one of his huge hands on my shoulder. "You just worry about figuring how to use that Shaft. We need to stop these things. There's been enough killing."

"I'll do my best."

The four Captains, Gaje and Guāng waited for me at the cavern's entrance. Each wished me a successful trip and a fast return. There was nothing but respect from each of these accomplished warriors. Thanks to their training, I was on the road to becoming like them.

Gaje came forward last and hugged me in a rough embrace. "Brother, I should be going with you, even though you will be returning." He pulled his Kukri out of its sheath and scraped a long cut across the palm of his hand so that the blood flowed freely. Reversing the knife, he said, "Would you honor me and become true brothers?"

Swallowing with pride and affection, I gladly took the offered blade by the hilt and marked my own hand. With the blood dripping from both our hands, we clasped each other, so the blood mingled.

"We are true brothers." He said with pride and emotion. With a laugh, my rough and humorous comrade shouted, "Father, you have a second son."

"And I am pleased to witness this bond," Gopi said and swallowed us both in a tight embrace. "My two sons have made me proud."

I have to admit, I almost lost it. There were so many conflicting emotions running through me; the grief of losing Ian, the worry for Freddy, the pride of acceptance and brotherhood. It almost overwhelmed me. But it was Guāng who saved me.

"We must go, Adam. The prophets wait."

I took in a deep breath and nodded.

"Yes, my friend, let's get going." I said aloud. "I'll be back. Don't fight this war without me."

As we left the cave filled with my two mortal friends and all those beloved spirits, I wondered how I would ever leave Heaven and my new family once this was all over.

"I think you remember how this works, Adam?" Guāng said.

Not waiting for a reply, he turned around me three times so that his light held me tight, yet safely and snapped straight upwards. We climbed beside the waterfall and then left it far below us as he crested the mountain itself. In a gentle arc, we slid over the mountains and in minutes left them behind as they tumbled down to the rolling grasslands of the prairies. From this high, the plains looked like a sandy-colored carpet with folds that held dark green woodlands following stream beds.

In the far south, I saw the settlement that Nita had called New Chicago. There were skyscrapers nestled around the tip of a deep blue bay of water that extended south.

Here and there we saw more evidence of the Klepton's raiding parties. Dirty brown smoke foretold of the devastation left behind their passage. At one point we saw a massive army marching out of the mountains, towards the main seat of power to Heaven, which is where we were headed. I felt anxious at the thought of being in the path of that juggernaut. Could the heroes of Heaven hope to hold back this horde or would it all be up to my friends and I?

I prayed that someone could teach me to wield this Staff of Moses in time to save everyone. I needed no more blood on my hands.

As if reading my thoughts, Guāng sped up, so I had to close my eyes to the rush of wind that flooded them with tears.

Chapter 30
(Adam)

In seconds we began slowing down as the familiar courtyard appeared ahead. Beyond, an Egyptian pyramid lay crumpled with its capstone collapsed into its interior depths. The remains of an ancient Sphinx lay at its base, the head severed from the stone body.

The giant golden Buddha had been defiled and one of its arms lay crumbled beside the two crossed legs so that meditation would have been difficult if not painful.

There were many other signs of the massive battle that had held the horde back to give us time to escape the capital weeks ago. So much had happened since that frantic time, it seemed ages ago now.

I had changed. We all had. We'd become warriors; maybe not as proficient as those who taught us, but we had enough skills to stand strong. The harsh training routine, the battles we faced and the tragedy that we had to endure hardened and tempered us.

Guāng circled the courtyard, bleeding off speed before gently touching down in the center of the smoke-stained, white stone. Once I had my balance, he untangled himself, allowing me to stand on my own. I stood holding the Staff of Moses in both hands, hoping that one of these Demi-gods would accept the burden.

"A child left us and a man returns," Mohammad said his voice deep and heavy with respect. "You have succeeded and proved that the God of gods choose the right person for the task. Welcome, Adam."

I nodded, acknowledging his compliments but held my tongue waiting to see what guidance they would offer.

"He has also grown wiser," said the Son of God from Galilee with a warm smile. I once again felt the flow of love and calmness sweep over me that took the edge from the anxiety of standing before the greatest deities on Earth's religions. "We will talk afterwards, Adam. I believe I have a surprise for you that will erase some of your pain."

"My Grandpa...?"

His gentle eyes closed, and he nodded. "Among others." He pointed to the path that wound through the apple orchard and led to my Grandpa's fire pit.

His words left me confused. My grandmother was still alive, unless she had passed since I arrived here and my mother's parents lived at their cottage each summer before fleeing to Florida during the colder months.

Some trees on the edge of the orchard showed damage. Broken limbs and burnt bark had devastated a couple of the neat rows of trees. It was clear the battle had come close to my Grandpa's home.

The old man stood waiting for me beside the fire pit. "There's my boy," he said pulling me into a warm hug. He pushed me to arm's length. "Let me look at you. It seems you've done some growing in the short time you've been gone. Lost all that baby fat."

I must have gone red because he slapped me on the back with a laugh. "Come on, sit and tell me about your adventure. It's your time to do the story-telling."

We talked for an hour until I finally told him about Ian's death. It choked me up, but he sat there listening and giving me the time and space to tell the story to its completion.

"I know you're hurting and I think I can help with that a little. I have someone I want you to meet. He's been waiting for you."

From behind me, a timid voice said, "Hi, Adam."

I knew that voice but it couldn't be. Twisting in my seat, I almost collapsed the folding lawn chair. Standing not ten feet from me in his black shozoko, his sword strapped to his back, was the very subject of my grief.

Ian.

He gave me that familiar shy smile before he said, "Miss me?"

I don't remember crossing to him but I had my arms around his slight form and the tears were flowing like they would never stop. By the time I finally could talk, the fabric of his shirt was more than just damp.

"How…? I watched you die."

His smile was gentle but tinged with sadness. "Remember where we are?"

It hit home, and it staggered me. He had died and like grandpa had explained, had been reborn here in Heaven. He saw how it affected me and guided me back to the chair.

"Nice deep breaths, Adam."

I was shaken but at the same time conflicted. It was so fantastic to see and talk with my friend who I thought was gone forever, but it also meant that he was dead and when we returned to Earth, he wouldn't. It tore my mind and heart. It would take time to sort out my feelings so I tried not to dwell on it.

"Did it…" I groped for the right way of asking.

"Did it hurt?" he said, his hand rising to his chest. "Only for a few seconds. You grabbing the egg was the last thing I saw. The next thing I knew I was here across the fire from your Grandpa."

"Why here and not with anyone from your family?"

"Because," Grandpa said. "We lost Ian's kin in the last battle. He had met me when you boys first arrived, so they asked me to welcome him. After all, we have you as a common bond. We've become good friends in a short time."

I shook my head, amazed. "Rob and Freddy will freak." I filled him on Freddy's reaction and my worry that he would try something stupid.

"Then as much as I wanted to visit longer," Grandpa said rising from his seat. "You better speak to the Prophets about that Staff and head back. You need to protect Freddy from himself."

"He's right, Adam," Ian said. "Time to get back to our crew."

"You're coming back?"

"Definitely," he said with a tight smile. "Freddy might think he has a reason for payback, but mine trumps his."

I laughed but could tell he meant what he said.

Both of us received a hug from Grandpa before he walked us back to the courtyard.

ENTERING THE COURTYARD, we found it empty except for three men. An ancient man with a long flowing beard stood between Mohammad and Jesus of Nazareth. Like the other two men, he wore a long one-piece garment that fell to his sandaled feet.

"I hope being reunited with your friend has eased your grief, Adam," Jesus said, his gentle smile making me feel loved.

"Yes. It was quite the shock, but after all my friends and I have seen and done since we got here, I should have realized that he would be reborn here. It just never occurred to me."

"The pain of losing someone you care for can blind us all," said Mohammad.

Gesturing towards the old man, Jesus said, "Boys, this is Moses and, in his time, God entrusted him with the Staff when he led the Israelites out of Egypt."

"You're the actual Moses that split the sea?" I said in astonishment, remembering the story from the Old Testament.

The three Holy men chucked at my surprise. Seemed like I was forever being shocked by what was happening to me.

"Yes, I am that Moses," the old man said in a deep baritone voice.

"So, we can bring plagues onto the Kleptons with this?" I said holding the Staff towards him.

"The power came through the Staff directly from God. I only wielded it."

"So, are you saying it won't work because God is not here to power it?" I couldn't believe what he was implying. If that was the fact, then why were we sent on a fool's errand in the first place?

"No," he said. "When you first picked it up, you felt the power that came from the Shaft?"

I nodded remembering the tingle as I first lifted it from its resting spot in the Queen's chamber. I had been bursting with power.

"The power is there to be tapped into, but you must learn how to do so."

"You've used it before," I said in frustration, "so why don't you use it to stop the aliens."

"When I was called on by God to free the Jews and worked all those incredible and amazing miracles with the Staff, it was because He had asked it of me. Because of the prophecy, it'll be through you. God named you as the leader to bring balance to the Heavens; not me."

There was no escape for me. If I didn't learn how to use the power of the Staff, there was no hope of ever beating the aliens. The heavy weight of overwhelming responsibility was once again threatening to crush me. Everything came down to me. If I failed, all the souls of Heaven and possibly Earth would be lost. The tightness in my chest made it difficult to breathe, and I felt light-headed.

As he could sense my inner turmoil, Moses stepped forward and placed both of his hands on my shoulders, looking deep into my eyes. "I know what you are thinking, Adam. I too felt unfit for the task God entrusted me with, but He would never ask of you more than you are capable of. I was one man who went against not only my brother but the entire might of the Egyptian civilization. Do not for a minute, think that I was unafraid. I was terrified the entire time. But I believed in my God and I believed in myself."

His hands squeezed my shoulders with affection before he stepped back.

His words eased some of my anxiety and I could breathe again.

"Also remember, my young friend," Mohammad said, "what you have already accomplished. That in itself shows your potential. When you first came, you didn't think you were up to the task of retrieving the Staff and yet, here you are holding it. You've become an accomplished warrior and leader and have invaded the enemy's stronghold. From what we have seen, there's nothing you cannot do if you believe in yourself."

His words made realize how far I had come in the weeks since we ended up here. I was not the same, pissed off kid with a chip on his shoulder.

Nodding my appreciation at his words, I looked at Moses. "So how do I work this thing? I don't see a button or trigger."

He chuckled. "It's a little about what we have been talking about. It's believing in yourself. When you want something, you must picture it in your head and focus that picture from your heart and mind through the Staff. The raw power of the Staff does the rest."

"So, I just picture what I want and it happens."

"To a degree. Your reasons must be true as well. When I separated the Red Sea, I focused on the sea dividing but it was to save my people as God had wanted. My reasons were not selfish nor were they malicious. I did not wish for my brother's army to perish. Unfortunately, his wounded pride would not allow us to go."

"Remember, Adam," Jesus of Nazareth said, "The prophecy said that you would bring balance to the Heavens. That implies both ours and the Kleptons."

I stared at him in surprise. I had not considered that. Thinking we were being trained to bring the battle to the aliens, I never considered that there was more to it than that. I had seen that the alien world was a savage environment that would have shaped their society differently than ours, not that humans hadn't proved their ruthlessness in the countless wars and conflicts throughout history. So, their behavior was dictated by surviving all the savagery of their own environment. They were not necessarily evil. It was just their nature. That understanding changed my perspective completely.

It still upset me they had killed my friend and countless others. My mind flashed to the two I refugees that I had ordered killed before the creatures within them hatched. They were no different than a grizzly bear that kills a hiker who crosses paths with the beast. It's unfortunate, devastating even, but there is no evil in the attack.

Those gentle eyes watched as the realization came to me and he smiled knowing I understood my role.

"Moses, when you first used the Staff, did it work right away?" I asked still not sure I could wield it.

He shook his head. "No, it took a lot of practice on my part. Start small, like moving a stone. Once you feel the connection between you and the Staff's power, you'll be able to do more and will learn faster. It's a little like meditating. Clear your mind of all distractions and picture what you wish to do as clearly as possible, putting as much of yourself into it."

"What do you mean?"

"You can add part of yourself by adding your feelings into the makeup of the picture. Like an artist puts his heart and soul into a painting. Think of your feelings as an important piece of the picture, like your feelings for your friend here," said Moses indicating Ian.

Ian blushed at the attention and flashed a smile.

I think I understood what he meant. It would be a matter of practicing. I was just worried that we might run out of time. I was sure the Queen was planning retaliation for killing her one egg and threatening the other.

When I mentioned this, Mohammad nodded. "It's already started. Guāng has been there and back to report that a steady flow of Kleptons soldiers have been making the trip through the riff. The Queen seems to be sending every warrior she possesses in a last-ditch battle."

I looked at him and wondered aloud, "Why did she take the Staff in the first place. Is she able to use it?"

It was Jesus who explained. "We believe that her soldiers felt the energy coming off the Staff and felt it was something they could tap into. We also believe that if she were to understand how to use its power, she would use it to gain entry into other Heavens and their home worlds. We must stop her once and for all. There are too many souls at risk."

I felt that weight getting heavier again, but refused to allow it to crush me again. I needed to figure out how to gain the power of the Staff, and had no more time to feel sorry for myself. It was time to put on my big boy pants and buckle down. There was no way I would allow the Kleptons to kill any more of my friends.

"Where do you suggest I practice? Here, or back with our band of warriors?"

"Your group has found a great hiding spot close to the riff," Mohammad said considering the question. "There will be much bustle here as we put together our own army and march to meet the horde. You would find fewer distractions in the mountains."

I nodded, relieved that I would join my friends, even though I would be busy attempting to gain access to the Staff's power. That would need seclusion and silence.

As if knowing it was time to leave, Guāng entered the courtyard, spinning with anxious energy.

"Remember," Jesus said to me as his warmth flowed outward. "Trust in yourself, Adam."

"Thank you. The faith you all have shown in me has helped. I will do my best."

With that Guāng twirled around Ian and I, pulling us in a tight embrace and rocketed towards the west.

Chapter 31
(Adam)

Guāng dropped us off beside the pool having explained that he would continue on, in case his movements were being monitored by the Scavengers. He had informed those inside the cave of our arrival and we found the door opened for us.

As expected, Ian being with me, alive and well brought an entirely different reception than normal. Freddy's tough guy facade fell apart, and he bawled like a toddler while Ian held and comforted him. Rob pulled us all into one of his signature group hugs, almost crushing the air out of us.

The most heart-wrenching reunion was reunion was Riku dropping to her knees before Ian. "I failed to protect you, so offer my life in repentance," she said exposing her neck to him.

"Warriors fall in battle, Riku," Ian said, his hands on her shoulders. "I let my guard down, fascinated with the eggs, instead of focusing on the Queen. The fault lies with me, not you." He pulled on her shozoko making her rise. Without another word, Ian hugged her. Riku stiffened for a second, and then relaxed in acceptance.

Once things settled down from our homecoming, I met with the Captains and the original eight and filling them in on what had transpired with Moses concerning the Staff.

"So, I need to learn how to tap into the Staff's power. And I must be alone to do so."

"It sounds like you need to release your Ki," Hattori said, his eyes narrowed in thought.

"Ki?"

"It is your life force. The Chinese call it chi, while the Hindus practice prana, and the Hawaiians name it mana. Most civilizations have some way of dealing with the concept. You can gain chi by meditation, exercise, and certain foods. The more energy you have the more you can focus into your given task. Those with strong chi are powerful or successful while those with low energy are sickly or prone to giving up."

"So how do you gain Ki?" I asked wondering if this was the answer.

"You've been doing it ever since you joined us," Hattori said. "The knife drills that Gopi puts you through are repetitive therefore allows the mind to enter a meditative state that helps strengthen the Ki. Catholic and Tibetan monks do the same with their chants or prayers."

It made sense; the workouts tired me, but I always felt refreshed as well. If I could tap into that energy, I might be able to use it to energize the staff. I would start there.

"You can use the valley here for your practice," Iron Horse said. "I will post my men at the mouth to warn us of any enemy movement so you have time to get to shelter."

"*And I can watch from high above for any Scavenger presence*," said Guāng as he came through the high lookout tower.

Thus, began one of the most frustrating times of my life. I had thought my time before the court and the boot camp was difficult, but trying to reach for some mysterious force within myself was a nightmare. Of course, the harder I tried the worse it got. Every past failure sprung up in my mind, replaying like a bad movie. Pressure seized me, yelling that EVERYTHING was riding on me.

The rock was a small smooth river stone which Gaje balanced on a taller one so it would tip and fall at the slightest pressure. "Even if you can squeak out a little of the energy, you should be able to see a reaction," he said with encouragement.

I repeatedly went through the knife drills, my muscle memory overruling my need to think allowed me to sink into a calming nothingness. When I fell in that zone, I pictured the stone in as much detail as I could, and my mind's eye watched it tip and slide off its perch. But as I reached for the Staff, the picture would crumble and I would lose my concentration.

When I expressed my frustration to Hattori, he laughed. "I said that the knife drill allows you to find that quiet spot in your mind, but there are other ways. Through meditation, you need not hold your knife, but can hold the Staff." He turned and walked out of the cave and I followed him to where I usually practiced. He had me sit facing the balanced stone. When I was settled, he pulled a black cloth from one of the many pockets of his suit and covered my eyes, tying it with a snug knot.

"Now, concentrate on the sound of the falling water, block out all else. Every time your mind wanders, return to the water. Eventually you will find the same calm spot, that you can picture the stone."

He left me and I spent the next few hours trying to block out all sound and thoughts other than the crashing water. A few times, I entered that spot, but fell out the minute I tried to picture the stone.

Disheartened, I gave up as I felt the chill of the early evening pull me further way from the quiet place in my mind. I made my way back to the cave and after accepting the evening meal from Nabala settled down by myself on my bedroll.

Seeing me, Gaje strolled over and dropped beside me. "You trying too hard, Adam," he said after I told him about my lack of results. "Do you remember when you learned the knife drills?"

"Yes," I said between mouthfuls.

"We started the moves slowly until you could complete them with the proper technique. Once perfected, we began to move faster and then faster once again. I think you are trying to rush this and it might be more important for you to master each step before trying to put them all together."

He rose and left me to consider his words. He made sense, and the training had been as he said.

The following morning had me attempting to slow everything down. Each time I listened to the music of the cascading water, I slipped into the quiet zone more easily. I found that the longer I stayed in that contented part of my mind, the more readily I could picture the stone, but time after time, I could not move it.

For three days, I repeated the process, taking my time to allow my mind to ease its way through the stages but nothing seemed to give. The frustration of not knowing what missing ingredient I lacked to bring the task to completion was building and interfering with the other phases.

On the last attempt for the day, I pushed myself to complete each step with the required patience and attention to detail. Every time my mind threatened to drift away from the picture of the stone, I would concentrate on the water so it blocked out everything both inside of me and out. I did not feel the wind or the Shaft in my hands. There was only the stone. I willed everything into the stone, trying to weight one side of it so it would tumble or even wobble on its perch, but nothing happened.

Just as the vision of the stone began to slide away, my frustration bubbled up and I yelled in anger. I felt life energy surge through me and into the Shaft in an instant. The stone left the shattered calm of my mind and flew from the spot it stubbornly sat for most of the week. Shooting across the valley, it ricocheted along the face of the canyon wall. I sat trembling with excitement as I listened to the echo of its chatter among the other rocks before it fell still.

A howl high behind me roared over the crashing water as Gaje shouted a war cry having seen my success. My guardian angel had been watching from below, secretly cheering me on.

In seconds, others rushed from the cave, knowing they had missed something significant. Rob helped me to my feet as my legs were cramped from sitting all day.

"I did it," I confirmed to the group of warriors. The cheer that went up invigorated me and for the first time I knew we stood a chance. This was only the first step, I needed to be as proficient as Moses was during this time with the staff.

The lives and souls of many worlds were on the line.

MY SUCCESS OF YESTERDAY did not repeat itself right away. It took multiple tries to get the added emotion introduced at the proper time to be successful. After another two days, I was flinging stones with the velocity and accuracy of David when he faced Goliath with nothing but his sling.

I used an assortment of feelings; from anger to love and was surprised at the different reactions to the Staff's power. Anger created short and quick actions, where feelings of loyalty, respect and caring allowed me to do massive wonders. Using the feeling of love for my Grandpa allowed me to raise myself as high as the waterfall and then gently lower myself to the ground as easily as Guāng. In response, he danced around me in both delight and fear that I would fall.

Anything I could dream of accomplishing, the Staff allowed if I followed the proper sequence and used the right combinations of emotions. The more I practiced, the better I was at controlling the power of the Staff. The issue lay in how long it took to calm my mind, create the idea and feed emotions into my life force to achieve the desired result. I imagined how I would act in a situation like the ambush we had staged for the enemy raiders. Events happened so quickly, that I would need to use the power of the Staff with the same flexibility and speed.

And what would happen when I didn't have a waterfall to concentrate on?

It was Ian who gave me the clue. He had been waiting quietly, leaning up against a massive boulder that had fallen from further up the mountain eons ago. It had dug itself into the surrounding cliff and sported several forty-foot shaking aspen on its thick soil covered top. When the last stone went successfully flying across the valley, he pushed off the rock and walked towards me with the grace of a cat. My heart ached with the fact that he was another spirit and he wouldn't be returning home with us once this was all over. Because of his death, he only had Heaven left. Not that it was a bad place to be, but it had robbed him of many years on earth. He would never fall in love or have children.

He crouched down beside me, looking across the valley, fiddling with another smooth river stone. With a flick of his wrist, he sent the stone skipping across the pond till the falling water swallowed it.

"I counted six skips," I said, as I began to rise to stand with him.

He waved me back down. "I've been going over the conversations you had with Moses and the other Holy ones. They and you mentioned the power coming off the Staff."

"Yes. You can feel it for yourself," I said holding the Shaft towards him.

He reached out and held his hand inches away from the ancient wood, but did not accept it. Holding his hand there, he eyes flicked from it to mine, before nodding. "I can feel it. It is like a charge of static electricity waiting to be grounded."

I nodded.

"So instead of using the waterfall, why not use the energy from the Staff itself?"

He chuckled at the expression of shock that must have covered my features. I nodded.

Closing my mind to everything other than the feeling of the electrical charge coming off the Staff, I instantly fell into the calm state of mind, pictured the stone in front of me, the ancient slab that Ian had been leaning on, in combination with my concern for my friend. The jolt of electricity coursed through me into the shaft and I opened my eyes to see the massive, house sized rock, was flung like pebbles, trees and all into the opposite canyon wall with an earth-shattering crash.

He smiled a toothless grin at me as the others come staggering from the cave to see what had happened.

This was the turning point.

Chapter 32
(Adam)

Needless to say, things began to move much faster. For the next few days, I rearranged the rocks in the valley, the echoes of the crushing impacts caused many to cover their ears. I had my own fan club as they cheered with each successful demonstration of the power that flowed from the Staff of Moses.

But some of their comments disturbed me.

I knew they were all warriors and killing was what they trained for, but I kept recalling what Jesus had said about balancing both Heavens. If I just used the Staff's power to annihilate the aliens, there wouldn't be a balance. It would be one-sided and make us as bad as them.

I certainly didn't want to wipe out the entire race. But how was I going to push them back to their own world before I sealed the riff?

"Any ideas, Guāng?" I said hoping he was close enough to hear me.

"Concerning what, may I ask?"

"How do I force the Kleptons to return to their home without having to kill them all? I mean it would be easy to drop a mountain on them, but that was not the way the prophesy intended by the way they worded it."

"Possibly a show of force might do it." From on high, he dropped like a shooting star to hover at my shoulder. *"Have you discussed it with the others?"*

I hesitated before shaking my head. *"No."*

"What has caused you to fear asking for their opinion, Adam?"

"There is so much talk about revenge and teaching the aliens that they can't mess with us that I'm afraid if I show a reluctance to just kill the Kleptons, they'll consider me weak. Or worse, refuse to follow me."

"Then you must explain it to them so they understand. You might also repeat what Jesus emphasized about the actual wording. Coming from one of the Divine Ones will hold much weight."

"Both Freddy and Ian are itching to get payback for what the Queen did to Ian," I said miserably. "They will look at my reluctance as a betrayal."

With almost little though, I picked up another boulder and threw it skyward, launching it clear over the mountain. I blinked at what I had just done. I acted out like a spoiled child, not caring that the rock might land and kill something or someone.

I felt my face burn with embarrassment as Guāng simply hung there. He said nothing. There was no need.

"Sorry," I said aloud.

Picking up my water skin, I walked to the water's edge and refilled it with the cold, clean water before returning to the cave. Moving among the different groups, I asked to speak with each of the Captains and my small band of eight after our supper meal. They all readily agreed.

Supper was a few hours away, so I went to my bedroll and lay down, my arm over my eyes, trying to figure how I would explain my dilemma to my warrior friends. Practicing the different arguments did not help me gain any insight, but it helped me fall asleep.

I woke to Gaje's foot playfully kicking my side and the laughter of my nearby Gurkhas brothers. Groggily, I rose knowing I slept hard, not realizing just how tired I was.

"Throwing mountains around must be tiring work," my blood brother teased me, his smile flashing in the torchlight. "You sure were sawing logs. Almost didn't wake you for supper."

As I rose, my stomach rumbled its complaint, "Good thing you did," I said, clearing my throat.

Thanks to the Comanche scouts who had been watching for enemy troop movements, we were treated to a thick soup flavored with fresh partridge and quail. Afterwards, we each received a fillet of fresh trout that Nita and a few volunteers had caught in the small lake he had used in his earlier expeditions. The ladies had cooked them in lemon grass till the flesh fell off the bone. I marveled at the meal that most five-star restaurants would be envious of.

My hunger satisfied, I moved to the main fire and most of those I had asked to speak to were already there. Before long, I had no excuses not to bring forth my thoughts, looking for their comments and hopefully their cooperation.

"Okay," I said with hesitation, trying to find the perfect words. But then I decided that I had earned the respect of these people through my actions and not my words. I would speak plainly.

"What has been troubling me is the wording of the prophecy and my interpretation of it and what Jesus of Nazareth said when I met him, Mohammad and Moses. With the power of the Staff, I could crush the alien army and although I think they deserve it, I have some reservations."

Both Ian and Freddy reacted like I had slapped them. Before they could interrupt, I pushed on.

"The prophesy said that I would bring back balance to both Heavens, ours and the Klepton's. Jesus made a point of this when I was with him. I think this is important. As much as I hate the Queen for what she did to you, Ian," I said looking at him with genuine feeling, "I don't think wiping out the entire race of aliens is justifiable." My words had him thinking at least. He mulled over the idea, but remained silent. Freddy just smoldered, and I knew he would be the hardest to convince.

"The eight of us entered the riff and saw how every creature fought for survival. The entire environment dictated the eat or be eaten mentality, so I began to wonder if the Kleptons were really evil or just acting according to their way of life, which their world forced upon them. Nature at its fiercest."

I took a deep breath, looking across the group of warriors and I saw no hostility, except from Freddy. Rob, Gaje and a few others, nodded at me and I knew I had some support so I continued.

"I am looking for ideas on how to force the alien horde out of our Heaven and back into their own. If we can do this, then I can use the Staff to seal the riff stopping them from ever entering again without wiping out an entire species."

There were so many eyes staring back at me with no expression, that I felt that I did not convince them. I felt sick to my stomach and got ready to leave their company and do what I had to, alone.

It was Gopi who spoke first. "You have come a long way, Adam. From the innocent to the leader you are today. But you have also learned a lesson that many warriors fail to understand." He raised his arms to include all the fighters of our group, even those who were not sitting around the fire. "We are warriors because of necessity. In each of our cultures, they have tasked us with standing up to invaders, dictators or corrupt leaders. Some events happen within a man's lifespan, while others last generations, so that fighting become a way of life. Therefore, we have learned the warrior way."

He paused to look across the assembly of fighters. "Brothers, correct me if I speak out of place, but would not all of us grab at a solution that would not involve killing?"

Almost every one of those historical fighters nodded in agreement. I even watched as those on the outside of our group nodded yes as if this debate should allow everyone a choice. And maybe it should.

Hattori raised a hand to settle the muttering. Once the room calmed, he said, "I agree. Too much blood has fallen from my blade while politicians try to impress the multitudes by creating unnecessary unrest and chaos to fuel their own agendas. If there is a way to solve this without bloodshed, I will support it. I am soldier, not a murderer."

I felt vindicated by their support as both leaders and soldiers agreed with my position. Rob stepped beside me wordlessly showing his support. Ian came towards me hesitantly and I understood that he had lost the most, therefore might not be able to turn away from the raw wound left behind. But by the end of the evening, he pulled me in a deep embrace and said, "You've always had my back, so now I have yours."

The evening had been a total win, having gained the trust of each of my comrades, knowing that I would do my best to expel the enemy, with the least amount of injuries and needless deaths on either side. What general had ever put that noble thought in his planning?

I had worried for nothing, but after centuries of fighting, I should have considered that even the greatest fighter in history needed a break from the killing. They did it because they were good at it, not because they enjoyed it.

WE TALKED ABOUT MANY strategies that evening and I was happy I had had a nap. Even so, I was exhausted when we finished having concluded that we needed to join with the other human forces before the two armies met. To successfully end this without more blood loss, I needed to be in the vanguard to use the Staff to deal with the aliens and protect the advancing humans. Our band of warriors would stand by to keep me protected from any flanking action the Kleptons might attempt.

As we bedded down, Guāng left to rendezvous with the marching human army to brief them of our plan and discuss a meeting place where the two forces could meet. We would leave in the morning and try to circle around the marching Klepton's army which had already begun its ponderous parade towards the main human encampment.

Although he had fulfilled the task of leading us to the riff, Nita would continue to guide us even though his fear of the aliens was clear. I shuddered to think what they might have done to the grizzled mountain man. I think he understood that this was our last chance. If we failed, he would be at the non-existent mercy of the Kleptons. He might also have gained some confidence watching my new abilities grow over the past few days.

Dropping onto my bedroll, I felt satisfied with our plan and was eager to see it put into motion. My mind was bouncing with all we had discussed and I feared a long night, but I touched the Staff and concentrated on the current of power. Within seconds, I remembered nothing more as I slipped into slumber.

Chapter 33
(Adam)

I was packing my gear when Hattori and Kwegu approached, their tense expressions bellowed bad news. Standing, I said, "What is it?"

"Freddy and Ian are not in the camp," Hattori said abruptly.

I glanced at Kwegu and he nodded. "They left sometime during the night and have taken both their packs and weapons."

Clearly Ian's concept of "having my back" matched Freddy's need for vengeance. But were they just going off to kill Kleptons or were they planning on going after the Queen, herself? I shook my head knowing if it was the latter; they were both as good as dead. Freddy would be resurrected, but no one knew what happened to the soul when one of those living in Heaven died.

"Guāng has gone looking for them, but we're not sure how long of lead they have or in what direction they went," said Hattori.

"Well, you can be sure it's towards the riff," I said rubbing my fingers across my eyes. "But they could lose themselves in the mountains and we might never find them."

"Do you want to send out a couple search parties?" Kwegu asked.

"No. We have no time," I said feeling the start of a headache. "Both Guāng and Nita have told us we need to leave immediately if we have any chance of getting in front of the Klepton's main force. We can only hope that we can put an end to this before those two end up dead."

Minutes later, we set out at a quick march, each of us chewing on jerky that had been prepared over the time we called the cave home. My water bags were cold and heavy on my shoulder, but the temperature would keep me cool through the fast pace we would have to travel at. As per normal, the Comanche led the way, spreading out we filed out of the narrow valley.

I had seen Rob for a minute before he mounted this horse. He clamped his big hand on my shoulder in understanding and support. He said nothing, just his strong presence backing me up.

Gopi led the march and was kind enough to slow the pace to a moderate pace to allow limbs which had been dormant for over a week to stretch out and warm up. Soon after though, he drove us hard; the miles flowing beneath our feet.

As we approached the valley that led to the riff, we saw a long line of Kleptons marching steadily east through another valley that Nita had told us passed through the mountains. It was the only pass for at least a hundred miles in either direction. There were breaks in the enemy line as if to separate different divisions or companies. Overhead, the fliers darkened the sky in a long line like migrating birds looking for a new nesting ground. Gopi had us all down on one knee, hard up against the tree line so they would not see us. The Comanches stood holding their mounts just inside the trees, having pulled all the outriders in with the troops so we could move forward as a single group.

Nita waved me forward. I moved in a crouch towards where Gopi and the mountain man knelt. He wasted no time with niceties, but said in his forthright way, "We can hold up and wait for nightfall. Hopefully, their march line will stop because they are so blind in the dark, or you can do that show of force bit and see if you can scare the devils back to where they come from."

"Let's try a show of force. I have an idea that might help stop any more of their troops from marching east." I watched a column of Wizards march through the mouth of the pass. The gap to the next group of Kleptons was about three hundred yards back.

"Now," I said. Gopi gave hand signals and together everyone rose and rushed the opening of the pass. It took only a few minutes to close on the pass, but the higher fliers had spied our movement. Several of them buzzed our way.

Raising the Staff, I allowed myself to fall into its steady hum of energy and pictured the wings on the huge dragonfly replicas. In my mind, I snapped one wing on the group that moved to swarm us. Instantly, their flight faltered, and they slowly fell to the ground, their bodies twisting uncontrollably to the ground like injured helicopters. More came as the ones further back in line saw their brethren fall from the sky. Wave after wave of the insects tried to swarm us, but using the Staff's power, I snapped their delicate appendages forcing them to the ground, until none remained aloft.

The alien soldiers behind milled about in confusion, their path blocked by their fallen aerial allies, not understanding what had transpired. Gaje and two others who had stood guard over me ran to catch up with our troops who had disappeared into the next valley which led through the pass. They waited just inside, not wanting to march too much farther and risk being spotted by the division of Wizards ahead. As I joined them, we moved together as a group. Once we were far enough into the valley, we stopped so I could use the Staff as a ground relocation division. Before their astonished eyes the mountains that stood apart creating the entrance to the pass, pushed together with Teutonic force. Loose rocks tumbled and thumped to the ground raising a massive cloud of dust.

In my mind's eye, I saw the jagged cliffs come together blocking the entrance and effectively cut off the rest of the Klepton's army. When I lowered my trembling arms, I breathed a sigh of release. The billowing clouds of dust were so thick that we couldn't see the end of the new box canyon I had created, but I knew for certain that the pass was closed, for now.

Gaje slapped my shoulder in delight, "Brother, that was the most amazing thing I've ever witnessed. Big difference from flinging stones around the valley." He made it sound so trivial as if it was normal to throw house-sized boulders in the first place.

I pulled one of my water-skins off and took a long pull on the spout. It had been a bigger thing, and I felt drained even though most of the energy came from the Staff. Obviously, some came from me as well. I would have to take care I didn't overdo it. Maybe it was because I used the Staff so many times without a break. I had downed fifteen to twenty waves of fliers.

The Captains recommended that we wait awhile before moving up the valley to allow the front end of the enemy column to get well ahead of us. Hattori had already sent two of his ninjas after the column of Wizards to ensure they knew nothing of what transpired behind them and to keep track of their location. Feeling the effects of the Staff, I had no issue with agreeing.

I was getting used to afternoon naps.

IT TOOK THE REST OF the day to pass through the high mountain pass. We came out at yet another valley that ran at an angle to ours. In the distance we saw the tail end of the enemy column disappear into another of these endless canyons. Rather than follow them, Nita pointed our small group towards a valley running parallel, to a southward valley.

"They take a way that is wide and empty of ob-stacles," he said with a cackle that echoed in the clear mountain air. "The path we take is narrow and per-ilous, but will cut three days off the march." Not waiting, he turned in the opposite direction, pulling his mule after him.

The narrow valleys did not allow us to have out-riders and without knowing where the old man was leading us, the scouts could not venture too far forward. A few covered our back trail, but most fell in line with the main column.

For a change, there was no wind. The high peaks of the range sheltered this new slope from winds from easterly and westerly winds, so we felt the late afternoon sun.

"Easy on the water fellows," Nita said in warning. "We won't see any until we descend the other side of the pass. It's dry this time of year at this altitude."

The path Nita followed was a game trail. There were only subtle hints of a trail in the tall grass that covered the slope, but it was all the mountain man needed. His mule protested the steepness of the grade and echoed the burn in my thighs. We were sweating freely now and the high altitude strained our breathing forcing frequent breaks.

We camped that night on the open ground under a star-laden sky. The clear alpine air was crisp once the sun sunk beneath the western peaks. Most pulled out a blanket that was at the bottom of our sacks having never been needed. There was no need for meditation to help fall asleep. The long day of exercise coupled with the effort of working the Staff took its toll the minute I laid down.

The following morning saw another cold meal rather than having the light from a fire give away our presence. My stiff legs lurched as we attacked the slope. Thankfully our pace brought them to solid strength quickly. Three hours later we crested the summit. We paused to take in the vista that spread out in all its glory at our feet. We had left the trees behind shortly after breaking camp. Except for short grass that struggled to survive under the onslaught of wind and cold, the mountain was empty of vegetation this far up. Far below us, the trees rose as if to reach for us. I could see great cuts in the tree line, broken by past avalanches that snapped tree trunks like kindling.

Beyond the next mountain, the plains lapped at the foothills for as far as the eye could see. Broken lines could be seen crossing the sea of grass and Iron Chief said, "The Klepton's raiding parties are heading towards the main host to the north."

The mountains hid the main enemy army but four or five of the smaller lines were definitely pointed in that direction. We were much too far to see actual movement or figures, but the swath cut in the prairie was unmistakable.

We descended the far side, startling a herd of elk, their long rack of antlers stretched across their backs as they bugled a warning. It was obvious they were not used to sharing the trail over the summit. However, they didn't act overly concerned ambling away from the trail, staring as if they hadn't encountered humans before. Some of the Comanche wanted to try their luck at taking down a few, but Nita said, "There'll be plenty more herds below. Best wait until we're near where we will camp so you don't have to carry the extra weight."

We trudged down a long hanging valley where as Nita had predicted there was an abundance of animals. Being mounted, the Comanche scouts could see further ahead. Every once in a while, one of them would have us stand quietly as they had spotted a bear ahead of us. There was probably nothing to worry about with a group our size, but it was prudent to avoid the chance. It was easier to allow the massive beasts to make their way to wherever they were headed rather than face a confrontation.

Following the game trail which was much clearer now, we skirted the clusters of trees, still descending. At the lip of the valley, Nita called for us to set up camp. He gave a small group of horsemen permission to take down a couple of elk. These were huge animals and would offer us a lot of meat, the bulk of which would be made into jerky so that none was wasted.

By the time the hunters returned eight drying racks had been assembled from fresh, green wood and positioned around two fires that had been reduced to coals. The meat was carved up by several men and passed to the women who placed the meat on the racks ensuring that they wasted no space. Each man received a steak of his own which was positioned on a forked stick and then propped over several communal fires. It wasn't long before the entire camp smelt like a steak house and I was almost drooling in anticipation.

"Where do you think they are, Adam?" Rob asked his face pinched with worry.

I shook my head before replying. "There's no way to know for sure. Guāng is still searching for them but they've gone to ground, probably knowing that we would search for them."

"I'm almost sick with worry."

It was my time to give him my support, and I gave him a big hug. Of course, I didn't squeeze the life out of him.

We feasted and ate until we couldn't stuff another piece of meat in without the chance of being sick. After weeks with the bare minimum, it felt good to have a full stomach. We laughed and talked around the fires until the last light fled the sky. All the fires except the two which were smoking the meat were extinguished, and we all crawled to our bedrolls, hugging our blankets as the wind began to climb up the mountain.

Chapter 34
(Adam)

We woke to a steady rain that had everyone soaked. With no choice, we folded wet, heavy blankets and squished them into our packs. We distributed the dried meat so everyone carried the same weight. Fortunately, the drying process had finished before the rain started and the meat would keep. We handed out the last of the meat as a cold breakfast, so different from the night before.

Following Nita, we continued down the mountain. The hanging valley tapered out at a sheer rock face and I couldn't see a way around, but I knew the old man had a way. He brought us close to the face which blocked our way and near the edge of the cliff on the north side of the valley and stopped in front of a clump of juniper that hugged the face to the edge of the cliff.

"Stick close to the rock face and take your time. One slip up and you'll fall to your death. Iron Horse, I suggest you blindfold your horses so they don't get spooked."

The chief nodded and repeated the order to his men. When they were ready, the old explorer pushed through the trees. As we came out the other side, I saw immediately that he had not exaggerated. The rock shelf was a little over eight feet wide before plunging hundreds of feet straight down. Traversing the wet stone in water-logged boots made each step precarious. No one would survive the fall.

The mule was strangely quiet as if he knew just how important it was to follow his master's guiding hand. We walked in single file and kept some distance between each man so not to crowd or rush each other. At times the rock shelf rose while at other spots it angled downward but not so steep that there was a chance of falling off the mountain. The path made a slow hazardous turn around the mountainside—dicey footwork for the unwary. It was after midday that the shelf turned further south and widened into a long gentle slope to the mountain's base. The dry wind coming off the prairies was a pleasant change to the chill mountain air.

There was no sign of movement from my angle of view, but as we descended closer to the plains, we would have to keep a vigilant eye for the enemy. The nights of standing guard duty would begin again.

WE REACHED THE GRASSLANDS the next day and aimed our march towards where we knew the human army was located. Guāng had been traveling back and forth so that both sides knew of the other's progress.

From higher up Nita pointed out a river that stretched across the plains, twisting upon itself as it followed the low ground running south. "Wind River," he said. "We must cross it at one of two points. I'm guessing both are being used by the Kleptons; the north one for the main force and the southern one for all those raiders we saw."

The Comanches spread out around us as we pushed towards the southern crossing. It was back to the rolling hills, and it was easy to get into the rhythm of the march. We could finally refill water bags as there were plenty of creeks in the area, all flowing towards the larger river to the northeast. The cold, fresh water was delicious after drinking the warm stale fluid in our skins. I had to be careful not to over-drink.

Once everyone had hydrated, we kept moving; the land rising and following with little to see. My mind wandered, and I began to worry about Ian and Freddy, praying that both were still alive and free of the Kleptons. If they tried to return through the riff,

I wasn't sure I'd even know it. With the multitude of soldiers streaming out the valley, they wouldn't stand a chance. It only made sense that there be an equal number of soldiers on the other side of the riff.

If I was with them with the Staff, it would be another story all together. The power of the Staff would make the Klepton's superiority of numbers moot.

We crested yet another of the rolling hills and spotted the dark muddy water of a fast-flowing river. We had reached the ford. Three Comanches waited by the river bank, their horses grazing on the rich grass.

They held us in a column as Nita pulled out a long length of hemp rope from one of the cargo box-es that his mule carried. Giving instructions to one native he fed out the rope so it wouldn't tangle and twist. The man and horse descended the steep bank and pushed through the fast-moving water. Soon the water rose to the horse's chest, and he half walked and half floated across the torrent, continuously being dragged downstream. When he finally made the shallows, he walked his mare back upriver until he was directly across.

He tied his end to a large tree and gave Nita a wave. Picking up the slack the mountain man wrapped the end of the rope around another tree so it anchored the line to both sides.

"Listen up," Nita said pushing his voice along the column. "Stay on the current side of the rope. If you slip, the rope should be able to hold you until you get your footing. Take your time and make sure of your footing before moving forward. Slide your hands across the rope rather than crossing over. This way you do not let go of the rope. Soon as you reach the other side, climb up the bank and assume a defensive position fifty yards to the east. We need you out of the way for the others coming across." He slapped the first man on the shoulder to signal him to begin.

The man, a Ninja, strung his bow and pulled it over his head so he would not have to carry it, leaving his hands free. Gripping the rope, he used the anchor to drop down the bank and into the water. With no hesitation, the man slowly made his way to deeper water, the current pushing him tight against the line. When he was about ten feet from the shore, Nita nodded at the next man.

One by one, the ninja moved across the fast-flowing river, their black outfits making them look like moving stones that caused the water to cascade across their backs and shoulders. While I awaited my turn, I tied a couple of knots to the staff so I could carry it on my back. Gopi stood to one side and nodded to the next man in line, Gaje, forward. His son would lead the crossing while he followed to ensure each of the men under his command made it across safely.

Once Gaje reached the deeper water, I felt Gopi, tap my shoulder to signal my turn. I grasped the course line with gloved hands and lowered myself down the bank. Slashing through the shallows, I soon felt the cold current tearing at my legs. The rope helped with the balance as I moved my feet over the slippery rock bottom. The one time I slipped, the water pushed me tight against the rope cutting into my stomach until I could get my feet back under me.

I was about halfway across, our line looking like beads on a necklace when a high-pitched scream of an animal echoed across the water. It came from the far shore. All the warriors stopped short, waiting for a sign that it was safe to continue. There was a thrashing in the trees and more screams that sounded like one of our horses being savaged by another animal. Had he encountered a bear?

Suddenly the water on both sides of me exploded, sending sheets of water flying high. "Ambush!" someone yelled as I watched two bodies float face down past the anchor line. I managed to grab one man's pant leg and pulled him to me. Letting the rope hold me, I rolled him over so he could breathe and he sputtered and started to splash in panic. I grabbed one of his hands and pushed it towards the rope which he clutched like a drowning man. On the far bank, several ominous shapes appeared between the trees, their short bodies aimed at the line of men crossing the river. Two Wizards released their sonic blast and more men went flying, losing their purchase of the rope, the current dragging them downstream.

Looking the other way, I saw Gopi fighting with a fully-armored Klepton as their force tried to overrun the remaining warriors. The line was severed, and I felt the tug of the current pull us downstream, even as more sonic blasts hit the surrounding water. The line acted like a pendulum with only one side attached and although we were swept with the current, we also swung to the eastern shore.

I tried to stand, leaning into the current and pulled the Staff off my shoulder. I felt the familiar energy surge through me and as pictured my own blast to either side of the river; I was hit with a double blast from either side of the river, knocking me under the surface, so that my back raked the jagged stones beneath. Feeling my skin tear, I twisted in pain, pulling my arms around my sides, it didn't even register that I let go of the Staff until it left my grasp. Feverishly, I reached for it, but it bobbed out of my reach; the current pulling it downstream. Lunging ahead, I groped for the only thing that might save us all, but the current quickly pulled it away from me.

Further downstream, I saw a massive Comanche riding a gray mare, almost black with its hair wet with sweat, dive off the steep embankment and plunge into the river. It was Rob. The animal and rider disappeared beneath the waves for a split second before rising and continuing for the far shore. I tried to wave at him, but a group of sonic blasts chased him to the shore. The last I saw of the Staff was it bobbing in the rocking water, moving even further out of reach.

Suddenly a massive force hit me, lifting me from the river, dropping me into darkness.

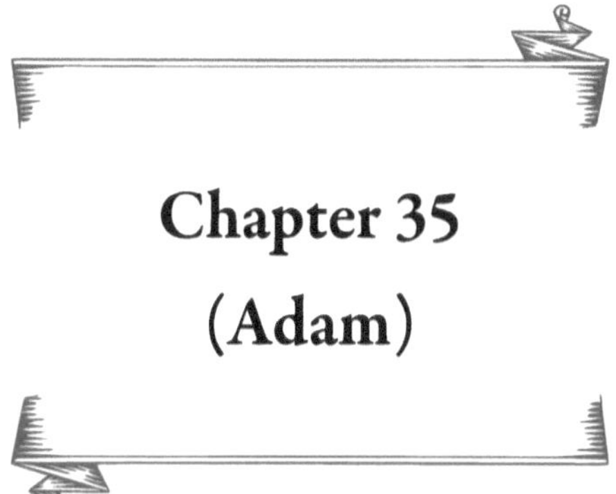

Chapter 35
(Adam)

I groaned at the pain that ran through my entire body. My arms were wrenched behind me and it felt like my limbs had fallen asleep; the numb tingling sensation causing my fingers to ache. Opening my eyes, the ground bounced back and forth as I was carried, face down. I could feel the pressure of blood in my head and knew I would have to contend with a massive migraine once we stopped.

My clothes were mostly dry, so I knew it had been some time since the ambush

Looking around, I saw that many of my companions were also bound and strapped over the shoulder of a massive Klepton. Although I knew these people, I could see none of our leaders, Gaje or Rob, which gave me hope that they were alive. If that was true they would pull the impossible and rescue us.

The beasts ignored the groans and cries of our injured. Looking around, I could see blood dripping from many of our warrior's ears signifying the sonic blasts had struck them, but also there were a few with severed limbs that spoke to the savage encounters with the Kleptons.

This march northward to the main alien host dragged all day. My mouth was parched, made worse by the fact we traveled beside the river. The constant swaying was making me sick, and I lost my breakfast in bursts of gagging vomit. As ragged as I felt, I accepted a small victory seeing the gross bile slide down the back of my captor's legs. However, I don't think she ever felt it through the hard shell.

I must have blacked out at some point because the next thing I knew, the sun had lost its harshness and angled towards the mountains we had just crossed. I prayed that the march would stop once the sun went down.

Someone must have heard my plea, because we marched into a large bend in the river where a makeshift camp had been set up. My captor dropped me unceremoniously to the ground. Fortunately, I landed on my shoulder rather than my head. I came to rest half on one of the other prisoners who matched my groan. Rolling off of him, I whispered my apology. All together eight soldiers had survived the ambush. A Suri and Ninja both had lost an arm to a Klepton's claw, but the bleeding for each had stopped for now

Looking around, I saw that we were not the only group of prisoners. Another group was being pushed into the center of the camp, a ring of Kleptons would ensure we didn't escape. This group comprised of men, women and children and they looked worn out as if they had been marching for months on little food.

A few guards moved forward and tossed a bunch of packages on the ground and the worn-out prisoners dropped onto them, pushing and shoving as if their lives depended on it. Like animals, they tore into what looked like raw meat with their bare teeth, snarling at any who came close. Even mothers pushed their children away until they had their fill. It revolted me to see humans act in this savage way.

They threw a handful of similar packages at us and the other group started towards our share. Our soldiers snapped the packages up and glared at those thinking they could steal our share until they returned to their own group.

Opening the linen packages proved that it was raw meat, still partially covered with the pelt. I recognized the color pattern of the pelt as one of the horses our Comanche brothers rode and we all exchanged a worried look. I remembered hearing the scream of an animal at the river crossing thinking it was being savaged by an animal. I was partially right. It was an alien. We had no Comanches among us so hoped they had escaped.

I shook my head when a piece of meat was offered to me, the gore rising in my throat, but the Suri tribesman said, "You must, Adam. To stay strong. When the others come for us, you must be ready to run."

"What difference does it make?" I said unable to look the man in the eyes. "The Shaft is gone, the river took it, so there's no way for us to win."

He grabbed me by my shirt and shook me violently. "You're a warrior, not a child. You never give up until you're dead."

The other men around me nodded, and I felt my face burn, shamed by the man's words and was grateful that it was dark.

He shoved the meat into my hand as if the argument was over. Forcing my mind away from the task at hand, I put the piece of meat to my mouth and bit off a small piece. The flesh being raw was tough and chewy and I had to swallow hard to keep my stomach in place. The second bite was bigger and the tribesman's teeth flashed a smile at me in the dark.

Unlike the other group of prisoners, we shared the meat, passing it around so everyone ate. Once finished, they led us to the river to drink handfuls of water. They then led us back to our holding area to rest for the night.

Unable to sleep as my stomach gurgled and turned, I ran over the ambush in my mind and the last I saw of the Staff. How could I have dropped it? If I could have used it, we wouldn't be in this situation. But the attack coupled with the current, the rope, and the sonic blasts all played against me and our group.

The others might attempt to save us, but without the Staff, we were just postponing the inevitable.

THE MARCH CONTINUED the next morning after another offering of raw meat. This time I didn't refuse and the Suri warrior nodded but said nothing more. They herded us like sheep amid a circle of Kleptons. Just behind them, a Wizard skittered after them as if backup to an escape attempt.

The river arced to the northwest and our party left it to continue almost straight north.

Around midday, an object seen from a distance came flying at us a tremendous speed and I thought it might be Guāng, searching for us. My hopes died as it closed on the raiding party and I saw the familiar dark skull of a Scavenger.

The dark orb raced to and hovered beside a Wizard near the front of the column. The two seem to be in communication, not that I would have been able to understand them. After a few minutes of exchange, the skull zipped and examined each of the prisoners that had been caught the day before at the river. I lowered my head, trying to hide my eyes which had been recognized by the first Scavenger I had encountered on Earth, but one of the armored beasts grasped me around the throat with his huge claw and lifted my head for examination.

As soon as the orb saw my eyes, it began bobbing excitedly, and I knew they had found me out. I braced myself to be killed on the spot which would have destroyed any chance of the prophecy being fulfilled. If they killed me, I would rise again at the main capital of Heaven, being reborn. At least I would be out of their clutches.

But they had other plans.

The skull left us, racing back to its masters in the north, while the march resumed. I didn't know what they had planned but my gut said that the worst was ahead. With no way of predicting the future, I could only put one foot in front of the other as we trudged towards the main host.

The sun became angry and the ever-present breeze tapered out as if holding its breath at the epic confrontation that was looming. My skin chafed from the friction of my sweaty damp clothes. The pain was like a hundred hornet stings. I could see my fellow prisoners gritting their teeth from the same affliction. There was no water to be had, and we panted like dogs in the heat. It drained the energy from us and we staggered over the rough ground.

Several prisoners dropped from weakness or the heat. If they could not stand up and continue, even with rough nudging by the guards, they were killed on the spot; the bodies torn apart and handed out to the Klepton soldiers for food. The horror of seeing humans rendered in this manner, forced all of us to keep moving.

Knowing that the aliens planned on either mating or eating us made it difficult to continue, but what choice did we have?

I couldn't guess what the aliens were experiencing with this environment, their own was so humid. Being aquatic, the dry heat of these grasslands should be roasting them, but they showed no outward signs of discomfort. Perhaps the armor shell protected them.

It was late afternoon when we crested a slight rise in the prairie and caught sight of the enemy force. The horde was gigantic, stretching as far as the eye could see. It was distressing to see the legions they could field in our world. How could anyone stand against such a foe?

As the initial horror sunk in, my fellow soldiers and I exchanged dumb, empty looks at each other and their expressions must have mirrored mine. This wasn't just one world against another. It was the ancestors from all time from two different Heavens come together to destroy the other. The unsettling thought was their entire race was warlike while only a part of ours was. We had artists, entertainers, philosophers and writers who wouldn't stand a chance against such a brutal adversary.

A Scavenger came rushing towards us and gave a series of orders to the lead Wizard. In turn, the guards around us dragged my men and I forward to push on at a faster pace. Someone wanted to see us.

TWO OF OUR MEN, A GURKHAS and the other a Suri dropped before we reached the main enemy camp. Both had lost a limb and plenty of blood before their wounds had been attended to. Even though we had pushed more of the raw meat towards them during our meals, the blood loss, trauma and exertion took its toll.

Their orders must have included a directive of speed, because instead of tearing them apart for food, they mercifully dispatched them and left them to lie in the tall grass.

They ushered us through the camp, many of the aliens ceasing from their duties to stop and stare as they paraded us, unarmed and weakened through their ranks.

There were legions of the Kleptons which we were familiar with. Hundreds of thousands spread across the horizon. There were fewer Wizards in the mix compared to their counterparts, but it seemed they might just outnumber the humans with their ranks alone. The dragonfly fliers were nested farther to the north, but the constant hum from that direction proved just how outnumbered we were. It was like being hemmed in by a field of bee hives.

As for Scavengers, they flashed back and forth across the camp. Presenting orders and returning with replies as the army readied itself for the final battle.

Deep in the center of the camp, a large tent rose from the multitude to hover like a beacon. The structure looked light and emerged with a subtle fluidity to three or four stories in height. Interior lights shone through the fabric so that everyone for miles around could see the presence. The bright light had a welcome feel to it but, as our guards pushed us in that direction, my perspective shifted.

Around the camp, Wizards shot multiple flares from their deadly scorpion-like tails to light up the night, making wavering shadows throughout the camp. It allowed the Klepton's army to function even when they would normally be blind and helpless. With the entire camp lit up my hope of escape disappeared. I had to keep recalling what the Suri warrior had said about not giving up, to just keep walking forward. The fear inside me was frenzied.

After a hundred twists and turns, we reached the central area of the camp, standing nervously in front of the colossal tent. The guards stepped behind us and forced us to kneel on the hard-packed ground.

From within the tent came a sequence of clicks and clacks but at a much higher and seemingly grander scale than I ever heard before. A line of silver-armored Kleptons marched out of the tent with quick movements, each holding a sword looking appendage strapped to its smaller and secondary claw. They marched towards us, but then turned left and right, every other soldier turning until the entire rank stood in front of us in a solid, formidable line.

Behind them, what sounded like an empty straw sucking at the last dredges of a Slurpee, continued to grow louder, and I felt the tingle of fear crawl up my back. When the creature appeared, I understood why they hadn't killed me immediately.

The Queen wanted that privilege for herself.

Chapter 36
(Adam)

Her hunger for revenge was clear on her alien face as her eyes swept over the prisoners on display for her until they settled on me. I could understand her hatred, but to make the journey from the safety of her citadel to lead her army in another world spoke of a greater animosity.

As she moved towards me, I bit my lip tasting the coppery tinge of blood. I could feel myself swaying on my knees as the horror that awaited me hit home. At a command, the soldiers parted before her but remained vigilant. Reaching with one of her sword-like claws she gently raised my chin and glared into my eyes. The hard carapace caressed my cheek the way a lover might, and I shuddered, knowing it to be the opposite.

She conferred with her guards and turned towards the tent and the wet slurping followed her as she secreted a slime which she slid on. One guard lifted me to my feet but my legs would not hold me up, so a second grabbed me from the other side. Together we followed behind the Queen, my feet dragging in the foul-smelling slime.

We entered a large domed chamber similar to the citadel's throne room, with a large podium littered with cushions. While the Queen settled herself on the throne, her guards bound me to a wooden stake that another rammed into the ground in an exhibit of colossal strength. It was no wonder that one blow from its massive claw either killed or incapacitated our warriors. Two aides wet the Queen's pale skin till it shimmered, then left the room.

Once secured, the guards were dismissed, and it was just the two us.

The Queen stared at me; her eyeballs perched on top of slender tentacles which moved with a mind of their own. Unable to communicate, I didn't understand what the point of this session was until she reached out and slashed my right thigh with the side of her pointed hand. The same which had gone through Ian's chest, so easily.

Pain flared and I could feel the blood seep down my leg. Reaching for a vessel I hadn't noticed before, she slowly brought it towards me and tipped it over my leg. When the fluid poured onto my limb, I screamed as it ate at my wound. It felt like acid burning a hole right through my leg. The searing pain made time stand still, and drained me until my cries were a whimper.

This amused the Queen as she clicked and cackled like an unholy demon. She showed no impatience as the pain went through me. I was gasping for air, my head hanging as the pain mercifully faded. Looking at the wound, I saw no difference to the cut; no burn marks, no scarring.

One of her silver armored guards presented himself at the entrance. In his grasp was a human woman, her clothes torn and dirty. She could have been one of those who traveled with us, but I was unsure. The guard dragged her towards the throne.

The Queen, rolled backwards exposing her vast stomach which opened like a pouch. The guard hoisted the wide-eye woman and before she could understand what was happening, deposited her into the pouch, the skin flap closed on the screaming woman, her cries muted but still audible in the close quarters of the tent. The Queen rolled back, her eyes watching my expression.

I screamed at the horror of what I had just witnessed, crying freely so my vision blurred; tears and snot flowing down my cheeks.

Once my breathing settled, the Queen lashed out once again, this time slicing my left upper arm. My lips trembled as she casually lifted the vessel and held it over the cut. She said something in her foreign tongue which I was sure was a taunt before slowly tipping the jar towards my arm.

Once again, I screamed, my throat felt as ragged as if I swallowed razors. The pain in my arm made it impossible to think about anything other than the agony. When this bout of suffering eased off, I realized this is why I had been taken alive. She would torture me like she tortured Nita when he first found the riff to her world. That time she did it to determine how he made it to her world. This time she was doing it in retribution of my attack on her children. The realization that they were her children tore a hole through my soul. Being an alien, I had never thought about that before. Had someone killed or threatened a human child, I would have been the first to condemn them as monsters, yet that was exactly what I had done. It might have been in retaliation to her killing Ian, but it was her I should have attacked, not her offspring. I understood her hate. I deserved it.

The next cut was to my neck and mercifully, my body and mind shut down, unable to deal with the pain. I fell unconscious.

When I came too, the throne was empty and I was completely alone. My blood-covered pants were dry and my limbs numb from hanging off the pole so long. I braced myself with my feet to take up my weight. As I stood, the gash on my thigh ripped open when my pants tore away from the wound. An involuntary groan rose up, and I gritted my teeth to finish my movement as silently as possible.

I worked my fingers and was rewarded with more pain, pins and needles from the fresh flowing blood. As feeling slowly returned, I struggled with my restraints but they remained secure.

The sound of clashing steel and loud battle cries off in the distance startled me. I took a huge gulp of air, praying my side was coming to get me. I pictured Thor and the rowdy Vikings hacking their way through the Klepton's defenses and mentally cheered them on. My need to escape was so desperate that I began to sob uncontrollably.

Minutes later, a Klepton soldier shuffled across the throne room and continued into the next section of the tent. A loud barrage of clicks and snaps followed and then the alien came shuffling out, heading into the night.

The slurping sound which signaled the Queen's movement started for the throne room and I came close to losing my bowels, so afraid of her that I barely held on when she slid into the room. Thank God her focus was what was happening out in the night and not me. As an afterthought, she reached out and dragged her razor-sharp claw across my chest, cutting through my shirt and skin. It was a reminder of what was to follow.

The noise of battle increased and I could hear screaming far off. It sounded like the entire human army was attacking Klepton camp. They would certainly have the advantage of attacking in the dark.

From behind me, I heard fabric tearing. Seconds later my restraints came loose, and I twisted around to see Gaje's smiling face. Silently he shoved a Kukri into my hand and motioned me to be silent. We slid though the hole he had made in the tent to find two ninjas, their faces masked and another Gurkhas standing guard, swords at the ready.

Without a command spoken the one Ninja took the lead, darting from shadow to shadow. Gaje pushed me to follow. The other two covered our retreat. I pulled Gaje close enough to whisper that there were more of our people being held prisoners. He nodded and had me follow the black-garbed assassin. They must have had a second team going for the prisoners. The surrounding area seemed emptied, and I expected all the Klepton warriors had headed towards the fighting. But my group took no chances, ensuring that they moved unseen through the night.

When we finally left the camp behind us, Gaje threw his arm around me and said, "You sure gave us a scare, brother."

"Trust me, I wasn't having a good time," I said unable to hide the tremble in my voice. "The Queen has crossed over to avenge her children."

"We saw. Once the main army made their attack, we had to wait for her to leave before we could come for you."

"How did you know where I was being held?"

"Guāng had done a high-level search for you and the others and found the compound where they were being contained. One team rescued them and they informed us that the Queen had you in her tent. Thanks to Guāng's mind link, passing the information to my team was child's play."

After saying that, he reached out to Guāng to ensure him I was safe.

Immediately he called me. *"Adam, thank God you are okay. We were so worried."*

"Thank you, my friend. And thank everyone who helped save me. I had almost given up. I wouldn't have lasted much longer. The Queen -" I couldn't articulate, even in the safety of my mind. It was too fresh, too raw.

"It's okay my young leader. She cannot hurt you again."

"But I lost the Staff..." But he broke the link.

WE CIRCLED AROUND THE enemy camp and eventually met up with the other prisoners; both our soldiers and the other refugees. Relieved that they were all free, we continued on to our army's camp, arriving shortly after dawn. Gaje informed me that we lost six men at the river crossing. Two had drowned while the others sacrificed themselves to hold the enemy in place while our people fled.

A stampede of howling Comanches reined in their horses just before they were on top of us.

Rob jumped off his Moonbeam and grabbed me in one of his legendary hugs. He broke away when I yelped from the pain of my chest wound opening up again.

"Oh my God, I'm so sorry, Adam. I was so happy to see you alive..."

"It's okay, buddy," I said clapping my hand on his shoulder. "You didn't know."

Iron Fist flashed me a rare smile and nodded a welcome.

The horse flanked us and we hiked the short distance to our own army's camp. As large as it was, I recognized that the enemy encampment dwarfed it.

"Are the two forces still fighting?" I asked Iron Horse.

"No. They only attacked to cause a distraction so the others could free you. They have pulled back, but we know the Queen will launch her forces soon."

I definitely agreed. That she had not done so at first light surprised me. Perhaps, our force did some real damage. Once she finds that I'm missing, she'll kill every defender to retrieve me as her plaything.

Jesus of Nazareth met us on the outskirts of the tent city that had been set up to house the army. He greeted me with a gentle hug and a soft smile. "We are so happy to see you safe, Adam. Come see the others that await your return." He led me through the camp to its center where several Deities sat in council. Guāng was there as well, and he circled me in a delightful dance.

"Well met, Adam." Mohammad stepped forward and clasped my forearm. "It is gratifying to see that the plan Hattori and Gopi put together worked so well."

"Thank you. But I'm afraid it might have been for nothing," I said stepping back.

His expression darkened and he said, "Explain."

"When we were attacked at the river, I lost the Staff. The last I saw of it, the current was taking it downstream. For all I know, it might have reached the sea by now."

"Do you mean this Staff, Adam?" said a familiar voice behind me.

I twisted and Rob stood with the Staff balanced in his huge hands. I dropped to my knees at the sight of it. Those around me chuckled at my surprise.

"Your friend chased after it," Mohammad said, his hand on my shoulder, "and caught up to it a couple of miles beyond the ford. By the time he returned, they had already taken you north to the enemy's camp."

I put my hand on my chest, smarting at the cuts beneath and blew out a breath of relief, knowing Rob's quick thinking had saved us all.

Moses stepped forward. "Guāng has told us you have mastered the Staff and have preformed some incredible miracles," he said. "Well done, my young friend."

"Thank you," I said feeling my face heat up.

He leaned in closer and under his breath he said, "Can't wait to see the show." He winked and walked away.

Leading me out of the circle, Jesus said, "Adam, you've been though a great ordeal. We have a place for you to rest and clean clothes for you to wear. Those wounds will also need tending to."

"But the Queen..."

"If she makes her move today, one of us will come for you. It's important that you are ready."

I allowed him to guide me to a tent that looked like it belonged in the desert with its billowing light fabric. The walls were partially rolled up to catch the wind, and it was shaded to create a pleasant atmosphere. Sitting in a chair by a table, my Grandpa stood and gave me a hug. "Good to see you, my boy. Heard you had some more exciting adventures."

I turned, but Jesus had already disappeared.

"There's a washbasin over there. Once you're clean, I'll bandage those cuts up. Don't want you bleeding over your new clothes," he said pointing at bundle on the bed.

After he finished, I slipped into the bed that was so comfortable it must have been made in Heaven. I was asleep in seconds.

Chapter 37
(Adam)

I held the familiar weight of the Staff in my left hand the next morning. I stood on a single rock that rose six feet above the prairie. Guāng informed us that the Queen's forces had been getting into marching order since before first light. Our forces had quickly assembled, but stood far enough back that they would not interfere with any of the Staff's magic.

Surrounding me were those fighters I had journeyed and fought with. Of the original eight men, plus the four of us, we had started out with eighty-five. We were now down to thirty-four, two of which had suffered a severed arm, now holding their weapons in the wrong hand. My group demanded the position surrounding me as personal guardians. I felt honored and relieved. I trusted these men and women with my life.

My Grandpa had woken me early enough so I could eat. Rob joined us for a traditional bacon and eggs breakfast that Grandpa pulled out of the air along with a delicious cup of dark roast coffee.

I had discussed my ideas with the Captains and there was no argument as long as the Staff allowed me to do what I hoped. Now we waited for the time that the "show" would begin.

At some unheard command, the front ranks of the alien horde began their ponderous march towards our position. The heavy armor of the Klepton's infantry didn't allow for anything faster. Like steamrollers, they crushed the tall grass under their weight.

Beyond them a battalion of Wizards waited to bombard our position. Further back the Fliers hovered in a cluster, waiting for the command. Why they hadn't attacked simultaneously was beyond me. I looked over at Hattori who must have had the same thoughts because he shrugged his shoulders.

The realization that these enemy soldiers were the Queen's children tore a hole through my soul. Being an alien, I had never thought about that before. Had someone killed or threatened a human child, I would have been the first to condemn them as monsters, yet that was exactly what I had done. It might have been in retaliation to her killing Ian, but it was her I should have attacked, not her offspring. I understood her hate. I deserved it.

This is a Mother avenging the murder of her child.

Not until the enemy was at one hundred yards, did my men unsheathe their weapons or notch their arrows. Although their hope lay in what I could do with the Staff, they were there for my protection. If I fell, or lost the Staff, it would be over.

I waited until their first division was fifty feet away and from my raised platform, could see the entire formation. I raised the Staff, sunk into its power and pictured the entire division removed to the valley in front of the riff. With no noise or warning, the entire group of Kleptons disappeared.

"Adam, it worked," Guāng shouted in my head. He had left at first light to stand over the entrance to the riff, high enough to be unnoticed. *"The whole group just materialized and they are milling around, totally confused."*

"It worked," I said so everyone around me could hear.

A cheer went up. That victory cry was carried back to the main force so that now everyone in our standing army knew of the results.

In front of us, the brigades of Wizards were rising to see their storm troops, realizing that nothing stood between us and them. A few threw sonic blasts towards us but a simple shield from the Shaft absorbed the threat. With no choice, they began their crawl forward, rear tails posed threateningly like the scorpions they resembled. I absorbed any blasts they sent towards our lines with ease. I even started experimenting with the power to catch and send the blast back at their ranks. When the first blast exploded among their ranks, their entire line faltered. Whoever was calling the shots for the Klepton's army had a difficult time getting the line to advance after that. This time, they held off firing their blasts, obviously not enjoying being on the receiving end. Once again, I raised the Staff when they were less than fifty feet to my front, and the entire group disappeared; this time to the valley hideout with the huge waterfall. I only hoped Freddy and Ian weren't there.

"Bingo."

I was moving the recipients of each group to a different spot, so they would not materialize in or on another of their kind. My intention was to reduce the loss of life. Using memories and images that

Guāng sent me, I could accurately picture the location for each jump.

Ahead of us, there was a pause in the enemy's movements. It was obvious that they didn't understand what was happening. They might theorize all they wanted, but I guessed that the Queen's need for revenge would force them forward regardless of the cost. It was part of their nature.

We waited for a couple of hours. I sat down on my rock and chatted with my warrior brothers. Grandpa and a few others walked through our ranks offering cold water and snacks. He squeezed my arm, either in pride or support before moving on to the next soldier.

The sun beat down on both armies but a breeze carried most of the heat away and I sighed at its cool kiss. I squinted in the bright sunlight, wishing I had a pair of shades, but no one else wore them so I swallowed my complaint as childish.

Finally, the Klepton's began to move across the field towards us. Another group of Wizards pushed to the side to flank our forces while the armored monsters marched forward. Above them the Fliers hovered, their wings creating a hum that could be felt and heard. The command came, and they launched themselves at our lines.

I put up a shield to deal with the sonic blasts that came at a steady barrage. The Fliers flew over their earthbound comrades, heading towards my men and I. Taking in the entire attacking enemy, I pictured the group in the valley where the Scavenger had found us weeks ago.

It was as if someone blinked, because the entire force disappeared, leaving the Queen exposed. It was her giving the marching orders. I dropped my consciousness into the power of the Staff and focused on the Queen. Part of me wanted to rip her in half for all the pain and suffering she had caused me, but I stuck with the plan.

Using the Staff's power, I lifted her squirming mass, so it hovered over her army. I spun her like a child's toy over their heads, imagining her bewildered screech. Her army parted like the Red Sea had parted for Moses and I pushed her further away. As every one of her subjects watched her humiliation, I sent her to the valley of the riff with a command that I hoped she'd follow.

"Go Home!"

GUĀNG REACHED OUT TO me, *"She has arrived, Adam."*

The Klepton's army, which still out numbered ours, still stood paralyzed by what they had just witnessed. With no guidance from their monarchy they were helpless and unable to decide what their next move should be.

Lifting the Staff, I gave them a little incentive. Similar to the Wizard's sonic blast, but on a much larger scale, I tossed three blasts towards their ranks. Bodies flew and were bowled over like tenpins. I wasn't worried about killing them, as I knew their thick armor would protect them. We could hear the hollow clacking of armor striking armor.

It had the desired effect. As they picked themselves up, some needing help because they lay helpless on their backs, they began retreating. At first it was a small trickle but as the fear spread, it turned into a torrent. As they pushed through their own ranks, colliding and crashing against their comrades in haste, they rolled into their armadillo-like shapes and raced westward. Even at the speed they could achieve, it would take days for them to reach the riff.

Behind me, the human army cheered, the sound tore after the fleeing horde in joyful thunder.

But it wasn't over yet.

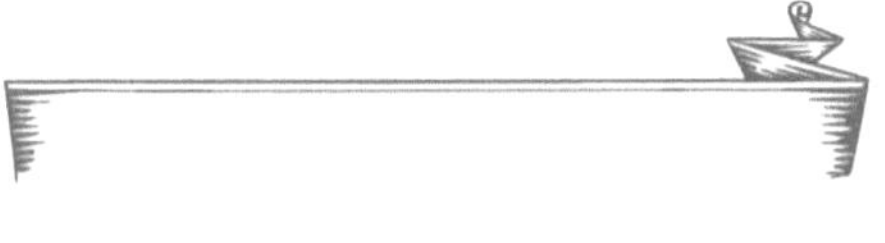

Chapter 38
(Adam)

Guāng lowered me onto the rocky ledge, his light uncurling from around my abdomen as we touched down. Below us, the Klepton's forces stretched across the mouth of the box canyon that held the riff. It was obvious that the Queen had not heeded my suggestion to return to her Citadel.

Her main host was still traveling towards the mountains and would be here in a couple days. I would have to reopen the mountain pass to allow them through, but first I had to make room for them. To accomplish that, these soldiers had to return home.

I pushed my hand through my hair, realizing for the first time how much it had grown in from the shaving I had received at the bootcamp. It also proved how long our stay in Heaven had been. With luck, this would be over in a few days.

Raising the staff, I tapped into the energy and fired off several sonic blasts at the neat formations that stood waiting for their Queen's command. The energy blasts hit the Klepton's ranks, scattering them like seeds. They milled around, trying to find the source of the attacks, but the sonic energy left them no clues.

I casually sent blast after blast into their ranks, knowing they wouldn't be hurt. The commotion had its desired effect, and the Queen showed herself. She slid on her mucus trail, her body secreting the slick goo as she advanced. She looked small against the rock wall which towered above her. I could see her massive head looking across the open valley in both directions, searching for a cause to the attacks.

Tapping into the Staff, I allowed myself to lift off the cliff and drop towards where she stood. Halfway across the valley, I was spotted and all eyes and tentacles swung towards me. Other than the wind, there was no sound as I floated towards the Queen, landing fifty feet from her. The formations of Klepton soldiers stood on either side of me waiting for a word from their monarch.

With the Staff, I pointed at the Queen and then back towards the rear of the canyon where the riff stood waiting. She glared at me, her black eyes trembling in fury and hatred on the ends of her tentacles.

For an answer, she pointed one of her long spiny hands towards me and in a rush of clicks ordered her army to attack. From behind her, the drone of a thousand wings echoed off the canyon's walls as the dragonfly like insects swarmed over her towards me. Both formations of armored Kleptons stormed towards me, the ground shaking as their heavy feet stomped.

I waited until all three forces were almost on top of me before I raised the Staff and used its power to freeze the attackers. Everything but the breeze stopped. Soldiers in mid-stride looked like statues while above the Fliers hung like grotesque decorations. I had left the soldiers their awareness so they could see and understand what was about to happen.

Only the Queen and I remained unaffected.

Her head jerked from one scene to another as she was unable to contemplate what had just happened. When her eyes returned to me, I once again motioned for her to return to her home. For many minutes, she stood still and I could tell she was trying to formulate some way to stop this forced eviction, but finally she turned toward the rock-face and spun slowly in the opposite direction. She entered the box canyon, and I followed to ensure she complied.

Without warning, two figures launched themselves off the rock-face to drop onto the Queens back. Freddy's long spear skewered the Queen so her back arced in agony. Before she or I could respond, Ian rammed the blade of his Ninjato into the creature's neck to the hilt. The Queen's body thrashed, throwing my two friends clear to land in a roll on the canyon floor.

I stood in shock at what they had done. I was trying to do this without bloodshed, but in a second, they took that away from me. The Queen's pale green blood pumped out of her wounds in a gush and her flailing slowed until she was still.

Freddy and Ian had picked themselves up from the ground and were giving each other high fives at their successful attack. They turned towards me.

"Why?" I said the disbelieve making my voice sound hollow.

"Payback," Ian said defiantly his face forming a tight snarl.

"But she was leaving. It was over."

"It wasn't you she killed, Adam. I'm the one that will never go home. Never see my mother. All because of her!"

Freddy said nothing, but stood ready to defend Ian against me.

I nodded my understanding and walked towards the two, ignoring the frozen aliens above and behind me. Both tensed up when I reached out, but I wasn't worried as I pulled them together in a hug.

"I'm glad you guys are okay. Rob and I have been sick worrying."

The two hugged back. I'm not ashamed to say, there was some unmanly tears going on.

"Come on," I said finally. "Let's finish this."

"Guāng. Can you give us a lift?"

My spectral friend streaked from on high and wrapped himself around us and carried us back to the rock ledge. Once we settled, I used the Staff to unfreeze the horde below us. The Fliers surged forward before coming to a confused hover. The two formations put on the brakes to avoid colliding with each other. As they collected themselves, their attention went to their Queen, who lay slumped over in death.

Whatever their culture said about a Queen's death I would never know, but there was one egg left at the Citadel and maybe that was the reason they began marching into the canyon towards the riff. It took hours as the multitude made their way to the spot that would allow them to return home. The three of us sat on the ledge watching quietly, sipping on milkshakes which Ian conjured out of thin air.

The sun was waning as the last of them disappeared into the mouth of the canyon.

I lowered myself to the valley below and using the last of my strength, reopened the pass by pushing the two mountains apart. My arms sagged with the effort and Guāng had to carry me and the others to the cave behind the waterfall. We would camp here to wait for the rest of the retreating Kleptons. As a favor to me, Guāng also fetched Rob so he could witness the closing of the riff and the end of the invasion.

The reunion was good for us. It allowed us to fill in the gaps as to what had transpired since the party had split up. Not discussed was the fact we would soon go home to Earth and our real lives, minus Ian. There was too much pain there. The goodbyes would be hard enough.

Two days later, the exodus continued as the main force reached the mountain pass. It took a day and a half to march the massive force through the canyon and through the riff. I had Guāng make a pass of their route to ensure everyone of them was through before I turned my attention to the riff.

Using the Staff, I squeezed the riff closed. To ensure it would never reopen, I pulled the mountain on top of it, burying it under a massive rock slide that filled half of the valley.

Finally, Heaven was safe. Grandpa was safe and all the other worlds were free of the danger.

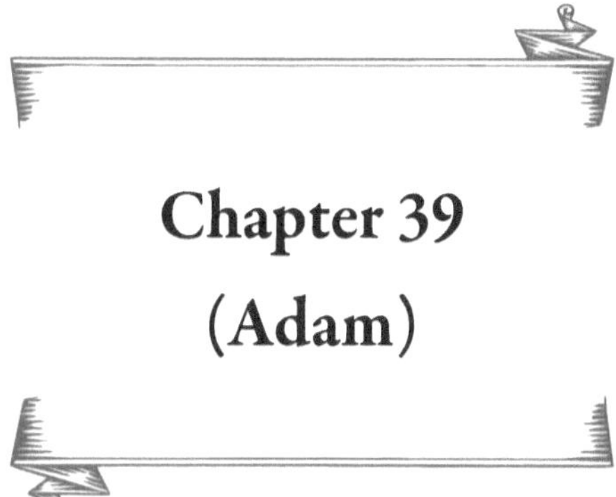

Chapter 39
(Adam)

Our return to the center of Heaven turned into the party of the universe. Hailed as heroes, they put together a massive feast in our honor. All our favorite foods were there for the asking, served exactly as we enjoyed them. I admit to getting a little tipsy after exchanging cups with Thor and his men. As I staggered to my Grandpa's cottage, I found him waiting for me.

"Some shindig, eh?" he said with a smile.

I plopped down in the chair next to him. "Oh yeah. I think if I eat any more, I'll burst," I said patting my stomach.

"Sure made me proud to see you being toasted by all of Heaven. Not that I didn't think you had it in you. You just had to believe in yourself."

"I will miss all this," I said surprising myself. "I met some great people and made a bunch of new friends. Even have a blood brother."

"It'll all be waiting here for you. Just don't be in a rush to get here. You have a whole life to live for yourself and you make more friends; maybe a girlfriend or two."

"But Ian won't," I said. I don't know if I was tired, or it was the Viking ale, but the heaviness of the loss of Ian hit me acutely.

"I know that, Adam," he said with a gentle voice. "Why don't you talk to Jesus in the morning? He might be able to put things into perspective. He always helps me when I'm missing you and your Grandma."

Knowing the calming effect, he had whenever we spoke, I agreed to meet with Him.

THE ACHE IN MY HEART eased the minute Jesus took my hands in his. "Peace be upon you, my young hero," he said his eyes warm and welcoming.

We sat on cushions under the tent flap. He offered me dates and figs before returning to the reason for my visit. "You are a loyal and good friend, Adam. It is natural for you to feel remorse and regret of losing someone you love. It was the same when you lost your Grandpa, although you had a harder time coming to terms with his death because of your youth."

He sighed and continued. "But there might be a way of bettering the situation, especially because of your contributions for all the souls of Heaven."

I sat up wondering what I could do.

"During my time on earth, the power of God allowed me to perform many wonderful miracles, including the raising of Lazarus."

My eyes were riveted on Him. Could He restore Ian, even though he had been killed. "But his body is in the Klepton's Citadel."

"The power of God transcends all things, you have used the Staff, have you not realized the power you wielded?" he said with a twinkle in his eyes.

"Do you mean...?"

He nodded gently.

"I have to get the Staff."

He held up his hand to slow me down. "Hear me out. Although you forced the aliens from our Heaven to theirs without bloodshed, there still is the idea of balance that the prophecy spoke of. As you think of helping your friend, also think of all those who suffered and were lost."

The enormity of what he was implying staggered me. But if the power of the staff was truly infinite, it could work. As I thought it through, I fingered the scab on my thigh from where the Queen had cut me. It was healing but would definitely leave a scar. The itching was distracting.

"It is a massive undertaking," he said. "Ensure you are well rested."

THE NEXT MORNING, I grabbed the Staff for a final time and made my way to the same rock I had stood on when I faced the Queen's army. I took the time to calm my mind enjoying the warm sun on my skin.

When I was ready, I stood and lifted my arms; the Staff held high. I tapped into that immense torrent of energy, letting it fill me to capacity and then I solidly envisioned what I wanted, picturing my desire for the good of both Heavens. Finally complete, I released the power of God one final time.

There was no explosion, no fanfare to show I was successful, and I looked around wondering if it had worked. Grounding the Staff, I reached down to scratch my thigh only to realize that the wound was gone. I opened my shirt and the cuts on my chest had disappeared.

Running back towards the courtyard, I met one of the men who had lost his arm during the ambush at the river. He waved the now restored arm at me in excitement.

"I don't know how I can thank you, Adam" He was weeping with joy and it overcame me.

I was at a full sprint when I spotted my three friends talking excitedly with Grandpa by his fire. I raced, and they turned at my advance, ecstatic smiles across their faces.

"Adam, what did you do?" Ian said.

"I visioned that everything returned back the way it was before the war with the Kleptons began. The Staff did the rest." I took his hand. "How do you feel?"

"Strangely alive," he laughed.

"It was the coolest thing in the world," Freddy said in excitement. "One minute he was talking to me and the next a glowing, blue copy of Ian materialized and the two merged together. He jolted like lightning had hit him, but then he was fine."

"It was awesome," Rob said nodding. He looked up at me, his eyes widening. "Does this mean the Queen is alive as well?"

"Yes, the Staff allowed me to return to before the Riff was opened."

"You've restored the balance, Adam. Well done."

"Extremely well done," said a deep voice behind us.

We turned as one to find Mohammad and Jesus standing there.

"You have fulfilled the prophesy, and all is right in Heaven." Mohammad said bowing to my friends and I.

"But it is also time to say your goodbyes and return to your real lives."

Boy, that seemed abrupt, and I was startled at his words.

Jesus smiled. "Much time has passed here in Heaven, but it has been only two days in your real life. If you are to re-enter, you must leave now."

Grandpa grabbed me and hugged me hard to his chest. "Love you, boy. I'll keep the fire going and you give your Grandma a kiss for me."

I swiped at the tears but could say nothing as it died my throat. I just nodded.

As my friends all said goodbye to Grandpa, I turned to the Prophets. "Thank you for trusting in me. I think this should remain here," I said handing the Staff to Mohammad.

"Thank you, Adam."

They led us to the courtyard where all our warrior brothers waited to bid us farewell. It was emotional but gratifying to know that they would be all here when it was my turn to return. The last to say goodbye was Gaje. We clasped hands as we did when the blood flowed confirming our commitment to each other.

"Live large, my Brother," he said pulling me in a tight hug.

"You as well. I'll never forget you."

Our goodbyes complete, Guāng wrapped around us one last time we lifted skyward. As we sped towards the portal to our world, I noticed that the massive gilded Buddha was no longer destroyed; the Mosque was prestige and inviting. All the buildings had been restored as well.

We entered the blinding nothingness of the portal and were then zooming through the mine shaft until Guāng gently unraveled himself in the mineshaft's front where he had first met us.

"Thank you Guāng. I will always treasure your friendship." I said though our mind link.

"I, as well, my friend. You all did so well. Enjoy your lives. We will be united another day."

With that he was gone, leaving us standing in the mining camp wondering which way to go.

Epilogue

Without warning, the mining camp began to fade away under a blaze of bright white. I had no choice but to tightly close my eyes at the intensity of the glare and yet could still see it through my eyelids.

"What the...?" Freddy screamed.

"Be at peace, my friends," said a voice in my head.

I could sense my friend's thoughts and knew we were all connected to this new mind link. The voice was rich and warm and I knew it was from Heaven.

"You didn't think I would let you go without thanking you for helping me with that little problem

with the riff, did you?" said the voice filled with amusement.

"You... you're GOD?" I asked.

"That is one of the names they have called me. There are thousands more from across space and time."

"But, where have you been? We could have used your help." Ian asked.

"What would have been the point of that?" he said with a chuckle. *"I wanted to help you grow stronger and learn new skills which you will need in the future."*

"Why?" I asked out loud hesitantly. "What's going to happen that will require a ninja or Comanche warrior?"

"The future is yours to discover. You might not need the fighting skills, but it may require you to lead, to stand together and take the right path rather than the easier one, and you'll need the confidence in yourselves to succeed."

He let that sink in. I had a thousand questions, but he cut me off.

"Your adventure is not over; it is just beginning. And I'll be watching."

With that, the light faded as did our connection to each other. The mining camp came back into focus and the four of us stood blinking at each other.

"Just beginning?" Ian said. "What the heck does He have in store for us?"

"I don't know," said Rob. "But it sounds like we'll be doing it together. And I'm good with that."

NOT KNOWING WHAT KIND of reception, we would find, we were hesitant at which road we should follow; return to the bootcamp or try to reach civilization. There was no sign of the "D's" or a search party as we would expect to find, although we heard a helicopter in the distance.

"Dwight had last seen us on this mountain," Ian said. "It makes little sense they wouldn't be combing the mountain if they had launched a search."

"Let's get to the ridge that overlooks the lake. We might be able to see some sign of what's going on," I said.

Taking the lead, we followed the trail out of the mining camp and climbed the slope until we reached the ridge. Below us, the pool where I had encountered the Scavenger reflected the afternoon sun, and looked inviting. Beyond it and the forest which slid down the mountainside, the lake spread out in its magnificence with the bootcamp on the far shore. I could see flashing police lights among the barracks and kitchen buildings. Beyond the camp, two helicopters crisscrossed the forest in what was obvious a grid search.

"Why would they be searching over there?" Freddy said. "Especially when Dwight last saw us, we were standing in this spot."

Rob chuckled out loud. "It's obvious. He doesn't want us found. That would open the door for the feds to question us why we left. The three "D's" have much more to lose than us."

"Our parents will be worried sick," Ian said looking at all of us.

"Then we shouldn't cause them more anxiety," I said with a grin. "Besides, I'm eager to see how Dwight and the other two dummies will try to wiggle their way out of this. They won't be dealing with a pack of delinquents offended by the world anymore. Those guys are long gone."

The End

DEAR READER, THANK you so much for joining me for this adventure. I hope you enjoyed yourself. Reviews are extremely important to authors and I would ask that you take a couple minutes and leave a review where you purchased your copy or at www.Goodreads.com[1]

---

1. http://www.Goodreads.com

About the Author

Dave Wickenden has spent time in the Canadian Armed Forces before the Fire Service, so is as comfortable with a rocket launcher as a fire hose. He has brought six people back from the dead utilizing CPR and a defibrillator and has assisted in rescuing people in crisis. He has learnt to lead men and women in extreme environments. He loves to cook, read and draw and write. Dave ran his own home based custom art business creating highly detailed wood and paper burnings called pyrography. One of his pictures of former Prime Minister Jean Chretien graces the walls of Rideau Hall in Ottawa.

After 31 years in the Fire Service and attaining the rank of Deputy Fire Chief, Dave retired to write thriller novels full time. He is a member of the Writer's Union of Canada, the International Thriller Association, and the International Screenwriter Association. His works include IN DEFENSE OF INNOCENCE 2018, HOMEGROWN 2018, and DEADLY HARVEST 2019 and MAD DOG July 2020 through Black Rose Writing. He has adapted all four stories into screenplays.

Read more at davewickenden.wixsite.com/dave-wickenden.